These Dividing Walls

Fran Cooper grew up in London before reading English at Cambridge and Art History at the Courtauld Institute of Art. She spent three years in Paris writing a PhD about travelling eighteenth-century artists, and currently works in the curatorial department of a London museum. These Dividing Walls is her first novel.

Fran Cooper

These Dividing Walls

HODDER &
STOUGHTON

First published in Great Britain in 2017 by Hodder & Stoughton
An Hachette UK company

I

A CIP catalogue record for this title is available from the British Library

Hardback ISBN 978 1 473 64153 2
Trade Paperback ISBN 978 1 473 64154 9
Ebook ISBN 978 1 473 64155 6

Typeset in Sabon MT by Palimpsest Book Production Limited,
Falkirk, Stirlingshire
Printed and bound by Clays Ltd, St Ives plc

Hodder & Stoughton policy is to use papers that are natural, renewable and recyclable products and made from wood grown in sustainable forests. The logging and manufacturing processes are expected to conform to the environmental regulations of the country of origin.

Hodder & Stoughton Ltd
Carmelite House
50 Victoria Embankment
London EC4Y 0DZ

www.hodder.co.uk

For Anne, a dear friend.

And for Alex, always.

Prologue: The Building

Far back on the Left Bank, there is a secret quarter. Beyond the neon-lit slopes of Montparnasse, the winding cobbles of the fifth arrondissement, a warren of quiet streets lie sandwiched between boulevards. Little traffic comes through here.

Number thirty-seven sits at the meeting of two streets in this forgotten corner of the city. It is much like the buildings that surround it – late nineteenth-century, pale stone. But for its turquoise door it might slip from view altogether.

On summer nights, its residents return home as the sun sinks over the city. Lights are turned on, windows opened; dinners cooked and babies put to bed. The smell of garlic browning in a pan drifts into the courtyard, along with a child's cries and snippets of conversation caught on the breeze.

Within its walls, people kiss. They talk, they laugh; someone cries, perhaps. A few are glad to sit alone. Others wish that they did not.

As darkness falls, the lights are gradually extinguished again. On such a heat-soaked, airless night as this, number thirty-seven's residents lie in their beds, listening to the rise and fall of neighbours' breath. Life is measured by the scrape of strangers' plates, the tinny ring of someone else's telephone, the grunts of sex (and other functions), until all is finally quiet again.

Number thirty-seven has its stories; in this it is like any building. For what building doesn't have secrets? How much does anyone know of what goes on behind their neighbours' doors?

I

Edward wakes with a shout in lung-crushing panic, palms slammed flat against the wall, feet scrambling up the bed towards him. *Where am I?* His heart thunders in his open mouth and he does not know if he is still screaming. He flings an arm out in front of him into the darkness – *a light, there must be a light* – but finds only a glass of water that his elbow sends flying. It is momentarily airborne before he hears the clunk, the wet shatter of it, and when his sleep-fattened fingers finally locate the light switch the rug is laced with shards of dangerous glitter.

Things swim slowly into focus, a pool of orange light beating back the shadows. He is in a bed, in a room, under the eaves of a building. Under the roof's slope he can make out a desk, the outline of his backpack, a mirror reflecting a blur of light. The window is open – banging against the wall – and the pale curtains are sucked in and out by the wind, rushing up into the room on their release like long, ghostly fingers.

Avoiding the glass, Edward makes his way across the space on unsteady legs. His palms are slick with sweat as they fumble with the ratty loop of rope that's been used, for years it seems, to tie the window open. It's come loose while he's slept. These fiddly moments bring with them a sense of calm, of focus. The air that whistles along the rooftops is cool, the knot of dread in his stomach is loosening, and by the time the work is done he has remembered that the terror was a nightmare, that he is in Paris, and that this is Emilie's apartment.

Apartment. He looks around him; the room is smaller than

his friend had implied. A single bed in one corner, the 'kitchen' in another, its electric hotplate just six diagonal paces from the clown-print pillow. Edward's lips twitch as the fabric face leers back at him. It's typical Emilie, this jumble of childhood bedsheets and snatches of paper thrown up all over the place. The wall by the bed flutters in the night air: patterns, postcards, sketches, pinned together like butterflies' wings.

Edward returns to the bedside and collects pieces of glass into an ashtray. The wind has quieted a little now, more breath than shriek as it ruffles the wall of paper, whispers over the bedclothes. His breath is still rattling in his chest. Just before four, according to his watch, but the blood is too high in him to think of sleep. He is in the grip of that sharpness that follows fear – the sudden cognisance of every cell, the microscopic rush of blood through each capillary.

The night terror sits just out of sight on his shoulder, a dark bird dancing its feet along his collarbone. Always the same: his sister's face smiling at him, the moment before the car hits stretching into an eternity in which he can't move, can't speak, can't tell her to stop . . .

The glass rattles beneath his fingers as Edward's hands start up their shaking again. He strains his ears but hears no noise from his neighbours. He hates the thought that someone might have heard his cry.

Opening the kitchen bin he is met with the warm rush of decomposition: rotting fruit, cigarettes, the queasy staleness of beer that's spent hot days at the bottom of old bottles. This is typical Emilie, too. He'd pushed the piles of dirty laundry out of his mind – and into the cupboard – when he'd arrived; tried not to think about the balled-up lace knickers by the bed, or how crisp they were underfoot. But he hadn't checked the bin, and in the pre-dawn murk the sweet putrefaction turns his stomach.

He pulls on jeans, trainers, yesterday's T-shirt. It cloaks him in eight hours of bus journey, the baked sweat of a

Channel crossing spent on deck, but it's better than the bin bag, which he ties and walks out of the room at arm's length.

Four o'clock, and Edward stands outside his new building, in a new city, breathing damp summer deep into his lungs. He doesn't know where the bins are yet, so he's left his bag of rubbish out on the deserted street. No one stirs. There's no one to stir, just lines of buildings flanked by parked cars.

He thinks back to the conversation he had with Emilie, standing barefoot in thick grass, the scent of hay heavy in his nostrils, pollen dancing in the golden air.

'I need to get out, Em.'

'*Edward!*' That tone she uses in exasperation, usually accompanied by the flailing of a densely-bangled wrist. He'd imagined the clink and jingle of it down the phone, metal on metal via metal, her handset to his, cheek to cheek across hundreds of miles of ether. 'Use the apartment. *Please*. No one's going to mind, my aunt's probably not even there, I'll get the *gardienne* to let you in, or there'll be some old *voisin* with a key . . .'

Edward didn't know what those words meant, but in the sunshine, with the bright timpani of her voice, her laugh, the surety with which she described it all, he was swept up on it. Up on the cloud of her. And he'd agreed, and bought a ticket, and it was less than three days ago and now here he is on a street in Paris in the early hours of a Friday morning.

And not the Paris he knew about, either. This is no boulevard – no landmarks here. The night before, the bus had dropped him at the back end of a car park behind a shopping centre. Shrieking teenagers with backpacks, an Orthodox Jewish couple and their impossibly tiny baby, a crumpled old man with a stick who'd immediately struck out in the opposite direction to everybody else. Edward had followed the crowd as it trailed its way through back doors and featureless corridors down into the metro, where he jumped the stile like everyone in front of him, right in front of the guard, her eyes glazed and vacant, and then onto a train which hurtled past names that meant something to him (*Champs Elysées, Musée du Louvre*), before changing onto one whose names did not. He emerged into streets filled with end-of-day crowds, the directions he'd scribbled down smearing on his damp palm as he navigated old women with shopping trolleys, kids streaking past on scooters, greengrocers waving bags of overripe cherries in his face, their bloody juice dripping vividly onto the pavement while outside a butcher's shop two men hurled grease from a rotisserie oven into the road so that the ground swam with fat and soapsuds. Wide women waddled along wrapped head to toe in neon prints, a teenager rode a motorbike along the pavement, a friend standing up on the seat behind him, and Edward, a country boy, reeled.

Now though, the streets are quiet. Edward takes a few tentative steps, but the morning light is taking its time and unease coats the base of his still-jittery stomach.

He is turning back to the building, to the great turquoise doorway that leads into the courtyard, when he hears it, could swear he hears it.

'*Edward!*'

His name whispered quick, urgent, carried on the air from the empty street. He looks but sees nothing, hears only the rush of blood to his head. He slams the door, crosses the courtyard, and takes the five flights of stairs at a run.

If the adrenaline coursing through Edward's veins for a second time that night had let his pupils widen, had let his eyes linger a little longer, he might have made out the shape of a man sleeping in the doorway opposite. Or not sleeping, in fact, as the man has been watching Edward with interest. This street is his domain by night. From his bed he rolls an old cigarette between thumb and forefinger, his eyes flinty in the strike of the match, intent on the space where the young man has been standing.

And if Edward could see into the apartments he passes on his ascent, he'd see that not all his neighbours are asleep either, early though the hour is. On the first floor, a middle-aged woman fans herself, half-hearted movements ineffectual against the bedroom's stale heat. Chantal's husband will not sleep with the window open, so she passes the night in long, warm minutes, sweat beading along her breastbone, aiming an occasional kick at the lumpen form next to her. '*César*, you're snoring!'

On the second floor there are children dreaming. Milky, contented, a baby stirs in his crib and in his basket a dog stirs too, chasing the elusive rabbit holes of sleep. The children's mother, Anaïs, stands at the window. Sleep evades her, her fingers gripping the windowsill and its flaking paint as she wills the sky to darken again, wills the morning to hold itself at bay.

Puffing, wheezing, Edward winds his way up the building, past the third floor where a sleepy hand bats away a mosquito, the fourth where he sees a computer's blue light in an open window across the courtyard. A hunched figure is furiously typing and, pausing for breath, Edward can almost hear the percussive assault of fingers on keyboard.

Finally the fifth floor, and Edward stands in his room with his back against the door. Outside, the sky is swimming inkily from black to blue and over the furthest rooftops brown smudges are starting to appear. He locks the door, has to stop himself from unlocking and relocking it again (a maternal rabbit hole down which he does not want to disappear today). He regains the bed, the clown-print pillow which smells, now that he thinks about it, of Emilie. He turns it over, buries his head in it with unusual force, trying to sleep, trying not to think of his friend and the one night they slept together, a night where the only bits that bumped were the bits you didn't want to – a long percussion of teeth and noses.

Edward's cheeks burn in allegiance with the sun, which is stalking up now with a vengeance, turning everything red. When finally he dips below the surface, it is to the sound of shutters opening below, of cars starting in the street, and the building waking up to begin its day.

2

Frédérique rises with the sun. *Penance*, she thinks, hanging over the stove waiting for the flame to catch. All those youthful mornings slept through, all that daylight wasted.

She opens the apartment's shutters as the coffee rumbles, metal pot clattering its way to the boil. The *salon*, with its deeply piled fabrics and heavy furniture, has never been to her taste. Instead she sips her coffee at a small scrubbed table in the kitchen, bare toes *tip-tap-tapping* along the tiled floor in time to the radio.

Mischa the cat is also dancing, slinking around ankles and chair legs. Her miaows aren't quite in tune or rhythm though, so soon enough her mistress is up, stooping to dig the cream out of the fridge. And although Frédérique drinks her coffee black, some mornings (today is one of them) she treats herself to a dash of cream in the dregs, swirling the thick liquid around her bowl while the cat laps happily in the corner.

On these midsummer mornings she steels herself to leap under the shower's jet of icy water, gritting her teeth through the pain and pleasure of it. The cat licks her paws cautiously in the doorway, distrustful of the droplets that fly across the room. The long hair, as much silver as blonde these days, is unplaited; the lines around the blue eyes patted with cream, with resigned familiarity.

She dresses. The act of opening the oak armoire is a jolt, each morning, back to childhood. Mothballs, dust, the *swoosh* of hangers along the rail, though her loose white shirts have nothing on her mother's clothes; the heavy drip of embroidery, the thick oiliness of fur.

Away from the possibility of water, the cat is again winding herself around Frédérique's legs, rolling over to display her belly in the most alluring light.

Slipping amber beads over her head Frédérique murmurs, 'Not now, Misch.'

There's much to do today, and it is already getting hot.

Stepping out into the street through the turquoise door, Frédérique cranes her neck up to the sky. It is peerless, deep and azure. The sun's slant has not quite reached the pavement, but already the city is pulsing with it. Another hot day.

Across the street, the man who has been watching Edward sits in the doorway whistling. He has rolled up his bedmat now, neatly bound it to the trolley on which his worldly goods are piled. He wears shorts and a clean shirt. He is tying his bootlaces, a half-forgotten tune sing-songing through his teeth.

He raises his hand. 'Frédérique.'

She returns the gesture. 'Josef.'

This is their morning ritual.

She sets off down the street, her sandals clip-clopping in time to his whistle. Josef watches her go with eyes that do not quite line up. He turns to put away his shaving kit; a nick on his cheek betrays the razor's recent strokes.

Frédérique makes her way to the *tabac*, where she joins the queue for cigarettes. Nicotine: the great equaliser. Even at this hour (it is barely seven), there are women in suits, men in paint-splattered overalls, skinny teenagers all in black, an old lady with her hair in curlers. Rows of scratchcards glitter in the morning light and already the TVs are buzzing with the day's news and the afternoon's horse races. Patiently the crowd inches towards the counter. Frédérique watches pinpricks of sweat appear on the burly neck in front of her.

Out on the street she is heady with the day's first inhalation. Today, as she does most days, she slopes down the street to the local bar, where gold-toothed Claude has already set out her croissant and her newspaper. Normally she sits at the counter, starts the day with the cold caress of the zinc along her arms, but this morning the bar is airless, stale with beer and sweat, so she takes her paper outside and leans her face up into the light.

Claude brings her breakfast, his arms blurred with constellations of old tattoos.

''s terrible, no?' He hawks and spits into the gutter.

'What?'

Claude nods at the paper. 'Another attack. Up in Bobigny.'

'Jesus.'

'Little Jewish kid. Thirteen years old.'

Claude shakes his head and turns back inside. He is not a man of many words. Frédérique turns to the newspaper. The front page talks about the heatwave, big capital letters and a map of France in violent red. Austerity as usual – taxes, the doomed budget, the latest round of cuts. Buried inside, at the bottom of a page, she reads about Bobigny; a few sentences on a child beaten on his way home from school for wearing a kippah. The same small print tells her that there's been another attack on a mosque outside Lyon, that a homeless man has been smashed to a pulp near Châtelet. That the Far Right is promising more protests.

Although the sun is beating down on her shoulders, Frédérique feels as if a cloud is passing over. It settles in her brow, which furrows; in her stomach, which sets itself on edge. She doesn't stop as usual on the way home – not for bread or milk, nor for the plump strawberries that Mo the greengrocer always keeps to one side for her. She jangles her change in her palm, hot and sweaty, her footsteps urgent in the quiet street. She wants to talk to Josef, but by the time she gets back his trolley is gone.

Frédérique does not feel her almost half-century. Winding her way up the staircase, she cannot believe it is four decades since her child feet tramped these boards. She knows every worn-down curve in the wood underfoot, every chip in the plaster. Some of these scuffs were probably her childhood heels kicking. Her knee still bears the scar from when she tripped and that loose tile on the ground floor cut deep into her flesh. It was a summer day, hot like this, and she could taste iron in the dusty air as dark liquid dribbled onto her white ankle sock.

Mischa is lying belly up on the chaise longue, four furry legs thrust in the air. Frédérique sits next to her, rubbing absentmindedly at the old wound. Five stitches, faded now to ghost flesh. Still, all these years later, the feeling is absent.

That is how she thinks of this apartment, her childhood home: a place where feeling is left at the door. So many years seeking expanse, horizon, a space larger than this city, a world beyond the bourgeois formalities cradled within these walls. And then to have life made infinite: to have a son, and lose him, and to feel the universe in all its immensity within her bones. To become hollow and yearn again for the slim child-hood bed, the flowery walls, the heavy furniture and the grim-faced portraits – everything that had suffocated her before in its intensity turned now into a cushion against pain; scar tissue around her heart.

The cat rolls over and pushes her face into Frédérique's – round green eyes and fish-flecked breath.

'You're right, my love. No use dwelling.'

And she doesn't. She has learnt a quiet contentment here. She has her cat, her books, the bookshop she keeps on the ground floor. Although neither its hours nor its customers nor, sadly, its income are very regular, there is a pleasure meted out to her in the syncopated rhythm of her days.

Forgetting the pack in her pocket she walks over to the side table in search of a cigarette and sees that a light on the answering machine is flashing. 'How long has that been there?' she muses, cigarette between teeth.

The message begins as she inhales: a piercing beep and her niece's voice, garbled, nasal. She's outdoors, traffic and gusts of wind cutting in on her words.

'Freddie, it's Emilie! Hope you don't mind . . . a friend to stay. I told him . . . keys from Madame Marin, won't bother you at all. Just a break—' The rumble of a lorry passing. 'Lots of love. Oh, his name's Edward!'

Another beep, and then silence.

'Edward . . .' Frédérique exhales the name with a sigh, searching her memory for those candle-lit, wine-soaked nights when Emilie would return from university full of adventures and friends and boys, their names spilling casually out over the table as easily as the way her niece would flick her hair back and laugh – 'God, Freddie, the wine there is *awful*!' – and Frédérique remembers reading the shadows for a blush as this wonderful friend, the wonderful Edward, came up over and over in conversation.

Those university years were ones of rupture. Her niece had almost lived with her before that, such a frequent visitor that her absence was more shocking than her presence, and there was no surprise returning to the apartment to find Emilie in the bath or curled up on the bed or rummaging through the bookshelves. Frédérique had had to relearn silence when she left for university. Such closeness before, and it was resurrected, of course, during the holidays, but it is inevitable, she reminds herself, that such things taper. That was years ago and Emilie's life is there now, in London, with Simon the slippery banker, all wide smiles and nothing but distrust behind his eyes. It has been months since Frédérique has seen her niece for more than a ghastly formal coffee in a tourist-trap café that Simon simply *had* to visit. She can't remember the last time Emilie burst in unannounced. The last time anyone arrived unexpectedly at the door, in fact.

Sensing the slip into reverie, Mischa disentangles herself from her mistress and stalks into the kitchen, leaving

Frédérique to her cigarette and her ghosts. The cat pokes her nose under the table in hope of a previously overlooked morsel. No such luck, but the windowsill (her favourite perch) is drenched with sun, so up she hops and settles in, one eye closed, the other trained on the courtyard below.

3

As Mischa's purrs subside into warm, breathy snores, the building around her creaks and splutters. Paint flakes, doors bang; the train runs underneath at intervals and sets a buzzing to the residents' throats.

Perched atop the tunnels that mined out its own grey-cream stone, number thirty-seven is not so much finite as in a perpetual state of flux. Gaps regularly open up between door and frame, wall and window. On windy nights, cold air rushes up and circles the top storeys with a moan, while in the summer the windows are flung open, shutters lolling like tongues, and the building pants through the heat along with its inhabitants. Too far from the river to ever have been truly fashionable, it is technically two buildings, one fronting the street, whose apartments are rather more gracious than those in the other which sits across the courtyard, separated from the first by the width of a squat, metal-roofed cube in which the *gardienne* lives.

Few at number thirty-seven can recall how long Madame Marin has been the *gardienne*, nor how long she has had the hairdressing salon on the ground floor. For three decades or more the passage from the entryway to the courtyard has been her domain, filled with the smells of shampoo and burnt hair, and gossip about her clients. She is, though she would never admit it, the wrong side of fifty, her eyebrows painted the same pumpkin orange as the tresses that were once her crowning glory, and never without a stiletto heel. Horrified by the dowdiness of housecoats, Estella Marin owns a series of brightly coloured kimonos, dazzling swirls of fish and flowers that wind themselves tight around her. Beneath translucent stockings the backs of her legs display all manner of mottled veins, the years spiderwebbing secretly up underneath her skirt as she sweeps the courtyard, sorts the letters into the mailboxes and greets the residents as they hurry by.

Once, the *gardienne* would have known everything about everyone. The buildings aren't so large – only five floors, just over a dozen apartments – and before the doors were so stringently locked and voices lowered during arguments, Madame Marin's predecessors would have been in on it all. For many babies have been birthed at number thirty-seven, their mothers' howls rattling the stairways where bloodsoaked sheets were carried down and heavy perambulators lugged back up. Deaths too, of course: old heads sinking quietly into pillows, and other, less timely exits.

The first war took two boys from the building: Alfred Michel, a freckled nineteen-year-old just out of the *lycée*, and Guillaume Bertrand, a blonde, blue-eyed clerk who left behind a girl in trouble. She turned up at the turquoise door one day, to his parents' mortal horror. Quietly they housed her at the top of the back building, in the room next to Edward's, while they remained in their apartment overlooking the street, never acknowledging her, never speaking to her, Madame Bertrand fanning the flames of the building's gossip by whispering about 'these girls' and 'war babies' and 'trouble' with the other housewives, until one day the girl (her name was Sophie) upped and left in the night, taking the blonde-haired, blue-eyed baby with her. The Bertrands barely spoke again, silenced by this compounding of loss.

It was rumoured that Sophie, who was originally from Alsace, had run off with one of the Americans who flooded Montparnasse after the war, but in reality the fabled Yanks never reached the building or its environs. The great boulevards remained for many of its residents mythic places spoken of in hushed, disapproving tones. Illuminated lights, theatres, cabarets – a different universe to the streets they inhabited with the café, the *tabac*, the grocer, the butcher.

In 1943, a family was taken from the building. The Kahns, from the third floor. Number thirty-seven's residents watched and did nothing, said nothing, and a new quietness descended over the building. People kept themselves to themselves, kept their eyes lowered. After the war the Kahns' three children were commemorated on a plaque at the nearby school, one of the plaques that dot all the city's schools; quiet reminders of complicity. Many of the same families stayed on in the apartments, and people grew up, grew old, died, inherited as the events of the rest of the world trundled by.

Tumultuous decades have done little to shake up number thirty-seven: the chimneys continue to whistle in the wind, and the door to the basement still clangs mysteriously shut in the night.

Towards the end of the last century, the residents decided that the building should have a new lick of paint. This millennium project didn't actually happen until the sweltering summer of 2003, when ambulances rolled silently up and down the city's streets collecting the old and the forgotten who had died from the heat. The paint job went unfinished.

And so number thirty-seven's story is, in many ways, the story of being always a little behind the times, a little outside its time, hidden behind the turquoise door on a street with forgotten flowers in its name (they don't grow here now, if ever they did). Here it has hung on for years, and hangs on still, though the neighbourhood around it is gradually changing. The third floor of Bâtiment A is empty, and there is a consensus amongst some of its inhabitants that they'll have to vet the next buyers carefully.

4

'I SAID, WE'LL HAVE TO VET THE NEXT BUYERS CAREFULLY,' César Vincent bellows above the roar of the bathroom taps. He turns them off and surveys his shaving-foamed face with satisfaction. He is just turning the razor to that tricky bit beneath his nostrils when his wife appears unseen in the doorway.

'What buyers?'

Startled, César's hand jumps and a spot of shaving cream turns pink.

'The buyers, the buyers,' he is exasperated now, 'for the third floor.'

'Oh, that.'

And with that, his wife slopes back to the bedroom.

César has never understood Chantal's lack of interest in the building. As President of number thirty-seven's Residents' Cooperative (his chest puffs a few centimetres further out each time he reminds himself of that title), he makes it his business to be interested. Property prices aren't what they used to be. He doesn't want anyone . . . *undesirable*. Sighing, he turns back to the mirror and the red dribble that is about to drip off his chin.

In the bedroom, Chantal Vincent returns to her seat on the windowsill. It's not that she's not interested in the building – on the contrary, that's what she's been watching – but she has not slept well. César refuses to sleep with the windows open, so her night has been hot and restless. He, of course, woke bright and refreshed, the self-satisfied 'pom-pom-poms' of his smooth baritone booming over the rush of the shower, and she knows he will emerge any second now, pink and plump and ready for his day. Chantal, by contrast, is sapped, still in her nightdress, hair clinging to the back of her neck, and she is clinging to the hope that she might snatch a few extra minutes before her shift begins at ten.

Chantal works in the library of a private literary institute in the fifteenth arrondissement. She first drifted behind the librarian's desk in her twenties, when library studies were more appealing (and more financially gratifying) than the ten lonely years it was predicted she would spend on a doctorate. For a while she'd worried intermittently that she had made the wrong decision, mostly in September when pencil cases and school-bags filled shop windows, or when a distant acquaintance would invite her to attend his PhD defence. But now, all these years later, she loves the quiet calm the job brings with it; the smell of freshly printed pages, the pleasure of cracking open a spine for the first time and delving into the detail of some previously unimagined world. Lately she has been taking pleasure in a new co-worker too, and though she is not yet at the stage where she is able to admit it to herself, it is sometimes to him that her sleepless thoughts have turned.

Trying to catch the non-existent breeze, to garner some energy for the day ahead, Chantal gazes out from her window-seat perch onto the courtyard and the building opposite. She's already seen the silver-haired Frédérique moving around on the first floor. On the fourth, that foul woman has slammed the windows shut again. In the apartment above her own, a baby starts wailing. *Bloody child*, she thinks, as anxious feet hurry across the floorboards overhead, accompanied by the scratchy nails of a fox terrier.

In the courtyard, a small man emerges from the house between the buildings. It is Madame Marin's somewhat unex-pected husband. Unlike his brightly painted, kimono-clad wife, Augusto Marin is a symphony in beige, his beige jumper tucked into beige trousers that are belted high up around his ribcage. He takes a few slow steps into the courtyard, squints up at the sky overhead, and shuffles towards the bins at the back of the building.

'Bonjour, Monsieur Marin!'

It is Chantal's turn to jump now as César has joined her at the window, towel around his waist, copious belly on proud display. The man in the courtyard looks up, wordlessly touches his hand to his forehead and continues on his way, almost bumping into a younger man in a suit who is rushing out of their building towards the street.

'*César!*' Chantal's arms wrap instinctively around herself (she can't remember how see-through this nightdress is). 'Cover yourself up!'

'Don't worry, my love, no one's going to see—'

He stops himself in mid-sentence (a rarity with him).

'What?'

'Look, look!'

She looks, and sure enough, the door onto the street has opened and through it steps Madame Marin.

Chantal need not have worried about the respectability of her nightdress: Madame Marin is squeezed into a neon pink confection as tight as it is bright. The expanse between her painted eyebrows and her thick black polyester lashes is drenched in turquoise, her lips a violent red. She smiles extravagantly at the man in the suit who has, by now, reached the main door.

César and Chantal hold their breath. The feet above them have stopped circling. It is painfully clear that Madame Marin has not been home, that these are last night's stilettos. She takes a few teetering steps, craning her head in search of her husband. But Monsieur Marin is occupied with his bins, and the building takes a collective sigh of relief as his wife totters furtively across the courtyard and into her house.

'Well,' César Vincent says to his wife, 'that was a close shave. How does she do it? He must sleep in the living room.'

Chantal shakes her head. 'She'll get found out one of these days. Everyone always gets found out.'

In spite of the heat, a chill runs across César's shoulders.

Number thirty-seven is laced with ironies. They seep between homes, just as the smells of other people's dinners waft up the stairwells and private sounds escape beneath closed doors. While Chantal sits at the window, grateful that her husband is going to work, the woman in the upstairs apartment wishes that hers had not. It is her baby who has been crying, her business-suited husband careering into Madame Marin in the courtyard.

Mornings are the worst, Anaïs finds. These moments after Paul leaves. The knowledge that it is not even eight o'clock yet and she has twelve hours to get through before he is back, before she has another adult conversation.

Back in the Auvergne, before they moved to the city, she had been a nursery school teacher. *Maîtresse de maternelle.* That title weighs heavily on her now. She can't escape the irony that she had much more patience for other people's children than she does for her own. Much greater maternal instinct. A class of twenty didn't chip away at her identity; they built it up. There were games to be played, songs to be sung, boxes to be ticked, and a neat, tidy, satisfying handover at the end of the day. Her own children seem endless. '*Maman, maman!*' rings deafeningly in her ears around the clock, and lately at night, in her sleepless vigils, she's found herself filling the silence with reminders of who she used to be. Of who she technically still is.

For a few snatched seconds of silence, Anaïs looks down on the pale courtyard – two, three seconds at most – and already, inevitably, there is a crash from the other room, followed by a piercing wail. From his highchair, Louis has sent a cup of milk flying across the floor. Florence has her chubby hands deep in a jar of Nutella. The dog is yapping and the baby cries, the smell of faeces fills the air and the whole circus begins again.

Anaïs doesn't know how or why she keeps herself awake at night. It seems hardly possible that she can manage it. Some days she is so bone-weary that she wonders if she will just stop; if her muscles will fall slack and let her sink to the ground, if she will lie on the rug, dog and children running, crying, crawling, puking in circles around her, her stillness a magnet for them, an anchor.

But even as she wonders, she is walking mechanically into the kitchen. Scolding the dog, her son, her daughter. Wiping everything. Today is not that day, but she fears that it is coming.

Down in the courtyard, the day's waltz begins, paths criss-crossing through space. The residents greet each other in the non-committal singsong *bonjour, bonjour* that rings throughout the building when those who share its proximity meet face to face.

César Vincent trots down the stairs and strides across the courtyard, briefcase swinging confidently from his arm. A tiny old man from the street-front building potters off to play chess in the park. Monsieur Marin drags a deckchair into a patch of sun (he is one who appreciates life's simple pleasures), and Madame Marin is back in her kimono as her clients complain about the heat and the hairdryers start their chorus.

Later, Chantal leaves for the library, heart faintly aflutter at the prospect of encountering Adrien again. She and Frédérique reach the large turquoise door at the same time, for Frédérique has come down to check the street for the homeless Josef.

'Bonjour Madame Vincent.'

'Bonjour Madame Aubry.'

They pause awkwardly in the doorway for a moment, neither willing to be the first to pass. A few false starts, a polite spatter of laughter, and once they're out into the street Chantal remarks to herself, not for the first time, what a pity it is that César and Frédérique knock heads so much. Frédérique, in turn, wishes that Chantal's husband wasn't such a bore. Both are reminded that it would be nice to have a friend in the building.

As Chantal's footsteps recede into the distance, the street falls quiet again. Josef is not here, just the hot and empty concrete. Defeated, Frédérique decides to open up the shop, which is tucked away in the back corner of the courtyard. Today's as good a day as any; she might finally get those catalogues organised, and she'd be out of the glare of this oppressive sun. Crossing the courtyard she glances upwards, and wonders again about Emilie's friend in the attic.

5

He is in the garden and the rain is coming. Dark clouds scud over the hill: there is a stillness to the air, an expectation, yet the leaves shake in the trees, birds ring out an anxious chorus. There are sheets on the line. White. Billowing. He has seen them before, and the figure silhouetted between them, arms loose, adrift on a sea of sails.

'Mum!'

He is shouting, but maybe there is wind after all because the bedsheets are whipping up into angry surf, and he can't hear his voice, the figure doesn't turn. He starts out towards her as the first thunder rumbles up and down the valley, but he is caught in them now, and he is small again, a child tangled in the powder-freshness, choking in linen seahorses, white foam and thunder pulling him down, and all he sees in the twist and sink is his mother's hand rising up, wedding band loose around her skinny finger, and she is clipping a peg together, apart, together, apart, the plastic snapping with thunderous cracks.

Again Edward wakes with a start, his hand flying up to his open mouth. It is light now and hot, his skin damp and adhesive; he has to peel himself off the bedsheets. It takes a moment to locate the noise that's woken him, the peg-cracks of his dream receding as he realises that someone is knocking at the door.

He drags a T-shirt over his head and a hand through sleep-matted hair. As he reaches out to turn the key he remembers, with a sinking stomach, the woman who showed him to the room last night. It was Madame Marin, in a cloud of perfume and leopard print, her hair almost as red as the fingernails that wrapped around his forearm with disconcerting intensity.

The woman standing in the doorway now could not be further from that picture. Tall, thin, a lion's mane of silvery blonde hair that slinks silkily around her neck and gives her an ethereal, otherworldly look. She wears a long white shirt, strings of amber around her neck and turquoise gems on her fingers. Her eyes are the colour of ink.

Smiling, she says something he does not understand.

'Err . . . *pardon?*' His French is rustier than he'd remembered.

'Ah, I'm sorry, Emilie did not tell me you are English.' The woman's voice is soft like butter. 'I'm her aunt, Frédérique.'

'Oh of course, sorry. Edward.' He sticks out a hand in greeting and the corners of her lips turn up at the formality of the gesture. She leans in – a soft *swoosh* of her hair against his ear, the scent of freshly cut grass – and plants a kiss on each of his cheeks.

'This is France, Edward. No handshakes here.'

Her silver bracelets clink as she straightens herself and he recognises the clash and clatter of his friend's limbs, the looseness with which Emilie holds herself. Somehow he's still holding his proffered hand forward and, dropping it too quickly, he becomes acutely aware of his bare legs, his boxer shorts, his embarrassingly knobbly knees.

'I wanted to welcome you,' Frédérique continues, her fingers absentmindedly looping one of her long necklaces, 'to be sure you have found everything.'

It seems to Edward that he's found everything except his voice, because he's nodding long before the 'Yes, thank you' emerges from his mouth.

'I wonder . . .' And again she smiles, a glint in the pool of her dark blue eyes. 'Perhaps you'd like to come to tea. Once you have dressed, that is.'

Sinking into the velvet sofa is like sinking into a different universe – one whose elements are dark wood, the faded scent of incense, the scratch of heavy, expensive material along the backs of his arms. He can hear Frédérique tinkering with tea in another room, the metal chimes of cutlery accompanied by the tinny trills of classical music on a distant radio.

Edward is alone in the *salon* – her word, not his. He might have considered calling it the 'living room' if it had been half this size. It runs the full width of the building: along its length, four windows stand open, their creamy drapes drawn and scuttling against the wooden floor. The walls are cool, somewhere between grey and blue and dust, and the ceiling is a riot of plaster confections.

Frédérique has directed him to the sofa that dominates one half of the room, a great mass of faded blue that both sinks and springs beneath him. He thinks of horsehair, of manes poking up in tufts, and has to check that it is only the thick pile of the velvet that grates against his legs. Around it, a constellation of lesser chairs, a chaise longue in faded floral print and, *everywhere*, books. They line the shelves that run the length of the room behind him, lean in precarious towers against each vertical surface.

At the far end of the room there is a grand dining table. Even in the half-light he can see the wood's gleam, and there are embroidered strings of bells and mirrors gleaming on the walls too. They tinkle gently in the breeze and his eyes are adjusting now; he can make out dark portraits hanging at intervals; great blue and white vases filled with flowers; statues dotted along various surfaces – golden gods and Buddhas, rich and indistinct in the dim light.

Edward runs his hands uneasily along his thighs. He was

not expecting such grand surroundings. Frédérique had told him where to find her – down his staircase, across the court-yard to the first floor of the street-front building – but he hadn't taken her wry dismissal of his room as 'servants quarters' seriously. He's washed since they first met, his feet gingerly sidestepping the grungiest parts of the communal shower, but it is airless even in this huge space and the sweat is beginning to pool behind his knees. He left a trail of wet footprints along his corridor and doesn't want to leave a trail of sweat along these furnishings. He'd been feeling more human in a fresh pair of shorts, the least rumpled T-shirt from his backpack, but worries now that he should have worn a shirt. This room has the air of one that expects buttons.

'Here we are.' Frédérique emerges from a doorway at the other end of the room holding a tray in front of her.

Edward leaps up. 'Can I—'

'Sit, sit.' She waves him down with her head, weaving her way between the piles of books with easy familiarity. The tray is set down on a low stool, and she busies herself pouring tea from a porcelain duck into blue and white cups of different floral patterns.

'You'd like milk, of course.'

It's more statement than question.

'Yes, please.'

Frédérique smiles. 'When I first went to England, it was so *strange* to me, this milk in tea business. Everywhere, every-where –' she's waving her hand now, cup and saucer clinking precariously against each other while Edward holds tight-fingered onto his '– *milk* in the *tea*. It was terrible, I felt sure I could *see* the fat in it! But then,' another smile, one that's half pleased, half sad this time, 'you get a taste for it.'

Her accent is slight, a trace of something sweet draped over her words, and before they even speak of adventure Edward can see her in his mind's eye, running her fingers along the same strings of amber beads on a distant beach at sunset, at dawn in the Himalayas. He is spellbound, and it is only after a moment that he remembers to respond.

'Were you in England a long time?'

'Not a long time, no. I'm a traveller, I always wanted to be off somewhere exciting. India, Tibet, Nepal . . .' If her hands are still, it's her eyes that waver, tracing routes that Edward can't decipher across the room's expanse. 'But English was always much more useful. If you're in a police station in Rajasthan, much better to bribe your way with English than with French.'

She meets Edward's eyes for this last phrase, laughing, and he is unnerved by how easily he can imagine this, as if she brings spice and heat and colour with her on the air.

'But enough of me – what is your story, Edward?'

He loves the French pronunciation; the trace of a third syllable – *Ed-ou-ard* – slipped in and skipped over. But what is his story? Top of his school, prime Oxbridge material everybody said, a sure-fire candidate for success. And he did the exams and got in and went, but somehow all the success he was on his way to hasn't quite arrived yet. The dreaming spires were enchanting, and without his realising it three years stretched quietly into four, five, six, a bit of teaching here, working behind a bar there, and by then his mother was teetering on the brink, his sister . . . He has no idea what his story is, but happily Frédérique presses on.

'Have you travelled? What do you make of Paris so far? Do you know the city?'

He doesn't want to admit that all he's done so far is sleep, that the relief of being here has eclipsed excitement, the urge to wander subsumed by the need to sink into the squeaky bed.

'I have been before.' He's deliberately offhand. 'Schooltrips and stuff. The Eiffel Tower, the Louvre, but,' he shrugs, feeling self-conscious suddenly at how small the circumference of his world has been, 'it'd be nice to see more of the real city.'

This strikes a chord, for immediately Frédérique is off again, arms waving. He sees so much of Emilie in the woman in front of him it's impossible to think that this is her aunt, that she must be twenty years older than him . . .

'You must! And stay, stay as long as you like! Certainly long enough to see the city, not just Notre-Dame and the mobs up in Montmartre; the *real* city, that's exactly it.' Her tea sloshes from side to side while her cup and saucer do loops in front of her. 'People travel now and see nothing, they take photos everywhere and see nothing, don't you think? Of course it's always been a bit like that, all the Americans strolling Saint-Germain and the Seine and saying they've discovered Paris, but now, with all this technology – do you have one of these new phones?'

For once, Edward is grateful for the battered handset on the bedside table. 'No, no I don't.'

'Oh *good*, you're old-fashioned, I'm so pleased! The last time I went to the d'Orsay – nothing but photographs, click, click, click, running from one thing to the next and no one looking at anything except the screen in his hand.' She pauses, fixes her blue eyes on him. 'We all need to learn to look, I think.'

Frédérique certainly has no problem looking. Edward is unnerved by the directness of her gaze. It is intense, expectant, as if waiting for some dazzling statement to leave his lips. He shifts his weight again and, propelled by the heaviness of silent seconds, asks, 'So, you're Emilie's aunt?'

Frédérique leans back on the chaise longue and curls her legs around herself, cat-like. 'She's my favourite niece, I'm her favourite aunt – at least, I hope I am! She spent a lot of time here growing up. Her parents—' she shakes her hand dismissively. 'You've met them?'

'Err . . .'

Edward has met Emilie's parents, remembers the yellow pocket square poking out of her father's shirt, her mother shivering through the damp in a fur coat the day he and Emilie moved into their Oxford college. His own parents had been and gone by then; nervous, proud, 'very impressed, very impressed' as his dad kept saying by the college's welcome, struck dumb at the size of the chapel, the stained glass, the grounds. Emilie's parents had peered into the poky rooms with dismay, her mother declining to look at either Edward or the communal kitchen as if she feared she might catch something. The father was nice enough, genial, chatty, but with a tension in his jaw as if his teeth were permanently on edge.

Was it clear to Edward, even then, how much her parents disliked each other? Or was it later, once they started speaking about it, smoking together over it, all those cigarette butts piling up on the rain-spattered windowsill, trying their best not to set off the fire alarm? It's seven years nearly since that mizzling October day, and his mind is playing tricks on him.

'It's alright, you don't have to be the diplomat with me.' Frédérique's voice reels him back. 'I think Caro's a complete pig, god only knows why he married her.'

'Well,' Edward tries diplomacy anyway, 'everyone has a hard time with their parents, right? I mean, isn't that the point of university?'

'Aha! True. I went to the Sorbonne. It certainly took a lot of effort to persuade my parents to let me live elsewhere. I was the baby of the family, you know how it is.'

Edward does know. A moment passes.

'Did you grow up here?'

'This very apartment.' Her eyes sweep the room, seeing things he doesn't see. 'That's quite extraordinary I think, to still be here. Growing up, we had family living in the same building. Aunts and cousins on the third and fourth floors. If we wanted to play, we'd stick our heads out the windows or shout up the staircases. My aunt, she had a particular tune she'd whistle if she wanted my mother to come up. We had a maid who did for all of us, sleeping where you sleep – I can't believe that now.' She laughs and shakes her head. 'Can you imagine? Mealtimes together. Four, five baguettes at a time, it was us children who fetched them, so many and so long you could hardly hold them climbing up the stairs.' She tucks a strand of silver hair behind her ear. A breath of air drags the curtains across the floorboards. It seems to drag her back to the present with it. 'And your family, Edward? Where are you from? Do you have brothers and sisters?'

Now it is his turn to obfuscate, to look beyond the deep pile of the sofa and the piles of books to see his own ghosts taking shape.

'I grew up in Warwickshire. I mean, it's the countryside. A farm.' A pause. 'My parents still live there.'

Frédérique meets his gaze, and in the quiet moment of it, there is something unspoken between them. And he thinks she understands, this enchanting woman he's never met before, who's talking to him in her second language in the stillness of a hot apartment on a Friday afternoon in Paris. There is the familiarity of loss in her, so real and tangible to him he could almost reach out and touch it.

Somewhere, a door slams. Voices start up in the street below and the spell is broken. Frédérique walks to the window, peers down at the outside world as if looking for something. When she turns back to him her voice is bright, her eyes shining.

'How are you fixed for money, Edward? Perhaps, if you need something from time to time, you might want to work in my shop?'

6

The sun dips down but the heat continues to press on the city. It wraps its fingers around the Parisians and squeezes. Shops have long since sold out of fans and ice-cube trays. No one has much appetite. Produce wilts on market stands up and down the city, and people wilt in their homes, too.

Day and night 'My god, it's only *June*!' echoes in the entryway to the apartment building.

It's too hot to think of anything more exciting to say.

César Vincent sweats gently in his living room, an overripe beetroot. Chantal lies limp across the sofa.

'It's too hot to cook.'

'Too hot to eat.'

Chantal's hand half-heartedly flicks over to the next page of her magazine.

'César?' She scans the page, uninspired by bikinis and push-up swimsuits.

'Yes, love?'

'You haven't mentioned the summer party this year. Is the bank not having one?'

The ice has melted in his drink, but frozen shards seize César's innards. He has been fretting for weeks about the summer party.

'You know, my love,' he stands, draining his glass to hide the tremor in his hand. 'I just don't know. Let me ask Guillaume.' He walks to the sofa and plants a kiss on Chantal's warm forehead. He takes her empty glass and waves it in front of her. 'Another, my dear?'

On the floor above, Anaïs can hear the murmur of the Vincents' voices below. All, for once, is quiet with her. She took the children to the park today and stayed recklessly long, through naptime, through snacktime, the kids too delirious with heat and play to remember their *goûter*, the sticky sweet *pain au chocolat* they smear over their faces each afternoon on the walk home. They are, for once, exhausted. Even the dog has given up, tail hanging limp over the side of his basket.

Anaïs is at the window again. It is late, the sky taking on that luminous aquatic blue she loves, but Paul is not home. Again her fingers grip the windowsill, but it feels tonight that if she lets go she might fall off.

With each exhalation, Anaïs feels her shoulders round, the vertebrae in her back poke out. She does not recognise this body of hers: the hands skinny and raw, the pot of flesh at the belly, the hard sag of unnursed breasts (Parisian women, she has learnt, do *not* breastfeed).

Twenty-five did not feel young when they married. It felt old, actually, compared to some of her friends. It felt like love and adventure and the excitement of moving in together and moving to Paris for Paul's job, of buying toasters and pictures and cutlery together, of finally understanding the metro system, and making picnics to eat beneath the Eiffel Tower on summer nights when he'd tug his tie loose around his neck and drape his suit jacket over her shoulders when, at last, it turned cool.

She knew, she's always known, that Paul was the more religious of the two. Before, in their small town in the Auvergne, she'd always felt that she could live and believe and go to church on Sundays and help out with the church fete, no problem. But Paris is different, and the babies came faster than she was expecting, and Paul says it is a blessing and God's will and she knows somewhere deep inside this alien body that it is true, but if this is bounty she is drowning in it.

Church scares her here. The building is big and dark, the congregation full and anonymous. No one wants to get to know you; there are no church fetes in this city. Though she doesn't say it, she is afraid of the Africans; of the noise, the physicality of their devotion, dark hands beating against their breastbones. She is intimidated by the old Parisian women with their pearls and two-piece suits and tight-lipped disapproval. Once, rocking baby Louis at the back of the service, a homeless man stepped out of the shadows and grabbed her breast. She shrieked, Louis howled, and a hundred pairs of eyes looked disapprovingly over their shoulders while the priest tutted.

Anaïs thinks of that moment when the children claw at her. The homeless man, with his ragged clothes and matted hair, and the face she only remembers as the rotting stench of a toothless mouth. Flesh is flesh to little hands, and they grab without realising, but sometimes she feels under the same attack. She misses agency. Ownership. Her every minute is lived out for other bodies, bodies to be fed, clothed, washed, soothed, while hers aches and bleeds and morphs into some unfamiliar thing, a loose skin she wants to slough off, and there's no one there to soothe her.

The clock strikes nine, and still Paul is not here because he is there, in the cloying, candlelit, incense-darkness of the church, talking Judea, Bethlehem, Galilee. A privileged male circle of study outside of time and space, absorbed in their truth, their faith, unheeding as the city, which could not care less about their devotion, roars on around them.

Above her, heavy feet plod from one end of the apartment to the other. She has no idea to whom they belong.

Three years, and Anaïs still doesn't know how many people live in this building. She is unanchored by its proximity, adrift amongst the density of lives packed into such minutely measured square-metreage. Having grown up in a house, in a field, where birds or hay-rumpled cows lowing their way in from pasture told the hours, she is unnerved by the contingency of this home. How each wall touches someone else's. And how she doesn't know who that someone is.

Downstairs the Vincents laugh. Someone across the courtyard is watching television; she can see the blue light dancing across their ceiling. 'You're tired, you're just tired,' she murmurs to herself, the same consolation she offers the kids, because tears are pricking behind her eyes now, looking out on the dark building opposite and all the little traces of life in it – the shadow of someone walking across a room, the glimmer of a hallway light, curtains being drawn for the night – and it is there, in all its richness, and she is here, just metres away, and she has never felt more alone.

As a single tear trembles over and slips down her cheek, a woman appears in a window opposite. It is Frédérique, though Anaïs doesn't know that. She knows her only as Madame Aubry who waves at her sometimes as she passes the shop on the ground floor; who smiles politely enough at Anaïs but whose eyes stare at the children with a strange, haunted longing. Now the two women stare at each other. Frédérique has a telephone to her ear, is murmuring something to some distant someone, but their eyes are locked and Anaïs feels she could almost reach out across the dark courtyard, almost touch the older woman's hand, stroke the smooth skin of her cheek and find an ally in the blue night.

But suddenly the dog is lifting his head in the direction of the door, whimpering loudly. Reluctantly Anaïs tears her gaze away from the window.

'What is it, Beau?'

The dog is not jumping out of his basket, tail wagging, little feet scrabbling in the race to the door as he does when Paul comes home. Instead he cowers in his basket, one paw over his nose as if in hiding, a low plaintive wail rumbling from his mouth. Anaïs steps tentatively towards the door. Sure enough she can hear someone outside. Without thinking, she opens it.

There is a woman on the landing. Anaïs has not seen her before, but that doesn't mean anything in this city. The woman is young, maybe twenty, twenty-two. Her pale brown hair falls in a cascade around her shoulder. Its long ends dance along the landing's balustrade, against which she taps out a soft rhythm with her hand.

'Oh, sorry,' Anaïs says automatically, as if she is interrupting some private reverie. But the woman does not look around. She continues her slow ascent up the spiralling staircase, the fingers of her right hand tapping as she goes. It is only as she disappears around the corner that she flashes Anaïs a brief, sad smile.

Anaïs remains rooted to the spot, the air around her thick with reverberations that hum just below her ears' reach. Who was that woman? What did her smile mean? She is still standing there when Paul bounds, hot and breathless, up the stairs.

'Hello, what are you doing here?'

'Oh, nothing. There was a woman, I thought she was knocking but she went upstairs . . .'

Paul gives her a peck on the cheek in passing, paying little heed to this story, his tall frame filling the doorway. His hair is newly shorn, buzzed, the way she used to like running her hand across it. Anaïs closes the door, giving one last glance at the now-silent hallway.

'My word, it is *hot*.' Paul sits to unlace his shoes. There are shadows beneath his dark eyes and the smell of sweat wafts in with him. She can see the yellow-grey grime of summer along the inside of his collar.

'Kids asleep?'

'Yes.'

'Good day?'

What can she say? 'Yes.'

'Good-oh.' He tears the end off the baguette he's been carrying under his arm. 'I'm ravenous – got the last baguette, too.' Such triumph in his voice. 'Any idea on dinner?'

'No. Sorry. The kids, the heat . . .' She feels her voice trailing away. It never used to be weak like this.

'Not to worry.' He smiles, pulling the cork from a bottle on the counter top. 'I'm sure we can throw something together.'

Sinking into a seat, into the smooth Burgundy he's just poured, Anaïs knows she should be grateful for this man. For his cheeriness, his enthusiasm. She watches him pad around the kitchen in his socks, leaving wet traces of feet across the tiles, telling her about his day, the office, the smashing Bible study group, what he's going to concoct out of two slices of ham, a beef tomato, and some goats cheese.

'You're tired, you're just tired,' she tells herself.

But she feels nothing. Even as she sits there, she feels herself becoming more distant, drawing in, contracting; as if she might rise up out of the window and float above the rooftops, above these dividing walls, looking down on herself and her husband and the dinner they are eating, on the dog in his basket and the kids in their beds, on all these people living happily ever after, and that mysterious woman still in her mind, trailing her way up the staircase to the attic apartments.

7

'I don't know what to make of your young man.'

It is evening, but the air feels no lighter. Frédérique reaches for the cloudy glass of pastis at her side. Rolls the sharp aniseed of it around her mouth. Waits for the ice to cool her.

'He's not my young man, Freddie!'

'He's nice.'

Frédérique moves to the mirror above the fireplace. She has kept her old telephone; long, looping cord, solid body that can be carried from room to room like a rigid little handbag. She clamps the heavy handset between her ear and shoulder.

'He's just a friend!'

She can hear her niece's exasperation and raises an eyebrow at herself in the mirror. Oh, the childhood hours spent trying to do that, standing on chairs, on tiptoes, desperately seeking that sophisticated arch, pudgy fingers pressed against the glass, hot child's breath fogging up the mirror.

'He's not there to see *me*, he's there because he needs a break. I told him you wouldn't even be there – you're not inviting him to things, are you?'

'One cup of tea—'

Emilie groans.

'One cup of tea! I saw him slope in last night, looking completely bewildered, then I got your message and thought it only polite to introduce myself.' She reaches for her cigarettes, lights up. 'He looks to me in need of a good meal.'

Actually, she thinks as she inhales, the thing he most looked was lost. Not in the geographic sense, the fish-out-of-water sense, but deeply, profoundly lost. She exhales, menthol looping its way across the room in front of her. She could swear she hears the same lighter's click at the other end of the line, the same intake, release.

'You're not smoking again, are you Freddie?' Emilie gets her question in first.

'I'm too old to stop, love. You're too young to start.'

'Young!'

'Young to me.' At both ends, the same simultaneous drag and exhale. 'So, this *young man*—'

'Freddie!'

'Sorry, sorry, this friend—'

'You can call him Edward.'

'Ok, Edward—'

'I'd have thought you'd have been on first name terms by now, if you've had him in for tea. I'm surprised you haven't got him in the shop and coming round to dinner.'

A pause. At both ends, long hair tucked behind ears, these strands silver, those strands gold.

'Freddie, you haven't!'

'I just said he might like to help out if he needed some spare cash.'

'You don't have any spare cash.'

'Anyway,' another drag exhaled over her shoulder, as if, across hundreds of miles, her niece might smell it. 'When are you coming over?'

'Soon, I really hope soon, but Simon's doing something in Italy, I have to see Papa at some point when he's back in London, but then if I come to Paris there's my bloody mother. Classes are *awful* right now, the end of term can't come soon enough, but . . .'

Returning to the chaise longue, Frédérique lets her witter on. It is strange to her to think of Emilie as a teacher. Dreamy, well-spoken Emilie, with the French accent on her English and the English on her French, brought up between different cities, between parents who refused to divorce, refused to live

39

in the same country, not even teaching languages but drama to a group of inner-city teenagers who couldn't care less and then meandering her way around London to auditions every other waking moment.

'Have you ever had something like that?'

Frédérique has not been listening, but she covers it. 'Mmmm. It was all such a long time ago, love.'

The chaise is so comfortable, so exactly moulded to her form. Her eyes are heavy, her legs throbbing. She forgets, sometimes, that she is old. Old*er*. That the heat takes it out of her now. Having Edward over was such a rush, showing him the shop, gossiping about the building. She loves new people. Lanky, she thinks. Hungry, but not just for food. There's something else there, too. Something in him unful-filled, she thought she'd caught a glimpse of it. *But you're making this up, dear. It was one cup of tea . . .*

'. . . and then he bolted.'

'What?'

She hadn't realised she'd said the words. 'Sorry, my love. I was thinking about your friend. Edward. Is he . . . alright?'

Emilie pauses. 'I don't know. His family . . . There was an accident. His sister. A traffic accident and he was there, and they couldn't save her. Awful, so awful.'

Frédérique wanders into her bedroom and surveys the courtyard from the window. *So that's it,* she thinks, sprinkling ash onto the windowsill. *That's what I recognise in you.*

The building opposite is disappearing in the gathering dark, squares of yellow light against the gloom. She can't see up to Edward's room. Faint music spills out of someone's apart-ment. At a window, that woman with the children appears. *Anaïs,* she chides herself. *You know she's called Anaïs.* But Frédérique also knows that she cannot bear to be around those children, that every time their paths cross in the court-yard or in the street her heart contracts and it is too painful to say hello, even to smile sometimes, though Anaïs seems far from happy. Far from happy, tonight, as they stare at each other across the expanse of courtyard.

'Are you alright, Freddie?' Emilie sounds concerned. Perhaps she's been talking and Frédérique has missed it again.

'Yes, yes.' She leaves the bedroom window, and back in the living room the ice in her pastis has melted, wet drops all down the side of the glass onto the wooden side table. *Shit*. 'He's welcome to stay as long as he wants, your friend.'

'Thanks, Freddie. I'll let you go.' Still faintly worried. 'You're sure you're ok?'

'I'm fine, love. A big kiss to you.'

'Kisses to you! Speak soon.'

Frédérique lets the handset fall onto her lap. She is still for a moment, listening. The music plays. Chairs scrape on the floor upstairs. A motorbike pulls up in the street. Reaching for the pastis, the wet glass slips through her fingers and rolls heavily across the floor.

8

As his first day in the city draws to a close, Edward is also rolling a glass around, though his has so far stayed in his hand. He is sitting in the corner of a bar he doesn't know. He doesn't 'know' any bars in Paris, but he has absolutely no idea where this one is.

He has been walking for hours. Moving heedless through space. When he left Frédérique, he walked out of the building, turned left and just kept going. He feels bad now about how abrupt he was.

Her shop was magical, full of art books. He loved it, loved the heavy smell of dust in the air, the gorgeous illustrations glinting jewel-like in the half-dark, and he'd loved talking to her and looking at what she was showing him and he'd never seen an Ingres before, and then suddenly, out of nowhere, a portrait that looked so much like his sister it was as if someone had smacked a club into his knees. He stumbled and made his excuses and left and walked, walked down streets filled with pale-cream buildings, down streets crowded with shops and shoppers, down a boulevard wide and tree-lined, marked by the steady *whoosh* of traffic.

Eventually – and he has no sense of time, other than an ache in his legs and the way the sky has slipped from blue to milk – he found himself outside this bar. It seems pretty typical: too many tables, too close together, and a metal countertop behind which the waitress ducks to pour wine out of cardboard boxes. It's shabby and cheap, but for two euros a glass the red's not bad. He's on his third and, box or no box, it's lining his stomach like velvet.

The doors are flung open but still the bar is airless, thick with heat and sweat and conversation. Edward can make out very little beyond the occasional *bah non!* or *putain!* as a glass is slammed down on a table or a hand clapped to an astonished mouth. It makes little difference what's going on around him; the words he said to his dad are circling deafeningly around his head. He's been trying to drown them out, to walk far enough or fast enough or somewhere new enough that he didn't have to hear them, but it hasn't worked. He can still see his father in front of him. His mind has fixed in slow motion the way the brown eyes smarted behind their smudged glasses, the way his father turned from him, crumpled a little. He did not make a sound, and Edward's words were left to ring in the silent room.

That's when he rang Emilie. When she told him to use the apartment. It's one of the things he appreciates most about her – that she's never asked about it. Never asked what it's like to have a sister die, or to have a mother who's spent years dancing on the edges of dementia slide down the rabbit hole. What it's like to be left with a father so totally consumed with grief for both that he can do nothing but put a brave face on it and smile and act normal and ask 'Who wants baked beans for tea?' like he did when they were kids, as if nothing has happened, until you just want to scream at him.

Which is what Edward did. Which is what broke the camel's back. It's why he's here, hiding from himself in the corner of a bar in a city he's visited once before, and this neighbourhood, with the man lying outside in a pool of his own piss and an entire Roma family camped out on a mattress on the pavement – this is no Eiffel Tower.

Edward gets up in search of another glass and feels the wine settle behind his knees. A girl appears next to him as he waits. He catches her reflection in the mirror opposite. She's very pretty, her fingers stacked with silver rings, painted red nails bitten to the quick, and when the barman arrives

43

she pushes herself up to the counter to kiss his cheeks. They speak in rapid bursts, in French that Edward cannot follow. The man behind the bar starts pouring. The girl laughs. Eventually the barman turns his attention to Edward.

'A glass of red, please.' Edward's French is faltering.

The barman grunts and heads towards the storeroom.

'You should really ask for the Morgon.'

Edward turns and finds that the girl has turned her attention to him. Up close her eyes are startling, cat-like and green. They stare out at him from under thick black lashes.

'Sorry?'

She switches from French to English. 'I said, next time you should ask for the Morgon. At least it comes in a bottle.'

'Oh, thanks.'

'Better than the piss they squeeze out of the boxes.'

Her accent lends her vowels a sultry flatness; 'piss' becomes '*peees*' and exaggerates her red lips. Or maybe he was just looking at her lips already? Edward tries to think of something to say, but she gets in first.

'You're visiting? Just moved here?'

'Err, both?' He makes a face and laughs awkwardly. 'Staying for a while, somewhere—' he gestures, realising he doesn't know where, exactly. Luckily the barman returns, slamming two glasses down in front of them.

'Arnaud' – the girl taps him on the arm as he turns towards the till. She nods her head at Edward. He hears the word 'Morgon' and, sure enough, his glass is being replaced with an empty one and wine from a bottle poured in when a volley of shouts starts up in the corner.

A roomful of heads swivel in the direction of the noise. Two men are standing up behind a table, gesticulating wildly at a small mousey man in a checked shirt who's trying to make his way to the bar. The men are young and tall, shouting and flinging violent gestures. The other man is much older, diminutive; half-cowering from their shouts yet still determinedly forging his way towards the counter with what looks like a pile of leaflets in his trembling hand.

'*Merde.*' To Edward's astonishment the barman hauls himself up over the bar and bounds into the fray.

'What's going on?' Edward asks, but his question goes unanswered. Other people are joining in now, their shouts and jeers escalating as the barman pushes his way through the mass of bodies. The mousey man, whose wire-framed glasses are slipping sweatily down his nose, is jostled in a sea of limbs. He tries to hand out his leaflets but the voices around him rise to fever pitch, an arm reaching out of the crowd to push at him, another pulling at his lanky hair.

Finally the barman is in front of the altercation, and like everybody else Edward's eyes are glued to the scene as they argue, a brief and heated dispute. The crowd roars, baying for blood now, as the towering Arnaud grabs the older man by the shirt collar and hustles him towards the door. An appreciative cheer rockets around the room, a communal release, a moment of mutual back-patting. Everyone seems to feel that justice has been done, yet to Edward it's the underdog who lost this fight. His fingers grip the clammy bar uneasily, freshly aware of how out of place he is.

Arnaud reappears, parting the sea of drinkers again, sliding back beneath the bar to his post. As he finishes pouring Edward's drink he slams down a handful of leaflets snatched from the man's hands. The girl next to Edward leans forward to pick one up.

'What is it?' he asks.

She scans the paper, a deep frown folded across her face. 'The Front National. The Far Right.'

Edward just glimpses the words *ARABES* and *IMMIGRÉS* in large red letters before she crumples the paper in her hand. She lifts her glass with sarcastic cheer. 'Welcome to France.'

He touches his glass to hers. 'What's your name?'

'Charlotte.'

'I'm Edward.'

'Nice to meet you, Edward. What a welcome.'

In the alternate reality in his head where he is bold and brave, Edward says something witty or charming or both. He makes her laugh, then asks where she's from, what she does, and he is so fascinated and fascinating that she spends the rest of the evening talking to him and lets him lose himself in those green eyes. But in truth, he is tall and clumsy, too shy to let words escape his lips without thinking about them first. He stands awkwardly at the bar, filled with something that feels like loss as she walks away from him back to her friends. They're the ones who stood up shouting, just as loud now as they relive and recount the previous moment's drama. How many times has he been in a group like that? At home, at university . . . Today that camaraderie could not feel further away.

The bar is filling up again as people forget the incident and turn back to their drinks, the noise crescendoing to a heady peak. Someone has taken his table, so Edward drinks his glass (which does taste better than the other stuff) alone, squeezed awkwardly between someone's sharp elbow and someone else's muscled back.

Outside, night is falling, tightening its drawstrings around this exhilarating, disorienting day. Edward walks until he finds a map, realises that he is, by some circuitous logic, almost back where he started. *Rue des Eglantines*.

He is almost back at the apartment when he notices a faint light in the otherwise dark street. It is in the doorway opposite his own. There, by candlelight, a middle-aged man is lowering eggs into a kettle that he's plugged into an external power socket. Next to him, a metal trolley, a corner of tarpaulin folded back to reveal a world of meticulously organised possessions.

'Good evening.' The man looks up to greet Edward, one eye sliding gently to the right.

'Good evening, monsieur.'

'Go carefully,' the man cautions, dropping a third egg into the boiling water. His words resonate in the darkness around them.

By the time Edward has climbed the five flights of stairs and lain down on the small bed, he is no longer toying with the lines he could have used to persuade that girl to come back with him. Exhaustion washes over him, and he thinks of home, the smell of his bedroom there, the birds cooing outside the window. He thinks of his parents padding around in their matching slippers; the gentle murmur of the television, the smell of his dad burning toast. His sister's room with all her things, and the dent in the pillow that cracked his heart when he realised that one of his parents had been pressing their head into it.

This day and everything that has led up to it swells in his chest, a tight, suffocating bubble against which he is fighting, scrapping for breath. Yet even as he does he is already slipping into sleep, and it is only in his last moment of wakefulness that he realises there are tears sliding quietly down his cheeks.

9

César is exceedingly precise. He will tie his tie four times to achieve the perfect knot, to be certain that its fall is perpendicular. His shirts are always crisp, his shoes buffed to a high shine. His clothes are performative: with the stiff, structured shoulders of his suit, the clasp of its buttons pulling his stomach in, he is every inch the businessman.

'Goodbye, my love.' He leans over to kiss the nape of Chantal's neck. Still damp, the taste of sweat lingers on his lips.

She turns to him. 'No breakfast, love?'

'No, no, a big meeting with Guillaume this morning. I mustn't be late.'

'A meeting?' Chantal turns and looks at him quizzically.

César feels panic rising in him as surely as he feels a red flush creep up his neck.

'Yes, love?' A hint of uncertainty leaves his words teetering between question and statement.

Chantal lowers her newspaper and looks over her glasses at him. 'On a Saturday?'

Fuck. It's Saturday.

Every weekday for the last twenty-five years, César has marched to the metro, greeting the greengrocer, the café owner, the car mechanic on his way (two and a half decades have built a familiar camaraderie into this morning walk). He has descended into the metro, its air close and sticky, sickening proximity clinging to hair and skin. Without fail, the platform has smelt of urine and without fail César has joined the other early-morning commuters in wrinkling his

48

nose if a homeless person ambles past. Every day, he has followed his corporate comrades into the train, an army of navy, black and pinstripe. He has sympathised with the general malaise, partaken in the widespread loosening of collars, the ineffectual fanning with the morning's newspaper.

For twenty-five years, he has changed trains at Châtelet. It's a dog of a station, an impossible, inexplicable warren of tunnels and travelators that, in his experience, take you from somewhere you didn't know you were to somewhere you didn't want to be, without any sign of the destination you might be looking for. It is a station he knows by rote, by the methodical plodding from one train to the next.

For the last few months, however, when his pinstripe-suited, briefcase-wielding companions have turned left in the direction of the business district at La Défense, César has turned right. The trains on this side of the track are far emptier. They chug out past Bastille, out to the very edges of the city.

In recent weeks, he has taken the train to the end of the line, one of only two or three to head out onto the street. Always, the station is busy with people walking in the opposite direction headed to work, to desks, to jobs. César does not head that way.

He was laid off nearly five months ago. *The recession, tightening our belts*, the obnoxious, oleaginous Guillaume had said, pouting his lips in imitation of sadness. Guillaume who is twenty years his junior, Guillaume who knows nothing of what César knows of the company, Guillaume with his motorbike and his drainpipe suits who has worked at the bank for all of five minutes. Guillaume who thinks César is stupid enough to buy the recession as an excuse.

So for the past twenty-one weeks, César has got up, got dressed, arranged his papers in his briefcase, put on his freshly ironed shirt and his polished shoes, kissed Chantal goodbye and travelled to work.

But it is not work. It is a non-descript café near the Château de Vincennes. He chose it because it is far enough from the city centre, from anyone who might know him. Here, under the waitress's blank-eyed stare, he has whiled away cup after oily cup of coffee. He has taken brisk walks around the park after lunch. He has read the newspaper. And he has counted down the minutes until he can make this clandestine journey in reverse and return to the apartment and tell his wife about his fictitious day.

Now, he has tripped up. It's Saturday.

'*César?*' Chantal looks worried. 'Are you alright?'

César is not. His mind has frozen. All the lies, all the stories, all the little details to make it convincing, and now his brain is bare and quiet as Arctic ice. He can hear the floes creak.

'*César!*'

His wife's voice pulls him back, to the kitchen, the cool tiles underfoot, the closeness of this summer morning. He pulls out a chair and drops heavily into it.

'Sorry, sorry, my love.' There's a shake to his voice that he strives to control. 'I've just been so worried about this meeting, I—somehow I thought it was Monday.' He gives a little laugh, looking up nervously to see if she has bought this.

His lovely wife. Those dark brown eyes, he'd fallen for those before they'd spoken two words to each other. Her chestnut hair in wide curls, salt and pepper now; the laughter lines he's seen creep silently across her skin, taut not with laughter this morning but with concern.

'Well,' she reaches her hand across to his and clasps it, 'at least you'll be doubly ready come Monday, eh?'

'Yes, there's that.'

César smiles and Chantal smiles, but hers does not mask the concern below. He wonders what she discerns in his.

'Well,' he smacks his palms down on his thighs, 'can't waste the whole day, can we? Can't waste a Saturday! Why don't I get changed and we can go to the market together?'

'Lovely.' Chantal returns to her coffee and her newspaper, stretching out her toes on his newly empty chair.

He is halfway down the hallway when she calls to him. 'César?'

'Yes, my love?'

'Don't forget your briefcase.'

He gives a wan smile and returns the briefcase to its stand in the bedroom.

Alone in the kitchen, Chantal sighs and takes another sip of coffee. She has never been a morning person and hot flushes don't mix well with sweltering nights, but something about this incident rings very wrong. For César to get confused like that – her César, who's always been so orderly and organised, always waiting for her to get ready, always rolling his eyes when she forgets things or mislays them and never doing it himself; César who loudly laments the jumble of books and magazines and bedsocks on her side of the bed as he regimentally straightens the objects on his own nightstand until they're perfectly parallel. To mistake a *meeting* – it's so unlike him. Chantal wonders briefly if his mind might be going, but that is too big a precipice to tumble over on a Saturday morning so she pushes the thought from hers.

Something has been different lately though, but she can't put her finger on it. *Age?* His birthday is approaching, but fifty-one is hardly a major milestone. Any wobbles would surely have made themselves manifest last year? Although last summer was a strange one. César's mother had gone into decline, so they were spending every weekend up on the Belgian coast, first with her in the home, radiators blasting heat and amplifying the smell of urine, then clearing out her house. Damp picnics overlooking the grey sea. Coffee in a thermos, shared under a blanket. Thick slices of ham in fresh baguettes.

There in the family beach hut, in moderate drizzle, they'd

saluted César's half century, champagne fizzing in plastic cups, and they'd said what they were grateful for. Good jobs, good home, good marriage. It *is* a good marriage. Close, companionable, affectionate. They hold hands in public, they still make love, if not with the zealous regularity of their youth. Chantal knows from her friends that to live with someone all these years and not to become bitter or unfaithful or bored is an extraordinary thing.

Her fleeting thoughts about Adrien do nothing to shake Chantal's opinion on this, for she has a strict understanding of the boundary between imagination and reality; that is not something she would ever act on. She has received offers, over the years, inevitably from men who should have known better – once even from a friend's husband – and while she's enjoyed the flirtation, the thrill in the pit of her stomach, the re-assurance that she is still attractive, she has always recoiled in horror at the actual proposition, slipping home and into bed with César and always, unshakably, happy to be there. Her César – precise, predictable, dependable César.

And yet, there is this difference. This change she cannot identify. It worries her, places its grip at the base of her skull and, alone at the kitchen table, she shivers, shaking her head as if to shake it off.

Still, she thinks as she straightens the newspaper, she is organising a birthday party for him this year. Drinks, friends, music – everything that should have happened last year. Perhaps that will cheer him up. Though, now she thinks about it, she'd better get in touch with Guillaume and some of César's work colleagues. And badger the stationer about the invitations.

Oh, the invitations. Finest Italian paper, deep cream, so substantial between thumb and forefinger that each sheet seemed to hold a miniature landscape of hills and valleys. Blue edging, sharp but with 'a touch of dynamism' (the stationer's phrase). A calligrapher hired to write the names and then the menus in elegant scrolls. Chantal spent an enchanted hour making her decisions, and has passed many a moment since reflecting on how marvellous the invitations will be, how marvellous the party will be, with its cocktails, canapés, all their friends grouped around them, César speechless and moist-eyed as she makes her speech and raises her glass to him . . .

'Ready, my love!' César reappears in the doorway in his weekend clothes (still starched, still crisp).

'Coming, sweetheart. Now,' Chantal digs her feet under the table in search of her sandals, 'where did I put my bag?'

Real-life César rolls his eyes, which aren't in the least bit misty, back to his usual self. Chantal rootles around the bedroom to the sound of her husband's percussive tuts. Everything as normal, everything as it should be. In time, of course, the bag is located, as it always is, and they walk down the stairs together, crossing the courtyard hand in hand.

Down in the courtyard, Edward watches them pass. First husband and then wife raise their hands in greeting.

'Bonjour!'

'Bonjour Monsieur.'

'Bonjour!'

'Bonjour Madame.'

They could not look more French; the wife in a blue-and-white striped dress, fresh from a Breton beach, the husband in those dusky pink trousers that only European men wear, a wicker basket on his arm. Edward wonders if they wonder what he's doing in the courtyard. (Indeed, as the turquoise door to the street slams behind them, Chantal turns to César in a conspiratorial whisper: 'I wonder who *that* was?')

Edward is loitering in the courtyard outside Frédérique's shop, though it is not a shop in the normal sense of the word. It sits across the courtyard at the bottom of the back building. There's no sign on the door, no sign on the street, no way to get into the courtyard unless you know the entry code. You have to *know* the shop is there. In the time that he's been waiting Edward has wondered how this secrecy affects business, but there is something so magical and otherworldly about Frédérique that it doesn't seem to matter.

Edward waits. He hears a clock strike a quarter hour. Waits longer, and soon enough it is rounding out ten o'clock. There is no sign of Frédérique.

A little man in beige and bifocals walks slowly out of the courtyard house to the back of the building. So unlike the coiffed, perfumed, leopard-printed lady who showed him in, Edward does not realise that it's Madame Marin's husband. Somewhere a tap is turned on and soon water is trickling back into the courtyard as Monsieur Marin hoses his bins.

'Arrête, *ar-rê-te*!' A harassed looking woman emerges from Edward's building with three small children, one under each arm and another throwing a tantrum behind. Its nasal wail reverberates off the stone as the woman marches the troop of them out into the street. Up above, a window closes, a radio plays, and somewhere someone's phone starts ringing. Still no sign.

Eventually, Edward walks over to the street-front building, where the entryway proudly reads 'B. . .TIMENT A.' The first A is missing, its ghost etched in dirt against the paint-work. Edward wonders about buzzing – a list of tightly calligraphic names accompanies a strip of silver buttons – but it turns out the door to Bâtiment A is no more secure than that to Bâtiment B and that, for all three signs reminding residents to *please keep the door locked*, it opens with a push. Edward enters and climbs the stairs.

Even as his knuckles make contact with the wood of Frédérique's door, he feels like an idiot. What was he planning on saying anyway?

The door swings open, and Frédérique appears in a loose cotton dress, her hair swept up in a magenta towel into a tall pink turban. She looks like a priestess or some fantastical queen.

'Edward!' She looks delighted.

'Morning, I—' he shifts his weight. 'I wanted to apologise for yesterday. For leaving so quickly. The shop's beautiful . . .' He falters a little. 'I'd love to help out. If you still need someone, I mean.'

She looks at him for a moment. There is something so familiar in it, a distant sadness in the lines around her eyes. She smiles.

'How lovely! I wasn't really thinking of opening today . . .' She searches for a clock. 'What time is it? Oh well. If you're here . . . I'll make us some coffee.'

Edward quickly learns that there is nothing organised or orthodox about Frédérique's shop. It is an Aladdin's cave, its books jewels amongst rubble. Dusty, battered and piled thigh-high, he opens them at random to medieval stained glass; Byzantine icons in blue and gold; eighteenth-century minia-tures, their faces so filigree-fine he can see each eyelash, count the dot of every freckle. He's never thought much about art before but Frédérique's books mesmerise him.

Business is sporadic to say the least. It's an almost exclu-sively male clientele: old men shuffling through in moth-eaten cardigans, young men ('young' by dint of being less than seventy) also in cardigans, also shuffling.

'*Art historians*,' Frédérique tells him in a loud theatrical whisper, eyebrow raised.

And yes, Edward recognises it now. These men have the academic's grey pallor, the stiff limbs, the look of mild surprise at being outside the library's confines. They blink, unaccustomed to brightness, even in the courtyard's dim light.

That first day he ventured into the shop to help, Edward worried that he wouldn't know where anything was, how to answer questions in French, how to work the till. In the end, it doesn't matter, because no one ever buys anything in Frédérique's, and no one speaks, save Frédérique herself, greeting one customer a day like an old friend on an egali-tarian and rotating basis. It's '*Ah, Clément!*' on a given after-noon, while Gilles stands jealously to one side with a catalogue of Flemish painting. The next day '*Ah, Gilles!*' while Clément glowers over a Delacroix.

Out of place and out of time, some days there are no customers at all, and Edward and Frédérique read in compan-ionable silence. They keep the door open, raising their heads every time anyone emerges from the buildings, and Frédérique peppers the quiet with gossip about the neighbours.

'Poor woman.'

Anaïs is dragging her children across the courtyard again. The two oldest, refusing to walk, set up an orchestra of wails. There has been no let-up in the heat, though there are thick clouds strewn across the sky. If anything they make it worse, pressing down on the breathless city.

'Is she on her own?' Edward asks, looking up from a study on Impressionism.

Frédérique is by the window, a book clasped between her arms. She rocks her weight gently from hip to hip, eyes fixed on the courtyard scene.

'No, but she might as well be. He's hardly ever around, the father. I mean, just look at her. She could break at any moment.'

Edward joins her at the window and it's true, the woman in the courtyard is too frail for her years. She can only be a little older than him, yet the furrows are ploughed deep across her forehead; her clothes hang limp from her gaunt frame.

'Uh oh.' Frédérique whistles below her breath as Madame Marin appears from her salon. In a lime-green dress and sea-green eye shadow, the *gardienne* looks like a lizard today, as if a scrolled tongue might dart out between her lips at any moment.

'Hello my loves, hello my little cabbage!'

The painted fingernails reach out towards the children and the crying escalates. The eldest girl darts back behind her mother, while her brother is scooped up in Madame Marin's arms.

'Oh there there my love, my heart. Coucoucou!'

Edward wishes he had a camera; this scene would make a fantastic photo. Madame Marin's painted face distorts into all kinds of grins and gurns as the little boy throws his head back and screams harder, trying to pull his mouth wider than hers.

'Poor kid.'

Frédérique raises an eyebrow. 'Yes, I'm not convinced that's going to help.'

Undeterred, Madame Marin is now bouncing the flailing knot of limbs up and down, trotting around the courtyard. 'Isn't your papa a naughty boy for leaving mama alone so often?' She grins at Anaïs through bared teeth. Anaïs turns very pale.

'Oh god.'

'What?' Edward has understood the gist but not the detail. 'What did she say?'

'She's implying the husband's got other women.' Frédérique reaches for her cigarettes. Edward pulls out his lighter.

'Really?'

'Between the lines.'

'But didn't you say—?'

'I wouldn't say it to her!' They light up and exhale simultaneously. 'Isn't it funny how we put our own stories onto other people? Besides, I don't think he's out philandering.'

Edward loves that such quirky, precise words trip so easily off Frédérique's tongue.

'What, then?'

But Frédérique just nods and they turn their eyes back to the drama.

Anaïs is trying to extricate her son from Madame Marin's grasp. 'My husband works very hard, Madame Marin.' Her voice is reedy thin above the wails of her children. 'With his church commitments too, he's a very busy man.'

'Interesting,' Frédérique murmurs, one eyebrow raised.

'What?'

'She said they're church people. I had wondered. So *that's* where he spends his time.'

As she says this, a third woman appears in the doorway

to Bâtiment A. Edward hasn't seen her before. She is about forty, dumpy, with dark, straight hair and a mouth puckered like a cat's arse. Her whole face is clenched into a scowl.

'Excuse me?'

The woman hugs her elbows closely, the end of her long nose curling down towards her lipless mouth.

'I have a headache. I would appreciate it if you kept the noise down.'

Even the babies pause for breath. A chill passes across the courtyard and colour flares in Anaïs's cheeks. Madame Marin's are too thickly painted for Edward to see if she blushes, but she cocks one eyebrow and runs her eyes damningly over the woman's lumpish form.

'Oh yes, *of course*, Madame Duval.' Madame Marin sneers too, pulling her lips back to expose her pale pink gums. '*So sorry.*'

The courtyard crowd dissipates. 'Who was that?' Edward asks, returning to the counter, to his half-drunk cup of coffee and the Impressionist exhibition of 1874.

Frédérique sighs and turns back to the books she is half-heartedly sorting from one pile to another. He watches her fingers trail over their covers: an infant Jesus, a Madonna and Child.

'Isabelle Duval. Fourth floor. Bitch.'

There are many episodes like this – Edward and Frédérique standing at the shop's window or in its doorway, smoking their cigarettes to the rhythm of number thirty-seven's life and Frédérique's low-voiced commentary on the residents around them. Edward knows little about her, but he can recite her dramatic accounts of the building by heart. He knows that the little old man on the top floor is shrouded in mystery, that Madame Marin has much-talked-of affairs.

'Strange, though, because I do think she loves that husband of hers, beige as he is.'

'That's her *husband*?'

'Oh yes, didn't you know?'

'No, I mean, I, I didn't think about it. He's just so . . .'

'Beige?'

'Yes, beige. Does he know? Does he mind?'

'Who knows? He's after the quiet life, she wants a bit of excitement – who's to say it doesn't work for them?'

Very occasionally one of the residents will actually cross the sacred threshold, like when Monsieur Vincent bounded in, briefcase swinging wildly between stacks of books, booming over everything Edward said (or tried to say) during their introduction and instead giving a potted history of the building and his role as President of the Residents' Cooperative.

'So any time, Edmond—'

'Edward.'

'Yes, Edmond – any time you have any questions about the building, about anything to do with facilities or procedure, you can come to me. That's what the office of the President of the Residents' Cooperative is for.'

By the end of Edward's first week working there (though it's not really working and Frédérique's hours are too irregular for it to count as a full week), he feels he has a sense of most of the building's comings and goings; has absorbed the idiosyncrasies and rhythms that pattern its days.

It is a Friday afternoon and hotter than ever. Even the plants in the courtyard have given up and keeled over, leaves curling in the heat. Edward is alone in the shop, save Gilles tucked away in the corner. He has just watched Chantal Vincent return home with the evening's shopping, and that tiny old man totter up into Bâtiment A. Frédérique has been gone for some time – he has no idea where – and when fresh footsteps clatter across the courtyard he assumes it will be her. Out of nowhere, the girl he met on his first night walks in. The girl who bought him a glass of Morgon – it's the only thing he's ordered since.

The first thing he notices is that she's with someone. He's big and broad, his hair slicked back, his bare arms thickly muscled. Just glancing around the shop he exudes testosterone. Quickly Edward leans forward and catches her eye.

'Charlotte?'

If it takes her a second to place him she hides it well, and if she can't remember his name she glosses over it.

'My god, it's you!'

'Yes, I work here, sort of.'

In the corner Gilles glares. So does the man that Charlotte's with. Judging from the book he's picked up and the expression on his face he's about to make a joke about a fleshy Renoir nude, but she is already on her way over to the counter.

'I can't believe you work here. I never knew of this place before.'

'It's a well-kept secret.'

Gilles tuts. The other man looks furious, puffing out his stocky chest like a prizefighter.

'Charlotte—' the man beckons to her.

'Listen,' the words tumble quickly out of Edward's mouth. 'I owe you a drink.'

She laughs, looking back almost guiltily over her shoulder towards her companion. 'Ok! Sunday?'

'*Yessssss.*'

He means to say it under his breath but it escapes and *thank god* they've left the shop by the time it does. Gilles is surprised by this sudden exhalation. Edward is surprised too, so surprised that he knocks into a tower of books on Renaissance portraits. As he scrabbles to pick them up again, Frédérique wafts in, appearing, as always, on a slightly different plane. Gilles looks up expectantly but she glides right past him.

'Everything ok, Edward?'

'Everything's great, just great.'

Saturday, and the market traders are up before dawn driving into the city. Soon the streets will be lined with stalls, their produce bursting to ripeness, juice dribbling in sticky pools in which fat wasps will dance excitedly. Soon the air will be thick with peaches and fish and stinking cheese, with the smell of chickens roasting and galettes browning on the heat, vats of couscous bubbling, ready for the hordes and their sharp, argumentative bartering.

All over the city exhausted children stumble into school for their half day of lessons. Exhausted parents stumble into bed, make half-hearted love, sleep. Only the department stores have air conditioning, so there are those who take themselves to wander glassy eyed amidst exquisite furnishings and luxury fabrics, seeking any respite they can from this inexhaustible heat.

That's in the white city, of course, in the centre; the postcard Paris. Around the edges, in the suburbs, there are no such luxuries. Men gather in the street to pass time that is marked by little else. Women count their change anxiously in tatty discount supermarkets. The call to prayer goes out. Police cars circle lazily, windows down, just in case; just on the off chance.

Still the temperature rises and still the tensions bubble.

Mid-afternoon, and Frédérique is standing in the turquoise doorway as Edward returns to the building. He's been walking again, ambling his way around the airless quarter. Aimless. Hot and dehydrated, he's in one of those vicious moods where he wonders if that's all he is good for; if his life can be summed up in this directionless wandering – wandering around the farm for as long as he can remember, wandering through Oxford, through his twenties, now wandering through Paris. He is just beginning to bicker with himself when Frédérique spots him.

He is lovely in the pale light. Loose limbs and sandy hair, and surely more of those golden freckles creeping over his skin every minute that he's in the sun. He looks like a poet, a dreamer from where she stands. She wonders, quite unexpectedly, who he is dreaming about.

'Edward!' Frédérique flashes him a broad smile, and her greeting is loud enough to silence any murmuring in her mind. *Ridiculous*, she chides herself.

'Hello!' He looks surprised. 'Were you waiting for me?'

Frédérique watches colour creep over his cheeks.

'No, actually, I was looking for someone else.' She scans the street again. 'No luck. But I'm glad to have found *you*. There's a hell of a commotion going on and I need you on my side.'

Frédérique places her hand on his shoulder to usher him into the entryway. He's skinny, and the blade of it juts into her hand. Inside, in the gloom, they are faced with a gaggle of other residents. Madame Marin is there, the old man from the top floor, the woman with the sour face.

'What's all this about, then?' the old man asks, waving a piece of notepaper, his voice rasping like a cat's tongue.

'A meeting of the Residents' Cooperative.' Frédérique arches an eyebrow. 'Our dear Monsieur Vincent has a bee in his bonnet again.'

Edward doesn't understand, but Frédérique leads the charge and they all troop across the courtyard and up the stairs to the Vincents' apartment. Chantal hovers in the hallway as César's booming voice welcomes them in. To Frédérique he gives a sharp but civil nod, to Edward and the others a series of pumping handshakes.

'Come in, come in, monsieur, madame, welcome, welcome; please do come through.'

The Vincents' apartment is smaller than Frédérique's, but without the heavy nineteenth-century furniture and the mountain ranges of books it manages to feel more airy. The furniture is light; clean edges and pale fabrics. It radiates calm, even with a dozen or so residents piled into it. Most of them Edward knows by sight, but there's a girl about his age chewing gum who he's never seen before, a pale young man by the window who's awkwardly tucking his hair behind his ear. Anaïs is sat on the sofa, nervously turning a baby monitor in her hands. Frédérique sits next to her and beckons Edward to join them.

'It's good to see you, Madame Lagrange.' Frédérique cannot quite bring herself to meet the other woman's eye. 'I hope your family is well.'

'Oh yes, thank you.' Small and mousey, Anaïs's voice comes out with a squeak. 'My husband would have liked to have been here, but he has church business today.'

Frédérique smiles. 'Of course.'

Madame Marin follows her husband to two folding chairs in the corner of the room. Isabelle Duval sits away from everyone else, arms folded, lips curled. Chantal circulates, proffering water and olives. Edward takes one but then gets stuck with the pit.

Finally, César calls the meeting to order.

'Ladies and gentlemen, thank you for taking time out of your busy schedules to meet today. As President of the Residents' Cooperative, I felt it my duty to inform you that we have had some interest in the apartment on the third floor of Bâtiment A.' He pauses. Frédérique nudges Edward as if to say *this is it*, folding her arms to steel herself for the fight.

'The interest, friends, is from a couple who are . . . rather *different* to ourselves.'

'Different how?' the girl with the chewing gum asks.

'This is going to be interesting,' Frédérique mutters under her breath.

César, standing at the head of the room to address his audience, flounders. 'They are . . . *culturally* different, shall we say. Culturally unlike the rest of us.'

'What's that?' barks the little old man from the front building, who's sunk so far into the sofa that he seems to have folded in on himself. 'Speak up!'

'They're *Muslims*, sir!'

There is a moment's pause before César regains his poise, his narrative. A few residents shift uncomfortably in their seats.

'They're Muslims. Which is . . . shall we say, *new* for our building. So I have called this meeting to see whether . . . whether—'

He rehearsed this so many times in the shower this morning – to see whether that's something *we want* for the building; to see whether that's something *we're comfortable with* as a building – but now, in the heat of the moment and the heat of the afternoon, with all these eyes trained on him, he cannot reach for it.

'To see whether we mind living alongside a Muslim family?' Frédérique finishes the sentence for him, her tone icy.

'Yes, thank you, Madame Aubry. Now—' César rubs his hands together, ready to resume his speech, but Frédérique cuts in.

'What, exactly, would be the problem with having a Muslim family in the building, Monsieur Vincent?'

'Well, it's a very different proposition to the type of people we've had living here before.'

'Why?'

'Madame Aubry, I would have thought that was obvious.'

'I'm sorry Monsieur Vincent, I don't see how it is.'

'Madame—'

'Look around this room. What unites the people here? We're enormously, fantastically different from each other.'

'Yes but none of us is wearing a headscarf,' Isabelle Duval cuts in. 'Or cooking strange food that stinks out the hallways, or praying loudly at all hours of the night.'

'Indeed, thank you, Madame Duval.' César can sense his precious meeting running away from him. 'I merely *intended* with this meeting to suggest that perhaps priority should be given to a French family.'

Frédérique snorts with laughter. 'Who's French, César Vincent? You grew up in Belgium!' A suppressed titter of laughter runs nervously around the room. 'What you mean is a *white* family.'

'I never said that.'

'But it's what you meant.'

'No, and I resent the implication.'

'This would be laughable, if it weren't so hideous.' Frédérique is on her high horse now. Next to her, Edward can feel the excitement, like electricity to the skin. 'You, César Vincent, cannot, simply *cannot*, decree who gets to live in this building on the basis of skin colour.'

César draws himself to his full height and looks imperiously down his nose at Frédérique. 'Madame,' his tone is as cold as hers now despite the heat, 'I am merely giving people the opportunity to express their concerns, should they have any.'

'Well let's see, shall we?' Frédérique stands up, just as tall and far more authoritative than her opponent. 'Madame Marin, would you have any problems with a Muslim family in the building?'

The *gardienne*'s hands flutter nervously over her canary yellow dress, smoothing its imaginary folds, though in fact the spandex is so tight as to eliminate the possibility of folds altogether.

'Well, no, madame, but I'm not sure it should be up to me.' She breaks off into a half-hearted laugh.

Frédérique nods and moves on. 'Monsieur Marin?'

A sort of wheezy noise emerges from Monsieur Marin's

throat. For a few in the room, this is the most they've ever heard him speak. Frédérique is unrelenting.

'I'm sorry, Monsieur Marin, could you speak up?'

'Fine by me,' he grunts.

Frédérique, satisfied, turns to the young man by the window. 'And you, monsieur?'

'I don't see why it should be any of my business.'

'Good!'

Isabelle Duval tries to cut in. 'Madame Aubry, I do not see what this hounding of opinions—'

'Don't worry, Madame Duval, I'm getting to you, though you've made your thoughts on the matter perfectly clear. Monsieur?' She leans down to speak to the tiny old gentleman. 'Does it bother you who comes to live on the third floor?'

'Bother me? Why should it bother me!'

César cuts in. 'They're Muslims, monsieur, quite different from the type of residents we have currently.'

'I don't see why,' the old man wheezes. 'I was born a Muslim. Tunisia, you know,' he adds to Frédérique.

The room is momentarily silenced.

'No, sir, I didn't know that.' She places a hand on his forearm. 'Thank you for your sensible support in this matter.'

Next it is the girl on the sofa, whose smacking lips have formed the background to the debate. She continues chewing as she speaks.

'Absolutely fine by me. There are plenty of annoying people in this building already, and it's got nothing to do with their religion.'

'Well, I'm with Monsieur Vincent,' Isabelle announces from the corner. 'It'd be nice to keep the building how it is, even if it isn't always civil.' She throws this last comment at the chewing-gum girl, who nonchalantly shrugs it off.

Frédérique turns to Anaïs. 'What do you think, madame?'

Anaïs turns beetroot red. She doesn't know what to say. There are parts of this city she doesn't visit. She knows she

67

shouldn't be, but she *is* intimated by darker skin, by voices she doesn't understand, by the fabric that these figures are shrouded in and the hot, dangerous-smelling spices that cloud around them.

'I don't know, truly I don't. I'll have to discuss it with my husband.'

'As a good Christian, though,' Frédérique presses her point, 'he's hardly likely to discriminate on the grounds of faith? Do unto others, and all that.'

Isabelle snorts and César cuts in: 'Or, as a good Christian, he'd like the building kept that way.'

Frédérique ignores this, and moves instead to Chantal, who has been standing in the doorway. 'Madame Vincent, do you share your husband's views?'

All eyes turn to her. Leaning her head against the doorjamb, Chantal is at a loss for words. She has been lost for words since last night, when César found out about the new neighbours and found his words, a wild, angry, vituperative torrent that went long into the night and led to this meeting. She, herself, is not bothered by these people. She is bothered by her husband, cannot understand why he is so knotted up about it. Last night he was apoplectic, his eyes bulging out of his skull, spit gathering at the corners of his mouth, and she felt further from him than ever. But, in the light of day, with all these strangers in her home, she does not know what to do but follow him.

'Yes, I'll agree with César and say I have reservations,' she replies. Just don't ask me what, she adds in her head.

'That just leaves Edward, then,' Frédérique says, turning to him.

'Oh, I'm sorry Madame Aubry, I don't think we can take the opinion of a mere lodger on this.' César is standing tall now, regaining the authority of his imperial namesake.

'Why not? He's here.'

César smiles thinly. 'Madame Aubry, if we were to take the

opinion of every one of your lodgers and *friends on the street*, I don't know where we'd find ourselves, but it wouldn't be representative of *this building.*'

There is a deathly silence, in which it looks as if Frédérique might go for him. Luckily Edward steps in.

He has followed, it would be fair to say, the theme if not the letter of the meeting. The French is faster than he is used to; more heated, less schoolboy, less strictly related to transport or the weather. But he has caught snatches, and so, in faltering French, he replies.

'It is ok, Frédérique. I will not speak. But it seems, to me, that more people are in accord for these new neighbours than against.'

Another pause.

César glares, his turkey wattle neck turning redder by the minute. 'Well, Mesdames, Messieurs, it seems our English friend is right. I hope you understand why I called this meeting. And I do hope that our –' he purses his lips, as if even the words are poison to him '– *new arrivals* are not to the detriment of the building. Good day to you all.'

12

César's meeting is the talk of the building, even for those who do not talk. Madame Marin clucks about it in the kitchen, while her husband sits silently in the blue glow of his television. Anaïs murmurs about it to her children as they wake from their naps, glossy eyed and messy haired. They can barely string sentences together, but she relays it to them anyway as she makes their cups of juice, wondering why she is alone yet again, why Paul is taking so long at church. Isabelle Duval storms back to her apartment, rants to the four bare walls about the bloody socialists, then takes to her computer to vent her spleen.

Although she keeps to herself within the building, Isabelle's neighbours would be surprised to learn how much she knows about *them*. She often stands behind her blinds looking down on the activity below. She has surreptitiously gathered names from the letterboxes in the main entryway and, late into the night, has searched for them online. She is acquainted with her neighbours through absence not presence; knows them through profile pictures and comments, through the value of their apartments and the level of their jobs.

She is the only person in the building who knows these new neighbours by name – the only resident who knows that César's meeting was pointless, that it's already a done deal. Only she has been determined enough to call up the estate agent under the pretext of some administrative responsibility and ask the names of the buyers; to sort doggedly through the junk mail to find the first letters delivered ahead of their recipients. She found their names and then she sought them out. The Laribis. One more Ahmed amidst the millions, she jokes bitterly to herself; one more Amina.

As she slams her fingers furiously against her keyboard, Isabelle tugs down on the T-shirt that insists on riding up. Her stomach has ballooned this year; three times she's had people offer her a seat on the metro. The first time she refused and brought the carriage to a stony silence; on the two occasions since she's accepted and fumed, hating the assumption, hating the judgement, and yet it's something she herself does daily, only the people Isabelle makes assumptions about don't look like she does. She'd never think to put the two together.

Her heart batters in her lungs as she hits the send button on her favourite forum, pleased with her efforts, high on the energy expended as if she's just run a race or made a long jump.

Dirty Muslim immigrants moving into our building. Liberal neighbours say it doesn't matter. But we know it does. This is Paris not a souk in Africa and why should we be afraid in our own homes? Why should we smile and be friendly when they're praying to Allah five times a day for our destruction? Shootings, bombs, rape, murder. The Left says everyone has a right to live peacefully – liberté, égalité, fraternité. But what about my rights? My liberty? My equality? Am I right, friends? When are we going to stand up and stop the Islamicisation of France, the Muslimification of our neighbourhoods? Who's with me?

Slowly her breath returns to normal and Isabelle sits back, contented, waiting for the likes to start rolling in.

'You could have said something to support me!'

'I did support you, César!'

'Oh yes, a long pause and an "I'll side with my husband."' He mimics her voice cruelly. 'Fat lot of good you were!'

'César, what is wrong with you? You held your meeting, I'm sorry you didn't win, but it's people moving into the building opposite, it's hardly the end of the world!'

'It *is* the end of the world!' He slams his fist down on the table so hard that Chantal jumps. 'It's the end of *this* world, can't you see that you silly little woman? One Muslim couple here and the value of the property will *plummet*. They all stick together, so one day soon we'll wake up and it won't be one Islamic couple, it'll be twenty of them, and we're the only ones stuck here while they chant the Koran and make foul-smelling food and take us back to the tenth century! And you, a feminist!' He's pointing at her dress now. 'You think they'll like you walking round like that, flesh on show, legs out? Oh no. And you won't feel safe doing it either, we'll be prisoners in our own home!'

Chantal feels sick.

'César, *what are you talking about*? Where does this, this hatred come from?' Her voice wobbles as she pleads with him. 'You've never spoken like this before.'

He turns from her. 'Well maybe I haven't needed to before. Maybe before everyone's been kept in their right place, and they haven't been coming over in droves, stealing our jobs, our homes, our livelihoods. I haven't needed to make this defence before!'

Chantal drops into a chair, her head in her hands.

'César, you are scaring me.'

'Well Chantal, your complacency scares me. Am I the only one looking out for this family, this marriage?'

'No, of course not!'

'I don't know. You trot off to your library, buy your pretty little dresses and talk of going on holiday or redecorating the bedroom, and it seems to me I'm the only one with my head screwed on, the only one thinking about money and expense and the security of our future.'

'But we're doing fine for money. Aren't we? Why would you worry about money, César?'

'I'm just saying someone has to worry about these things. About the important things.'

'Like if a Muslim couple moves in opposite?'

'Yes!'

'César!' She is shouting now. 'How can that possibly affect us? We're probably never even going to see them!'

'I don't want them here! Elsewhere is fine, but not here.'

'Oh what are you going to do then? Turn out little old Monsieur Lalande into the street? What are your criteria for eviction, Mr President of the Residents' Cooperative?'

'Don't you think that's a dirty trick keeping that information secret? Don't you think it's suspicious that he's been hiding it all this time?'

'No, César, I think that's the sort of thing people are forced to do when they live next to bigots and xenophobes who won't employ them or talk to them if they find out they're Arabic.' She pauses, her insults hanging heavy in the stifling air. 'I'm sorry César, but I simply don't understand this. I don't understand it in you. It's so very ugly.'

Upstairs, little old Monsieur Lalande chuckles as he lines up crumbs on his windowsill. Born Hakim, he has spent forty years now as Henri. Pale skin – a blessing in youth and an aid to employment – has faded even paler in age. Clearly none of them knew his difference. 'Worth it just to see their faces,' he laughs chestily to himself.

One by one, his birds land on his windowsill. He feeds them every day at this time. Little spindly things, they're nothing fancy. 'Sparrow mutts,' he calls them affectionately. Over time, he has built up a rapport with them. Some will even sit on his hand.

When he was a child, his mother had kept canaries. Bright,

jewel-like little things. He had loved feeding them, loved the patter of their tiny feet, the swoop of their wings in flight. But one day he had left the cage open, and all four or five of them had flown away.

'Don't be a caged bird,' the old man says to the sparrow hopping along his wrinkled, liver-spotted hand. 'Learnt that a long time ago.'

13

Back in her own apartment, Frédérique crows.

'Did you see the look on his face? Huzzah!' She raises her fist high in the air and laughs. 'A victory against the small-minded, Edward, it's not to be scorned! And you were brilliant, with your French. It's definitely improving!'

'I figured I had to say something.'

'It was perfect, perfect! How dare he think he can decide who lives here. We're not quite back to the 1930s yet, thank god.' She disappears into the kitchen. 'Let's drink to that!'

The cat curls herself around his ankles as Edward takes in the *salon* again. He hears ice clinking in the kitchen as he edges his way around the portraits: aquiline noses, pale golden curls, severe black dresses cut right to the neck – almost into the necks – of what he assumes to be Frédérique's ancestors. One portrait, a woman with a glacial stare, has a Cyrillic signature curlicuing across the bottom of the canvas.

'White Russians.'

Edward turns to find Frédérique behind him, two glasses in her hands. The liquid in them is clear – he can smell the cucumber coolness of gin from here, the spritz of lime – and realises, feeling foolish, that the White Russian is in the frame in front of him.

'Russian émigrés, I should say. *Anastasia*.' Frédérique delivers the name in a heavy accent. 'She came to France during the Revolution. A dress, a suitcase, and that painting, nothing else with her. Got work as a dressmaker and ended up marrying a picture dealer.'

They touch glasses.

'That's extraordinary.'

'Mmm.' Frédérique reclines on the chaise longue. 'They were tough, that side of the family. Made money in paintings, but my god, they didn't give an inch.'

'Is that how you got interested in art?'

'Ha, I'm a poor shadow of their glory, I'm afraid. The money was gone by the time I was growing up. Someone made the decision to switch from paintings to books.' She shakes her head ruefully. 'Probably not the best decision this family ever made.' Pushing herself up on one elbow, she gestures in the direction of one of the bookshelves. 'There's an album over there somewhere. Photographs of them, the gallery.'

Edward dutifully springs up and follows the direction of her finger. On the bottom shelf he finds a run of dark, cloth-bound albums.

'No, not that one; to the left, with the gold trim.'

He locates the bulging album and brings it over to her. Sure enough, there are photographs of the painted lady, even more severe in the tiny monochrome prints, brow more furrowed, lips more pursed. She stands with a row of top-hatted gentlemen in front of a gallery ('Aubry Frères'), sits uncomfortably in a group in some unknown garden. Frédérique's fingers turn the pages eagerly.

'Oh, I'd forgotten these were here!'

Edward sits on the edge of his seat, watching the photographs spin through time. They leave the gallery behind and interleaved are Kodachrome faces from the 1960s, geometric prints and heavy glasses; a group of girls with 1920s bobs.

'My mother,' Frédérique says, gesturing to a young woman smiling on a beachfront, her hand shielding her eyes from the sun. On the next page, the same woman in later life: plump, permed, her face drawn in though the rest of her had filled out.

'There was a house,' Frédérique murmurs, flicking pages,

'in Normandy. Wrecked during the war, of course, but we went every summer. Yes, here—' Edward leans in to view the squat cottage, trees and tall grasses curving over it, blown to an angle by the sea breeze. 'A riot of cousins and dogs and family feuds, everyone laughing and fighting all the time—'

'Is that *you*?'

She's turned the page and suddenly they're in India, a young Frédérique in front of a stand of spices and coloured powders: mustard yellow, fuschia, turquoise, and she is the image of Emilie in a printed tunic, long blonde hair plaited down her back, smiling at the camera.

'Yes! Kerala, Rajasthan . . .? My god, I look so young!'

She is his age in these photos, Edward realises. They pore over them, heads together: a palace in a lake, a ruined temple, Frédérique laughing as she gingerly extends a hand towards a monkey. It's just her, he thinks, until he spots a figure of a man on a balcony. Out of focus, the man's eyes take in something the camera cannot see.

'Ah, I'm sorry Edward.' Frédérique leans back. 'It's no fun looking through someone else's memories.'

'No, it's fascinating! We don't have anything like this in my family. I haven't been anywhere half that exotic.'

'You have it all to come,' she smiles, taking a sip of her gin. 'Don't wish any of it away, Edward. Life is long, for most of us.'

Something distracts her. They've been sharing the weight of the album, and now the majority falls to Edward's hands.

'Shall I put this back?'

'You're sweet, thank you. Oh, this heat, I can't think.' She runs her wet glass (its ice cubes have already melted) across her forehead.

It falls as Edward stands, a single loose photograph. He picks it up, and even before he sees it his mouth is forming the words.

'Who's that?'

They're not off his tongue before Edward wishes he hadn't said them. Too late, his brain catches up, and he realises the little boy in the photograph is the spitting image of Frédérique, and that she has her arms around him, and that in this photo she is happy. This is it, he realises. This is what made those lines around your eyes; this is why I recognise loss in you. Why we are kindred spirits.

When finally she utters them, her words hang in the heavy air.

'That's my son.'

Don't tell me, he thinks. You don't have to tell me. I know all this. The pieces just fell together like a puzzle, and we can sit here in silence, because we both know there aren't words to talk about it. We don't even have to try.

'I'm sorry,' he says eventually.

'He was nine,' she replies. 'It was a long time ago.'

Slowly, Edward replaces the photography album down on the table in front of him.

'How did you know?' Frédérique asks.

'Know what?' He does meet her eyes this time, sees the tears threatening.

'That he died.'

'Because my sister died. And I recognise it. In you.'

Frédérique laughs low, drops her head into her hands. 'It's like a club.'

Edward almost smiles. 'Yeah. A really shitty club.'

Over dinner they talk frankly about loss for the first time.

'We were living in the south of France. Daniel was nine. Provence in the summer: cicadas buzzing, lavender on the air, ochre dirt underfoot. We'd found this beautiful, tumbledown farmhouse. My partner, he was a woodworker, so we were doing it up. Putting down roots.'

Frédérique pauses.

'There was a fire. They couldn't say how it started. They thought Daniel must have been playing, the way boys do; sun through a magnifying glass, or maybe he found some matches, they said, but I can't believe that, he was such a good boy, so well behaved. His father was working, sawing wood out in the barn, and he didn't hear anything, didn't smell smoke until it was too late. It was so hot that summer, dry as a bone, and by the time I got home it was all over. Fire engines wrapping up their hoses, the house charred beyond recognition. I came back along the lane and there was a huge cloud of black air over the fields. What's that novel? An English novel, you English have a novel for everything. Anyway, it was like that. I could see already that something was wrong.

'It was the smoke that killed him. Only thing that keeps me smoking these. Stupid, really.' She inhales. 'I came straight back to Paris. That very day. Dirt on my feet, nothing but the clothes on my back. I came home, back to this place, back to the apartment. My mother was still alive then, so I came home. And I haven't ever left.'

'What about your partner?'

She sighs.

'It is very hard to survive something like that. You know it, Edward. We still see each other, we rattle about. Can't be together, can't really be apart. I blame him. I know it's unfair but I do. So I smoke these, and he can't bear to be indoors, and we keep on. Keep going. That's the extraordinary thing about these bloody bodies. Somehow you just keep going.'

The lights on the terrace fade in and out of focus, and around them the hum of conversation continues: the affairs, the arguments, the debates, the mundane chit-chat of friends chewing over the day's fat. In the packed proximity of a Parisian restaurant people pour out their hearts to each other, elbow to elbow with strangers who hear every word.

Their moustachioed waiter, a model of discretion, eaves-dropping and efficiency, holds their plates until a suitable pause.

Frédérique looks at the boy in front of her and wonders, not for the first time, why she's telling him all this. His floppy hair, the broad smattering of freckles, they make him seem even younger. But his green eyes know. Somehow they understand.

Edward, in turn, looks at Frédérique, her silvery hair glinting in the candlelight. She had insisted on taking him to dinner. They had walked quietly through streets that stuck to the soles of his shoes, redolent of the day's heat. Frédérique had spoken firmly with the waiter, who'd immediately found them a table outside in spite of the line of people waiting. And in the public intimacy of this place, with this woman he barely knows, he is putting voice to things he has not been able to say elsewhere.

'I think my parents blame me. About my sister.'

He hides his trembling hands beneath the tablecloth. It has taken so much to voice these words.

For all that she has just said, Frédérique looks surprised. 'Why?'

'Because I was there. Because maybe if I hadn't run across the road first, she wouldn't have, she would have stopped, or would have seen.' Edward pauses to steady his breath. 'It was an accident. She stepped into the road, and there was a car. It was going fast, too fast, they said that, they did tell us that afterwards. But in this awful – I don't even know what to call it – this awful *parody*, the driver was speeding to get to the hospital because his wife was giving birth. So my sister is lying there on the ground, and at the same moment she is – ' he still can't bring himself to say *dying* – 'there's a baby being born twenty miles down the road.'

'But you know,' Frédérique's voice is soft, 'you know *logically* that it was not your fault.'

'Yes, but there's logically, and then there's here.' He taps his chest.

'Yes, I know that. That I know.' She takes a sip of wine. 'It must have been very hard on your mother.'

Edward's jaw hardens.

'Sorry, not the right thing to say. I see everything through my own eyes.'

'It's hard on everyone. There's no one it's not hard on.' He drinks too, cool wine swirling into the gin in his belly. 'But then, I don't know, I get so *angry* at all the other people – friends, schoolteachers—'

'Who want to share in it.'

'Yes!'

'Want to tell you how shocked they are—'

'How heartbroken—'

'Devastated—'

'Distraught—'

'Distressed they are!'

They laugh.

'Yes, I got angry at that too. Oh Edward, Edward.' Frédérique shakes her head. 'We're in Paris. It should be joyful.'

A peal of laughter rings out from the adjacent table.

'Isn't it?' he asks.

'It's not the picture postcard. Violence, tension, inequality, it's everywhere. And everyone has their secret to carry. How would you say it in English?'

'Their cross to bear.'

At last, their waiter arrives with their food, two pieces of white fish swimming in sauce. They eat and talk, and in each there is a certain lightness now, a weight that has lifted into the warm night air. They drink white wine with their fish, a spicy red with dessert, and when they walk home through empty streets Frédérique links her arm through his.

'Thank you for dinner.'

'Thank *you*, Edward.'

'What for?'

'For sharing your story with me. It does me good to talk with someone who understands.'

Just as they are approaching number thirty-seven she stops and tugs on his arm.

'What?'

'Look!'

Sure enough, the door to the building is open and Madame Marin is sneaking stealthily out of it in a tight red dress and matching heels, looking comically over each shoulder like a cartoon villain. Once she has tottered far enough down the street, Edward and Frédérique let out suppressed giggles.

'You see? It goes on. The same ridiculous, farcical, heart-aching life goes on.'

And it is true. Across the city people fight and make up; they cheat and scream and caress each other. There are those who are meeting friends for a drink, those meeting lovers; new lovers, old lovers, those who might, if the balance of the evening tips in their favour, become their lovers. There are tourists and visitors; people who hate Paris and people who can't stop falling in love with every pale, crooked building. There are old people and young; the topless men who bare their sagging flesh as they hurl *pétanque* balls across the dusty ground, the kids who cycle in the streets practising their wheelies, the prostitutes who line the seedier boulevards, the flower sellers who walk from bar to bar, restaurant to restaurant in the hope of selling a single faded rose. There are beggars on the pavement, thieves slipping nimble fingers into unknowing pockets. There are those who light candles in churches, mosques, synagogues, temples. In distant corners of the city there are those who meet with a darker purpose, plotting to bring this feverish metropolis to boiling point. All of it under the same blanket of heat and dust, the same dark sky, the same invisible stars drowned out by the sea of electric light.

Madame Marin's heels clatter off down the street and Frédérique pauses at the entry to Bâtiment A, planting a delicate kiss on each of Edward's cheeks.

'Goodnight, Edward.'

'Goodnight, Frédérique.'

14

Paris should be joyful.

Edward wakes at midday with Frédérique's words ringing
in his ears. He has slept undisturbed for the first time in
months. No nightmares, no night terrors (they are different,
the internet assures him, and he is well-versed now in the
fictional fright of the nightmare and the night terror where,
between waking and sleep, his worst fears are played out in
front of him in his very bedroom). Not today. Today he is
light.

Paris should be joyful.

Joyful even in the fifth floor's communal shower, where the
water is icy and rust stains drip down the wall. Joyful in the
bakery, where he buys a croissant *and* a *pain au chocolat*
because he's got coins in his pocket and it's a beautiful day.
Joyful meandering his way through the Sunday city, and even
more so when, with a jolt, he remembers his date with
Charlotte.

As Edward walks, he rehearses imaginary conversations
with her, out loud and in his head. He revels in the liberty
of being abroad, a tourist, a stranger. Frédérique told him
that foreign and strange were the same word here – *étrange*
– and what do any of these people care if he walks along
talking to himself? Eccentricity is permissible, even if his
words trail off in failure.

'I'm from the countryside, this is all new to me . . . I'm
just here to explore . . . I want to get to know the city . . .
Oh *god*.'

He discovers the Luxembourg, where desperate sunbathers

have already stripped down and bagged the best deckchairs. Fat ponies trot a short route between the trees, children bouncing up and down on them in fear and glee. Dust clouds roll across the gardens: across the tennis courts, where white-clad women with serious expressions tense themselves for play; across the pavilion, where men of all shapes and sizes sit playing chess; across the pond, where already spoilt brats are wailing to sharply dressed parents that they want to play with the sailboats. Sun dapples the water and the world is a dazzle of light and dust and sweat beading on even the most refined faces. Frédérique has told him the sixth arrondissement is snooty and Edward takes no small pleasure in identifying it as such.

Outside Odéon, he walks into some kind of meeting. A gaggle of people in pink T-shirts, some stood listening to a man with a megaphone, others handing out leaflets. A woman approaches him.

'Here, monsieur. We're the Manif pour Tous. We protest for everyone.'

She is in her forties, with cropped blonde hair and a face that simultaneously holds a smile and a deep frown.

'Who's everyone?'

'The children, monsieur. We have to protect the children. We have to protect families from these dangerous policies.'

'What policies?'

'The Left's policies! Gay marriage, gay adoption, it's breaking the family.' She breaks from him momentarily to shout across the square, 'Children need a mother and a father!'

The two men walking arm in arm at whom she's shouted yell back a loud 'Fuck you!' and continue on their way. She returns to Edward and thrusts a leaflet in his hand. He takes one, takes a long look at it and at the front of her T-shirt, which shows a stick figure family holding hands. Mother, father, son, daughter. He shoves the leaflet back in the woman's face.

'We're on the side of God, monsieur!'

As he storms down towards the boulevard, Edward wishes he were fluent. Wishes he could tell this woman, in her own language, what a loveless bigot she is. He remembers Emilie talking about this group. 'If you don't like gay marriage, don't get gay married!' she'd cried, throwing her hands in the air. Today, the best his French can manage is a bleated 'Fuck you', a weak imitation of the one that came before. The woman shrugs, runs a hand through her hair, and looks for a new target.

He is crossing the river before his hands stop shaking, outside Notre-Dame before he can admit to himself what it feels like to see those stick figures of the perfect family. Something his was, and now isn't. Mother, father, son, daughter. He doesn't mind who marries who but flopping down onto a bench outside the great cathedral, he realises the sting today was as much that perfect image as the intolerance behind it.

Still. He breathes in deeply. *Joy.*

Notre-Dame is buzzing. A huge queue snakes out of the great doors and across the square. Tourists of every nation, creed and colour clamouring to get the best photographs. An American tour group approaches him, all brightly coloured running shoes and shorts, either stick thin or loaded with flesh. Their guide is explaining the medieval layout of the city, how this square was originally crammed with houses and churches and thousands of souls trying desperately to survive.

'Oh look, Ron!' A loud nasal wail from a woman crammed into particularly tight shorts. 'Get a photo, get a photo!'

This is the general chorus for a few moments, until the guide raises his umbrella and gently ushers them towards the cathedral entrance. Edward hops up to take their place, traces their steps across the medieval city, whose filth-ridden alleyways are now commemorated in neatly inscribed paving stones, the kind of thing you don't see unless someone tells you to look.

He walks on, bumpier cobbles under his feet, stomach growling. He crosses the river for a second time, throws a centime into it for good luck (why did his mother teach him that?). Winds his way through medieval streets, buys a crepe from a man on the pavement, dislikes the crowds, particularly when he is almost caught in an altercation between an Orthodox Jew and a young Arabic man. The French is too fast, but he understands the punch that is thrown and, thankfully, misses; understands the fat oyster of spit that is hawked up and left threateningly near his feet. Later, he understands the armed police officers outside the synagogue and scurries quickly past them.

Edward walks on, less interested in the big clean monuments than the little grime-covered ones that seem to pop up on every street corner. He stops to look at the medieval Madonnas built into nooks in certain buildings; laughs at the Rue des Mauvais Garçons, wishing he could send Emilie a photo of himself on Bad Boys' Street. He doesn't know where he is going, but recognises that there is a rhythm to it: fancy cafés across the street from run-down stores selling cheap crap for expensive prices; homeless people lolling on the pavement in front of a Burger King, just next to a bright and fancy monument, lovingly restored. He watches a man and a woman leave a restaurant, their skin and hair as golden as the jewellery that drips from their wrists. They do not miss a beat stepping over the tramp lying prone on the pavement and into their chauffeured car. When Edward gingerly side-steps around him, the smell is fierce.

He does not understand this city. Does not understand it, but sees the residents of number thirty-seven everywhere. Here, a woman dressed up like Madame Marin (mutton dressed as lamb, his mum would say). There, a Monsieur Vincent, proud chested and tall. A gaggle of children that remind him of Anaïs's. Old men shuffling like those who frequent the bookshop.

He walks until the light turns the buildings to end-of-day gold. Charlotte had whispered 'Eight?' at him when she left the shop yesterday. He should get back. Panic flutters briefly in Edward's chest, not knowing where he is.

Chance takes him down a tiny street that leads, ultimately, to a boulevard where a bus is waiting. It is packed: old women with shopping bags, children in buggies, ordinary people looking cramped, hot, unhappy. He takes a punt on it, squeezing himself on, figuring that if it heads south, that'd be near enough. He doesn't pay (those coins in his pockets have gone on fresh baguettes and iced tea). He's in luck, it does head south, and the hot, lumbering journey back to the Left Bank is all the more enjoyable for the absence of a ticket.

Charlotte is more beautiful than Edward had remembered. Or maybe it's the kind of beauty that grows on you, he thinks; the kind that's magnified in animation. Her long lashes blink with extraordinary frequency, eyes bright beneath them, and the hands with the stacks of silver rings dance as she speaks.

She's a politics student, and much of their conversation revolves around the things he's seen today. Poverty. The rich– poor divide. Homelessness. The Right and its conservative doctrine. (When he thinks about it later, the evening takes on the air of a seductive lecture – Edward is not sure he says anything at all; she seems almost bored when he talks about England, Oxford, the world he knows).

'Paris is segregated,' she tells him, smoke curling seductively from her lips. 'Twenty rich, white arrondissements, and then the suburbs. That's where the poverty is, the immigration, the unemployment. Parisians don't want to see it – they *pay* not to see it. Each arrondissement is meant to provide some social housing, or they get fined. *Some arrondissements prefer the fines.* Would rather pay tax than see someone with different-coloured skin to them in their neighbourhood. It's fucked up.'

Edward thinks back to the canvassing for the elections back home, the men in pinstripe suits winning support by voicing ugly fears.

'I don't think it's much better in Britain,' he ventures.

'You don't elect MPs from a party founded by a Holocaust denier. Your most popular politician isn't the pretty blonde face of Fascism.'

'No,' he concedes, 'but there's also this tide – I don't know how to describe it – I have this feeling like it's somehow becoming okay to be racist again. When I was growing up people didn't say things like that, or at least not openly. I mean, my grandma would and she'd get shushed and told "you can't say that anymore", but she was ancient. If you weren't ninety and you felt that way it was all very hushed up. And now, a few joke politicians are on TV and on the radio telling everyone it's okay to not hire someone because of where they come from, it's okay to be scared of people with darker skin than you, to want them out of your country—'

'Whatever "your country" is in the first place.'

'Exactly.' He takes a drink, feeling like he might just have won back her attention. 'God knows where it ends.'

Charlotte looks at him darkly. 'Something's going to happen here. It's only a matter of time. Last week, Jewish graves desecrated, a mosque attacked, the Far Right retaliating against whoever they choose.'

He must look surprised because she quickly explains.

'Not in Paris, not where you'd hear about it. That happened in the suburbs, that's why we don't hear. But it's happening. Something bad is coming.'

She looks at him, and for a moment the fierce politico softens. A smile creeps over her lips and she is twisting the rings on her fingers.

'Sorry, I'm – how do you English say it? – *talking shop*. Here you are, Edward,' she raises her glass, 'here in beautiful

Paris for a holiday and all I'm talking about is everything that's wrong with it.'

'No, honestly, it's a lot more interesting than the stereotype. I saw so many tourists today, so excited for the fairytale they didn't seem to see anything else. Your version's depressing, but it's much better than The City of Lights, The City of Romance and Baguettes!'

She laughs.

'Well that's true, our bread is far superior to yours. I studied in London for a while and—' she makes a thumbs-down sign. 'But, you know, look around. This place is still beautiful, for all its flaws.'

Edward follows her gaze. They're at a tiny table squeezed onto a pavement that can barely hold them, let alone the people walking past. He's lost count of how many bags and elbows have knocked into his head. A steady stream of cars and bikes pass, their lights glowing, and up above the sky reminds him of a fountain pen that's bled across a white shirt. The air is hot and full of dust caught in the café's lights like motes of diamonds, and yes, even with the traffic fumes and the smell of dogs' piss, it is beautiful.

'Besides,' Charlotte leans in towards him, 'there can be romance even in the worst of times.'

In this moment, Edward falls hook, line and sinker. It runs from nose to heels, looping around his ribcage before tingling somewhere deeper. They share another carafe of wine, then walk. Charlotte shows him where Picasso once lived. They wander along the imposing walls of the Montparnasse cemetery, kiss in a deserted marketplace with the day's forgotten newspapers and lettuce leaves swirling around their feet. On Charlotte's initiative they peel off stickers that the Manif pour Tous has plastered all over the neighbourhood, and on Edward's they crush that perfect stick-figure family in their hands. They climb eight flights of stairs to her attic room and stand on tiptoe under the skylight to see the Eiffel Tower sparkle. They share a joint that makes Edward's chest expand and everything around him glow. Finally, they crawl beneath the sheets, and there is solace in her body, in the touch of someone else's skin.

Joy, he thinks, as his eyelids close.

15

Time does not cool César's rage. He fumes all that night, fumes the next morning, is still fuming as he slams his brief-case down onto the grease-smeared table at the café in the Porte de Vincennes.

'Muslims!' he growls to himself, wincing in pain. His anger has taken physical form in his belly, his guts hard and twisted with the injustice and humiliation of it. 'That bloody woman,' he snarls under his breath, and he can't tell if he means Frédérique or Chantal, the woman in the hijab who's getting ready to move in, or all women altogether.

Once, just once, he has been back to the bank in the months since he left it. 'You fool,' he'd told himself, 'did you not see this coming?' For the suited crowds of smokers gathered outside its entrance did not look like him any more. Skin like black coffee, skin like café au lait, and every shade in between. From his vantage point behind an awning on the opposite corner he had watched them come and go, these people who'd taken his place, who now sit at his desk. And what right do they have to it?

'For you, *Monsieur*?' the surly waitress asks, belly hanging out of her trousers.

'Coffee, *please*,' he replies, a veneer of politeness. They go through this ritual every day. As she slouches behind the counter, lip ring glinting in the sun, he's sure she thinks he's pathetic, sitting here all day in this filthy hovel, and he thinks the same of her. He wonders where she's from, with that accent and that dark hair.

The café is more crowded than usual today. A group of

workmen cluster round the table next to César's. At least, they look like workmen – rough hands, heavy boots – but César is sensitive to questions of employment these days, and workmen should be working on a Monday morning. César sips the cheap coffee that's been placed in front of him and tries to concentrate on his newspaper, but the conversation next to him is loud and raucous.

'They should go back to where they bloody came from – isn't that right, friend?'

César looks up to see he's being addressed by the ringleader, a grubby-looking man of about forty with a shaved head and tattoos on his hands. He's not sure he likes the use of 'friend'.

'Sorry?'

The man leans towards him. 'My friends and I were talking about the immigration problem. Putting good French people out of work. They should go back where they came from.'

'Ahh.' César's inherent snobbery prevents him from agreeing too readily, but his interest has been piqued. Sensing it, the man continues.

'Take Michel, here –' he gestures at a lanky figure in his early twenties opposite – 'can't get a job on a building site any more.'

'Wouldn't want to,' the boy cuts in, his voice high-pitched and churlish. 'Bloody darkies all over the place.'

'Ah!' The ringleader holds up his hand. 'It's not about skin colour, Mich. It's about the right to work, the right of French citizens to have French jobs.' He turns to César. 'There might be plenty of dark-skinned French citizens who have every right to be here. But it's the ones flooding in we have to worry about. The Roma, the Arabs – where does it end?'

César shifts in his seat. 'As you say, it's certainly very difficult.'

The ringleader nods towards the door. 'Go and have a

smoke, boys.' The five men around the table dutifully get up and trail towards the doorway. The ringleader holds out his hand.

'Sylvain.'

'César.'

They shake.

'Now, César,' Sylvain leans back in his seat, 'I don't mean to be rude, but you don't look the type to hang about round here. I've seen you before, just sitting here.'

César bristles.

'S'okay.' Sylvain holds up his hands as if César is a horse that might suddenly bolt. 'I'm just saying, with the suit, the briefcase, you're dressed pretty nice for this dump. What brings you here?' Then, more quietly: 'Lost your job?'

Unable to speak, César nods. Sylvain places a hand on César's forearm. César can almost overlook the dirty finger-nails for the relief of having told someone, the flood of gratitude for this stranger's empathy.

Sylvain shakes his head. 'That's terrible. You worked there a long time?'

Again, César nods. 'Twenty-five years.'

The other man whistles under his breath. 'Wow. And they turned you over for someone younger, someone they can pay less to do the job less well?'

'Yes.'

'Same thing happened to Damien out there.' He gestures towards a man in his fifties, slightly smarter than the others. 'Didn't work on the sites himself, but in the office, doing all the paperwork. He was brilliant, Damien. Then suddenly one day, there's a kid called Mohammed sitting at his desk for half the pay and Damien's out on his ear.'

'It's just not . . . *fair*,' César stumbles.

'No, you're right there, César. In fact,' Sylvain shifts a little closer, 'that's why my friends and I are here. We're organising to take part in a protest, a little march that's taking place against some of these injustices. Because it *is* unjust, César, to rob a man of his work like that. You married?'

'Yes.'

'Your wife work?'

'Yes.'

'She know about this?' Sylvain gestures at the walls around them, the greasy spoon, the whole sorry situation.

César shakes his head.

'I understand. It's a man's right to work. It's who he is. It defines him. It's different for women – they've got the family, the house, other things to be thinking about – but what's a man without his work? This government doesn't understand what it means to a man to have that taken from him. *Oh, the EU's great; oh, it's good for the economy to have migrant workers coming in* – well they're out of touch with the ordinary Frenchman, that's for sure. Why don't you join us, César? We could certainly use a man of your expertise.'

Much later, in the quiet hours of a different night, César will think about this exchange. He will think about Chantal, and what her reaction to this depiction of womanhood would have been. He will think about his Belgian passport. He will think about the word 'expertise', and what it could possibly have meant when not a word had been said about his career, or what was left of it.

But in the moment, he says yes. And, in having people to talk to, it is the best day he's had since leaving the bank. He listens to their stories, tells a potted version of his. They talk about politics, about which leaders can be appealed to, which should just be shot. As the sun arcs high overhead, they switch establishments, move from coffee to beer in the tiniest, dirtiest bar César has ever seen. He is, by nature, fastidious, yet he feels he belongs today, even amidst the grime.

Returning late, beer on his breath, César stops to straighten his tie in the hallway mirror. Chantal is already in bed.

95

'Where have you been, César?'

'Oh, out and about.' A little unsteady on his feet, he totters to the window and peers across the courtyard at the windows on the third floor. No sign of that new family. 'Sorry, they'll all be sorry,' he coos to himself triumphantly before stumbling into the shower.

In the bedroom, Chantal plumps her pillow and turns out the light. She has a big meeting tomorrow, lunch with a friend, *her* life to be getting on with. She can't just be the anchor to this – is it a mid-life? – crisis of César's. Falling asleep to the sound of the shower running, she feels herself adrift. When César eventually joins her, she stirs briefly, mourning the loss of their habitual entanglement. For César, it is the deepest, least-troubled sleep he's known in months, but Chantal is tossed on the waves of ill-omened dreams. They lie either side of an ocean of inches.

16

Gone two, and Anaïs is wandering the apartment again. Limbs and brain as heavy as lead, yet she cannot sleep. She is so tired she wants to cry, to weep and wail and throw her arms around like the children do, desperate for rest. But she can't. There's nothing there.

She remembers when she was younger trying to make herself cry. Sad stories on the news, tragic deaths, cruel acts against animals, and if she concentrated hard enough the hot salt tears would come. Not now. Now she is numb, eyes aching as if they were made of marble, bones fossilising inside her, heavier by the minute. But lying in bed in the depth of night is unbearable, the whirlwind of thoughts too loud to silence, and the silence itself too loud to bear.

In the children's room, hot little limbs are flung outside the covers. The window is wide open but there is no air; for weeks in this city there has been no air. Silently Anaïs tiptoes to her own bedroom, watches the rise and fall of Paul's chest in silhouette. Slow and steady, like Paul himself. In the living room she crouches down to stroke the dog's ears. Beau struggles to rouse himself from sleep, to give her hand a half-hearted lick. His little eyelids flutter, too tired to stay open. She leaves him and returns to the window.

The courtyard is in darkness. No Frédérique tonight. No one at all. No sound of cars in the street, no grunts of motor-bikes whirring into life. The world is eerily quiet.

How many other people have stood here? How many sleepless feet have trodden these boards? The floorboards were the most disconcerting thing to her when they moved;

real nineteenth-century floorboards that spring and squeak beneath them. To leave the solid stone of the Auvergne for these mobile, mutating surfaces, it makes her think the whole building is in motion; that everything, here, is always in motion.

1896 it says above the grand turquoise door downstairs; *Architecte P. Valentin-Legendre*. Who was he, this man who thought so much about the layout of these rooms, the width of these windows, the piped-icing flurry of decoration on the ceiling that makes Anaïs think of her grandmother's baking? *1896*. She imagines round-bellied speculators with white beards and white collars journeying out from their mansions in the sixth and the sixteenth, and this neighbourhood must have felt like the very edges of the city. Muddy still, and rural; dirt roads and hedgerows and she wishes it was still like that. She'd feel more at home with that.

Her toes wiggle, conscious of standing in someone else's ghostly footsteps. There must have been other women throughout the years who stood here. Mothers, maybe; other people who felt as blankly desolate as she does. She closes her eyes and in the breathless night she can almost hear the scuttle of long dresses across the floor, the clack of hobnailed boots, the *tsk* of a broom sweeping dirt into a pan. The noise of men returning from work, the smell of them; the smell of food kept in cool boxes, of soap and polish, of the sheets that must surely have been strung from these windows to dry in the breeze.

She is heavy with it tonight, those other lives so close and yet so distant; those other joys, losses, laughter played out in the same space, on top of one another, and yet entirely out of reach. Layer upon layer of them, and maybe if she could just cut through this thick air she'd find them.

Without quite knowing how, she finds herself in the kitchen staring into the cutlery drawer. Firm handles, sharp silver lines . . .

Once, when she was a teenager, Anaïs had thought about cutting herself. She was fifteen and anxious, and everyone was doing it then, all the girls at school with their sleeves self-consciously rolled up to draw attention to the dirty scab lines.

'What was I even worried about?' she murmurs to the empty room.

She hadn't done it in the end. Too scared of blood, of her parents, of what it might mean to permanently mark her skin. Three babies in, the fear of blood has long since left her. And in these endless, gaping, lonely hours, she longs for some kind of feeling, however perverse and raw the logic. With a trembling hand, she draws the flat edge of a knife along her skin.

'Ana?'

Suddenly Paul is in the doorway, and if she's been playing with the idea of opening her skin, she now jumps straight out of it.

'God, you scared me.'

Even in the dark she sees him flinch at the Lord's name. 'What are you doing?'

'I couldn't sleep. I thought I'd do the washing up.'

And it's true, there's a mountain of dirty dishes: plastic plates, empty bottles, tiny spoons.

'Ana, it's the middle of the night.'

She slips the knife back into the drawer, plunges her hands into the cold, soapy water. 'But if I don't do it now it won't get done, you know what it's like.'

'Alright, alright.' Paul switches on the table lamp, whose brightness momentarily stuns them both. 'I'll wash, you dry.'

Paul watches his wife out of the corner of his sleep-sticky eyes as they stand in silence at the sink. Anaïs has her eyes fixed firmly forwards, an absolute refusal, it seems to him, of any kind of intimacy. This is madness, he thinks to himself. Who does the washing up at two-thirty in the morning?

He's not really sure when these night-time rituals started. At first he would wake to an empty bed and think that she was feeding the baby, but the baby has been sleeping through the night for months now. Tonight he stretched out a hand and found her side of the bed stone cold, as if she had never been in it at all.

And they become one flesh. The Bible verse rings in his head as he scrubs at the dishes, feels the ends of his fingers wrinkle and pucker. *They are no longer two but one.*

There don't seem to be scriptures, though, for recovering this distance. For closing the gap that is growing nightly between them. *Husbands, love your wives*, the good book says, and he does and he tries but she is slipping through his fingers like so many grains of sand. And time – there never seems to be time to just hold her, to stroke her hair and ask what's wrong. Between work and church and children the days gallop past, and his legs are aching with how much he wants to be asleep right now.

But she wants him to wash the dishes. So he will wash them, and when they're done he'll pull out another tea towel and help her finish drying. He will turn off the light and plunge the apartment into darkness again, and he will put his hand on her shoulder to guide them both gently down the corridor to the bedroom. He'll wrap his arm around her in the bed, and if he's lucky she'll let him stay like that for a few moments. He might even dip into sleep before she slips away from him, clinging to the very edge of the bed as if to a life raft.

If it is the very rarest of mornings, she will even still be there when he wakes up.

17

Edward knows he is too happy. Filled with a joy that – like this heatwave – must surely, eventually burst.

In these first few days, in the freefall bliss of meeting, he forgets he has an apartment, forgets he should play it cool. They meet after Charlotte's lectures, after the library. He skulks outside every university building in Paris, it seems, waiting to get that glimpse of her as she saunters out into the street and smiles at him.

She is doing a Master's, she tells him repeatedly, because she believes in people. After a week or so he meets her friends, and they all seem to believe too. Amorphous groups sitting hunched outside cafés, immersed in clouds of cigarette smoke and liberal outrage. They're nicotine-thin and unwashed, and they shout passionately about things Edward half under-stands.

He concentrates instead on the smoke rings floating effort-lessly from Charlotte's lips. He loves the way she leans in to take the glowing embers from his mouth. They spend every night together, and when his night terrors jolt him upright the tangle of her arms and sheets pull him back. When he sees his sister's face in dreams, it is only for a moment. She haunts him, but more briefly.

He tells Charlotte immediately about the meeting he witnessed in the Vincents' apartment. Secretly he is thrilled about it – not the meeting itself, but the chance to tell Charlotte about something in which he participated, about something more real than his drifting hours between cafés and the bookshop. She is, as he predicted, appalled.

'That's vile. *Vile*. Thank god you spoke out! When do they move in, this family?'

'I don't know, but everyone's on tenterhooks.'

It's true, the building has been holding its communal breath since César Vincent called his meeting. People trot more quickly through the courtyard, heads down, avoiding each others' gazes, nervous of any interaction that might lead to conflict. Every time the great turquoise door opens, Edward and Frédérique look up from their books. 'Not yet,' one says to the other, and further up the building, in all the different apartments, the other residents whisper the same thing.

'Tenterhooks?'

He loves explaining the oddities and idiosyncrasies of English words to her. Her English is almost flawless and that makes him love these moments of confusion even more, where her brows knit together and lips jut forward in a cherry-ripe pout. The words become secrets held between them, holding them together. 'Tenterhooks', 'flabbergasted', 'nut-job' – they escape in the evenings when they drink with her friends, a lover's code.

Edward can't tell if it's the heat that amps up these conversations – this suffocating summer that leaves a perpetual sheen on his forehead, perpetual stains on his clothes. The French is fast, frenzied. He can just about follow it, but doesn't trust his own to stand up to the level of debate. Mostly he leans back, his arm loose around Charlotte's waist. Julien, the stocky friend who'd originally brought her to the bookshop, scowls at him.

'But isn't it the right of any democracy to be allowed to protest,' a pale blonde girl asks one night when the heat is so solid and compact that not even beer can cut through its grip, 'however hideous the opinion?'

'But what about my right as a Jew, a Muslim, a woman, an immigrant not to be hated in my own street?'

'It's not even that,' Charlotte counters, waving Edward's

cigarette across the table. 'It's that the extreme Right is mobi-
lising in ways we haven't seen before. They're making it okay
for ordinary people to feel like that. It was never like this
before, you know,' she speaks directly to him for a second
and his stomach leaps. 'When I was younger you never saw
people dare to show these opinions, it was hidden, secret –
this is out on the fucking boulevards.'

'Or worse!' a redhead chimes in from across the table,
flashing his phone in people's faces. 'Look what we found. A
Parisian forum for this horseshit.' He puts on a whining
miserable voice. '"*Dirty Muslim immigrants moving into our
building*", "*Don't feel safe on the streets of Paris any more*"
– that's someone *here*, in the city! Can you imagine!'

'I think we should ask what Edward thinks.' Julien's smirk
is greasy, patronising. Edward cannot think of a better word
than 'cocksure' as the other man flexes a muscled forearm
and settles his gaze on him. 'Or should we switch to
English?'

Happily his French holds up long enough to say it's terrifying, that he hates the anger, hates that it makes him angry
too. His reply is short, basic, he's pretty sure he gets a tense
wrong, but when he finishes Charlotte turns and plants a
lingering kiss on his lips. On the periphery of his vision Julien
shrugs and looks away, but when they leave hours later Edward
catches him whispering urgently in Charlotte's ear.

Walking home, to her home, Edward feels like he's won a
prize. The excitement effervesces, so much that he leaps up
onto a lamppost to tear down one of the latest protest posters.
Something big is happening next weekend and the city is
plastered with them: fierce slogans and the Right's typically
white, male, middle-aged face.

Charlotte hoots and hollers, claps her hands, but as Edward
crumples the paper face in his, he notices a group of men
further down the street putting these posters up. Looking
down he realises his hands are covered in wet glue.

Charlotte hasn't seen them and is still cheering him on.

'Shh, shh!' He pulls her into a doorway.

'What?'

'Look!'

The light of the next streetlamp catches three closely shaved heads, three sets of broad shoulders as they slap glue mixture from buckets up against the wall and spread their posters on it. Just as Charlotte is whispering 'Fucking hateful' under her breath, a fourth man appears out of the darkness.

'Oh my god.'

'What?'

Edward strains his eyes against the darkness and the many glasses he's downed tonight. 'I think that's my neighbour.'

'What? Which one?'

'That one, the one who has hair!'

They watch, and sure enough it is César Vincent waddling over, bucket and brush in his hands. He's swapped his smart, expensive clothes for a pair of old jeans and a white jacket. With his round glasses and his floppy schoolboy hair, he's completely out of place, but no less fervent slathering the walls with his propaganda.

'Him? The one who's angry about the Muslim family?' Charlotte asks as César's group finishes their work and heads off into the night.

'Yeah.'

'I'm going to fucking talk to him—'

'No!' Edward grabs her by the arm. 'What're you doing?'

'What are *you* doing Edward? Aren't you going to stand up to this, this awful man?'

'Charlotte, I'm not standing up to those guys. They looked like skinheads!'

'Yeah well, they probably are, knives in their pockets ready to slash anyone who gets in their way.'

'Exactly!'

'What, you're scared, so you won't say anything?'

'No, I mean . . . Look, *he's* not like that. Monsieur Vincent, he's old, he's . . . posh! He's a banker for God's sake!'

'Look at him! Look what he's doing.'

'I know, but . . .'

'But what?'

And Edward doesn't know what. Doesn't know how to say that in the village pub there are men who are like César Vincent, less well dressed than César Vincent, but men of his age who grumble about Europe and immigrants and the bloody migrant crisis. And he *hates* it, he's always hated it, but he's never done anything because they're not bad people, for the most part. Just different – different generation, different education . . . But he can't say this to Charlotte, so she stands and watches him flounder, eyes fierce under the streetlamp. When she speaks, she folds her arms tightly around herself, as if folding him out.

'You have to say something to him.'

'Come on.' Edward tugs at her forearm, but she holds firm.

'I mean it, Edward.' Her words hang like a threat in the humid air.

18

'César Vincent? I don't believe it!' Frédérique is perched atop a stepladder reorganising a pile of books on Turner. 'I don't like the man but I can't believe that.'

'I'm telling you!' Edward hurries over to steady the ladder, which wobbles every time she speaks. 'It was him!'

'César Vincent? Putting up fascist posters?!'

'I don't know if they were strictly fascist, but yes, César Vincent putting up posters for the Far Right!'

'Well.' Frédérique turns in her seat. 'I suppose we should have guessed something was wrong at that meeting. I wonder if his wife knows.'

'Maybe she feels the same way.'

'No, I don't think so somehow.' Frédérique has that faraway look in her eyes again. 'She looked very worried during that meeting. Besides,' she turns back to the shelf in front of her, 'she can't be that right wing – she works with books.'

'What?'

'She's a librarian. I refuse to believe a librarian could support the *Front National*!'

Her Turners organised – or at least less disorganised than they were when she started – Frédérique climbs down the ladder. Edward holds her hand for the last steps. She is about to thank him when a slip in one of their wrists allows one of her rings to scratch him.

'Oh, I'm sorry!'

'It's nothing, don't worry.'

'No, let me look.'

She cradles his hand as they watch drops of blood bead

along the skin. Their heads almost touching, each can feel the other's breath, damp clouds in the stifling air. They stay, perhaps, a moment too long, Frédérique pondering the weight of Edward's hand, Edward the softness of Frédérique's.

'Oh bloody thing!' Frédérique pulls away first, wrenching the offending ring off her finger. 'It's lethal. I am sorry, Edward.'

'Honestly it's nothing.'

They retreat in silence to their separate corners of the shop.

'Are you making—'

'Have you heard from—'

Their words clatter into each other. Frédérique strikes again first.

'Are you making friends here, Edward?'

'Err, yes, I guess so. Students, mostly.'

'Oh good, good.' Frédérique concentrates unusually hard on the Matisse monographs in front of her. 'Nice for you to have friends your own age.'

'Yes.'

Another pause. Edward tries again.

'Have you heard from Emilie recently?'

'Emilie? Not so recently, no.'

'She's always super busy.'

'Yes.'

This time the silence continues.

Sex, she knew it as soon as she saw him today. There was a looseness to his gait, a soft smile on his face. Well good for you Edward, she'd thought. That's what a young man in Paris should be doing. But now somehow it's shifted. The touch, the blood, it's brought a charge into the air, and there's no way to avoid it except this awful silence. *So British*, she tells herself, and yet she too keeps her lips firmly sealed.

Eventually, one of her devotees heaves open the courtyard door and totters into the shop, moth-eaten cardigan flapping in the breeze. With a third presence, the pull between them is dissipated, the air demagnetised, and they work on in quiet companionship until Frédérique looks up quite suddenly and says, 'I'll close up tonight, Edward.' Edward says his good-nights and Frédérique is left alone with her books. She sits down at the desk, head in her hands.

Touch had been the hardest thing to lose when Daniel died. She had not expected it, but tactility's absence had almost broken her. She remembers her son in clammy hands, hot skin, wet kisses against her neck, the silkiness of his hair when he fell asleep in her lap.

In the decade since, she has lived within the confines of her own skin. Self-contained. The return to Paris was a withdrawal from the senses, a refusal to be contiguous with anyone or anything. If, in that first desolate year, she sometimes rode the metro at rush hour just to feel the crush of other bodies, she has long since grown accustomed to her isolation. Touch is rare now, and this episode with Edward has shaken her.

Chantal Vincent appears through the courtyard door looking tired and drawn. In the moments before she looks up, Frédérique sees the slump of the other woman's shoulders, the downward slope of her lips. Their eyes meet, and Chantal offers an uneasy wave. Frédérique responds in kind.

It is unusual for any of number thirty-seven's residents to visit Frédérique's shop. Fairly unusual for anyone to visit at all, and those who live closest to it are the least likely customers. Many hardly know it's there, or, in the busy rush of their daily lives, have never stopped to think what might be in this space at the bottom of Bâtiment B. So it is strange that Chantal now diverts from her usual route across the courtyard, strange that she taps on Frédérique's door.

Laden with her evening's groceries, she stands awkwardly in the doorway.

'I wanted to apologise about that meeting.'

'Apologise?'

'Yes.' Chantal's eyes range over the books, flitting from one brightly coloured cover to another. 'César's behaviour was . . . unacceptable that day. I'm sorry you got caught up in it.'

Neighbours for some ten years, Chantal and Frédérique have rarely spoken this many words together. Proximity does not invite closeness, and all the years of polite *bonjours* and the waving at each other across the courtyard have really served to demarcate their own space, not invite the other in. It crowds around them now; the weight of friendship that might have been.

Frédérique holds her tongue. She senses the other woman has more to say.

'I really don't know what's wrong with him at the moment, or where these . . . *feelings* come from. But I—I wanted you to know that I don't hold them. And I don't think César does, really. He's not a bad person.'

'No.'

'No.'

Chantal smiles a wan, resigned smile.

'I should let you get on, I'm sure you've lots of things to be doing.'

'Not really, just organising the books.'

'You have lovely things down here.' Chantal trails a finger over a nearby cover. 'I'll have to come down and have a proper look sometime.'

'Yes, do.'

They smile at each other, the polite smile of people who have been strangers too long to make the leap to friendship. Both know that this meeting and its frankness are the exception to a long-standing rule. Tomorrow they will wave politely at each other again across the courtyard. Chantal will not visit the bookshop.

'Well, goodnight Frédérique.'

'Goodnight Chantal.'

Once again the door swings shut, and Frédérique watches Chantal make her way to her apartment. Instinctively, she goes to straighten the book the other woman has touched. It is the Ingres catalogue she looked at with Edward on his first day. She flips through it idly, wondering which picture it was that reminded him of his sister.

'Come on, dear.'

She gives herself a little shake, puts down the book, and turns off the lights. Stepping out into the street, she wonders what to do. She is restless. Cigarette? A drink somewhere? As she is deciding, she hears the strike of a match and sees a flame appear in the doorway opposite.

'Good evening, Frédérique.'

Crouching on his heels, the man with the off-kilter eyes looks up at her.

'Evening, Josef.'

He gestures to the step, where he has just laid down two cushions. 'Please.'

She sits.

'Were you expecting someone?' She gestures to the cushions, the two cups he has placed in front of them.

'Thought you might be coming by.'

She doesn't ask how he knows this. He pours a slug of red wine into each cup. 'Your good health.'

'And yours.'

They drink. The wine is big and bold and surprisingly good. Not for the first time, Frédérique wonders where Josef acquires such things.

'So what's new, Jo?'

'Getting harder to find places.'

'To set up camp?'

He nods, setting light to a meticulously clean campstove.

'Lot of folks getting abuse these days. Beaten up, spat at, even in the city.'

'I read about the attack at Châtelet.'

Josef grunts, a mixture of derision and phlegm. He cracks two eggs into the pan.

'What's new here?' He nods at number thirty-seven.

'Oh, not much. Emilie's got a friend staying—'

Josef nods. 'I see him. Young. Sad. Not from here.'

'No, he's English. Then there was a big hoo-ha last week. A Muslim family is moving in, supposedly, and the head of the residents' association went berserk.'

'You watch out for him,' Josef warns darkly, flipping his eggs. 'He's not right.'

'What do you mean?'

But Josef just shakes his head. 'Not right. In with a bad crowd.'

Frédérique waits, but nothing more is forthcoming. She drinks her wine. How does he know these things? How can he who is on the outside know more than those on the inside?

'And take care for that woman with the kiddies.' He's slipping the eggs into bread now.

'Madame Lagrange?'

'Three little ones. Keep an eye on her.'

'Okay, Jo.'

Frédérique sits in silence as Josef produces two tiny glass jars, one for pepper, one for salt, and carefully seasons his dinner.

'Do you need anything? Is there anything I can get you?'

He shakes his head and gestures at his trolley. 'Everything I need on these four wheels.'

'Alright then. Enjoy your dinner.' She rises to go. 'Take care of yourself, Josef.'

'You take care of yourself, Frédérique.'

19

Anaïs would be shocked to hear Josef talking about her. Shocked to hear he'd noticed her at all. Not that she has really noticed him, not beyond crossing to the other side of the street when she sees his trolley, not beyond thinking to herself that it's not nice having a homeless person opposite. In her eyes, the homeless are alike in their anonymity, and while she'd like to feel charitable towards them, what is there separating this man from the one who accosted her in the back of the church? They might even be the same person.

Paul, of course, would see things differently. Oh yes, Paul would want to sit and talk, give money and tell him the ways of Jesus. Bring him round to the fold. Typical Paul.

(And she's right, that *is* typical Paul. He's often dropped coins into Josef's cup on his way home, sat and spoken a few words until the other man has smiled and gently shaken his head.)

Anaïs wonders if she might have done that once, back when she felt her faith more keenly. But in her village growing up there *were* no homeless people. Most people *were* good Catholics. And if there was poverty it was on the farms, in farmhouses that hadn't been decorated for fifty years, mould running down living room walls, putrid toilets in lean-to outhouses, not people living on the streets. Mostly men on those awful farms. She remembers visiting them with her father and shudders.

'Ana? Everything alright in there?'

Paul's voice pulls her from her reverie. He is knocking at the door. For Anaïs is in the bath, practising holding her breath underwater.

A gasp as she finally breaks the surface.

'Fine.'

She almost wants to laugh. Looking down at her ribs, her jutting hips, it seems as if her body's shrinking daily. She doesn't sleep. She barely eats. She hasn't cut yet, but she dances knives along her skin, holds her breath underwater, wonders about stepping out quickly into busy boulevards, and Paul only notices when he wants to get into the bathroom himself. 'Everything alright?', however tenderly voiced, is inevitably code for 'how long are you going to be in there?'

She heaves herself out of the tub and stands shivering on the bathmat, her hair dripping rats' tails down her back.

It comes to her quite suddenly in the glare of the fluorescent light, the realisation that she's got her body wrong. A revelation so shocking that she has to grab hold of the counter to steady herself. Looking anew at the sag of skin, the blocked pores, the pimply gooseflesh, her fear changes. She sees instantly, with dazzling clarity, that there is no need to cut her skin. She is at breaking point already. Not a metaphorical breaking point either: surveying the push of ribs through papery skin, the bones that poke through raw and swollen knuckles, she suddenly understands that she might actually break. Crumble. Fragment. A knock or a touch would be enough to split her into oblivion.

Gingerly she takes her towel, and pats with utmost care at the water droplets on her skin. Her heart is pounding, caught between fear and exhilaration. She might break. She might break! 'You might break,' she whispers to the face in the mirror and even as her lips move she wonders if they too might shatter.

'Ana? You coming out?'

'Yes, I'm coming.'

With enormous care she wraps the towel around herself and unlocks the door. Her steps are fairy light – it takes huge concentration to walk without splintering – but eventually she makes it to the bedroom. Sure enough, she hears the slide of the bathroom bolt, the cacophony of satisfied grunts that follow.

Perched at the end of the bed, heart fluttering in her chest, Anaïs understands everything now through the prism of fracture. There was the first breaking, the wedding night with its sharp rip through that secret web. Her pregnancies, the obscene swelling of her skin into enormous, parasitic growths that did not hold themselves but were hauled and hung from her flesh as if they might simply break off. She remembers the bulge and burst of it, remembers the births themselves as pain so acute and all-consuming that it threatened to extinguish her. She remembers, near the end, the long, slow rip of flesh.

She looks down at her hands, and a fingernail she's been worrying loose for weeks falls off into her palm. Falls clean away leaving puckered skin beneath. As her hair dries, she feels its strands dropping out too, the feather-light tickle of fall down her back. Standing, her joints click ominously and everything foreshadows total disintegration.

From the other side of the bathroom door the familiar rumble-flush of the ancient toilet. The hiss of air freshener and now Paul is beside her again, wrapping his arms around her, nuzzling her neck the way she loved when they were newly wed. But she's not twenty-five any more and the thought of dissolving into his arms is terrifying. The lightest touch sets panic to her throat.

'Paul . . .' She steps away from him. 'Don't.'

'Don't what?'

She eyes his strong hands with new alarm. They would crush her.

'I don't want to.'

'Don't want to what?'

'Do that. Tonight.'

He drops his hands. 'Is everything alright?'

'Yes, fine, I just . . . can't, tonight.'

I can't have any more babies. I can't give myself up to you. I can't let anyone else maul at my body because it is simply going to shatter.

'I miss you, Ana.' This he says softly, in a low voice that catches in his throat.

'I'm here, I'm right here.' She tries to placate him, but he is moving towards her again and fear of touch is rising in her throat.

'I love you.' He catches her by the wrist and she tries to keep the panic out of her voice.

'I love you too, but Paul, please—'

'What?' He is trying to pull her towards him and she screams, more loudly than she intends.

'Paul, don't, I'm going to break, I'm going to break!'

His face drops into utter panic, but he doesn't drop her arm.

'What?'

'Please, Paul, please, please I'm going to break, you're going to break me!'

The wrist is dropped and he steps away.

'Break you? What does that even mean? Ana?'

Cradling her hand, she cannot answer.

'*Anaïs?*'

'I just . . . I just . . .' She cannot give voice to the words. They are the truest thing she's felt in months, but she knows they would sound ridiculous to him. *I think I am going to break. I am breaking.*

'*Break* you?' Paul repeats the words with utter incredulity, with anger rattling in his throat, and as they reverberate between them she can see in his face how strange they sound to him. People break up, they break down, they break out of prison, they break into houses, but to Paul's deeply logical mind they don't just break. He stands on his side of the bed, convinced that they do not. She stands on hers, convinced that they do – that she will – and she can see no way to bridge this gap. Everything between them, everything they own, everything they've made, everything they've shared together seems to evaporate, until they are just two strangers facing off across a void.

'Are you going to say anything?' he asks eventually.

'I don't know what to say.'

Slowly he turns on his heel towards the children's room and she is left alone in the empty bedroom, horribly, guiltily grateful.

20

The next day dawns close and heavy over number thirty-seven. The air is thick with tension, electrical and otherwise. A storm is coming.

Charcoal clouds race ominously across the sky, while, at their breakfast table, César and Chantal enact an uneasy ceasefire. He is back in his suit, chipping dried glue off his fingernails, his phone buzzing with news from Sylvain. She is reading the newspaper, pretending not to notice. She refuses to ask who these flurries of text messages are coming from.

Above them, the silence is deafening. Paul sought solace in the good book last night. He read in silence, prayed in silence. Now he sits in silence while Anaïs carries out the usual morning routine, her body carefully, fearfully going through the motions. His face has the anger of the ancient tribes and last night's words hang around them, much as Florence hangs around Paul's neck, and the baby growls in his crib, wanting to be picked up. Anaïs does not lift him. Paul prepares to leave for work and nothing is said. Words have ceased to work in this apartment.

On the top floor, Edward is waking up alone. It's the first time in weeks. He saw Charlotte last night at the bar as usual. They kissed and smoked and drank as usual, but she had an early meeting today, a project due, and he hadn't argued, but on his solitary walk home he'd replayed her explanations in his head until they took on a new, ill-omened weight. Over and over he saw Julien's self-satisfied smirk and waking now to dark skies, he is convinced that something is wrong.

For the first time in weeks, he thinks about his parents. Not just the half-hearted, brushed-off, batted-away thoughts. The difficult ones; the ones he's been doing so much to avoid. Home has receded to the periphery of his vision lately, a dark blur he catches at the curved edge of his sight, a blur he does everything to ignore. This morning, it rushes into full focus.

'Have a good time son.' His father's gruff voice, his down-cast eyes, mottled hands gripping the steering wheel. It had been the quietest drive of Edward's life. His dad, who always had a story to tell, who was always busy recounting what had happened to that ram, or who'd bought a duff heifer, or who was winning the darts tournament down the local pub. His dad, who couldn't manage more than a stiff wave as Edward walked towards the platform before quickly turning his back. His mum hadn't even managed that, twisted up in her armchair as usual, tears dripping slowly onto her dressing gown.

'I should be there,' he mutters, looking out over the pale, peaked Parisian roofs, watching someone walk through the courtyard with a baguette under each arm. 'I should be there.'

Down in the shop, Frédérique twists the rings on her fingers, jumps a little each time the courtyard door opens.

'Is everything ok?' Edward asks.

She looks up.

'Sorry, I'm on the edge today.'

'The edge?'

'On edge, on edge. It's this weather, and . . .' She pauses, wondering whether to tell him about Josef and his dark forecasts. 'It feels like something bad is going to happen.'

Edward looks up at the square of blackening clouds he can see above the courtyard.

'I hear that.'

It's Frédérique's turn now to look at him. This skinny Englishman has glowed in Paris. She's watched his freckles multiply and creep across his skin. She's watched the lines around his eyes fade, the taut grip of his shoulders loosen. He's come to life here. But today, the dark circles beneath his eyes are back. He's biting at the skin around his fingernails. He looks profoundly unhappy. Funny, she thinks, that Josef didn't have a prophecy for him.

'And what about you, Edward?'

'Me?'

'Your body's here but your mind is somewhere else.'

He looks at her. She can almost see the debate taking place inside his head, whether to brush it off or talk about it. A tightrope he is walking, and should he cling to what he knows or pitch into the abyss?

His voice is low. 'I was thinking about my parents today.'

'Why today?'

'I don't know.' A pause. 'I'm thinking maybe I should be there.'

'Do you think it would help?'

'I don't know. Maybe? Maybe I should be there whether it helps or not.'

Frédérique pulls her chair next to his.

'Edward, I can promise you truly that nothing helps.'

His shoulders slump and she can hear the sadness catching in his throat.

'I know . . . I just . . .'

The first tear falls onto the desk in front of them, and as it does Frédérique finds her arm reaching around his shoulder. Her hand strokes his soft, sandy hair as he buckles under the weight of his sobs. It is those things we lock away that come back the hardest, she thinks.

'I'm sorry—'

'Shhh.'

'I don't know why today . . .'

'It's okay. It comes in waves.'

'I miss her.'

'I know.'

And this is the first time she's stroked someone's hair in ten years. Sweet hay and meadows; how strange that it should remind her of that, of spring so definitely. When she came back after the fire she lay on the bed for weeks, her mother hovering awkwardly in the doorway, and how she would have loved to have felt someone's fingers in her hair back then.

They stay like this for some time. Gradually the racking of Edward's body begins to slow, no different from a child who has cried itself to sleep. Most people can only be distraught for so long.

He sits up, wiping his face roughly with the back of his hand. 'I'm sorry.'

'Edward, there is absolutely no need to apologise.'

She smiles as she says it and reaches to push the hair out of his eyes, and just as she does the door bursts open. It is Madame Marin, who pauses only momentarily on finding them in this strange embrace.

'I'm sorry to interrupt, Madame, but they are here, the new family is here!'

Edward is immediately up and at the back of the shop, wiping his face on his T-shirt. Frédérique is at Madame Marin's side in the doorway.

'They've arrived or it's just their furniture?'

'The furniture, Madame, but with things come people, no?'

Madame Marin is wringing her hands.

'I don't know, do you think I should tell the other residents, Madame?'

'No, absolutely not!' Frédérique is fierce enough for Madame Marin's painted eyebrows to climb a few centimetres higher up her face. 'They don't need to know their arrival has caused such heated debate here. No, as far as they're concerned and we're concerned they're just another family, no need to do anything out of the ordinary. Although –' she catches the departing *gardienne* by the silk of her kimono and says with a wink – 'I'm glad you told *us*.'

Madame Marin smiles her toothy, lipsticked, lipstick-on-teeth smile.

'Of course, Madame.' She winks conspiratorially, before her hand flies up to her mouth – '*Merde*, I left a client under the dryer!' – and she is trotting at double speed across the courtyard back to her salon.

A distant thunder crack rolls across the sky.

'Well, Edward,' Frédérique turns back to him, 'what a day this is shaping up to be.'

Edward is behind the counter, the book of Ingres portraits in his hands. She had not put it away last night.

'This is one of the books you showed me on my first day.'

'Yes.'

'*Ingres*.'

He pronounces it correctly, so it sounds like *anger* rolling off his tongue.

'One of them . . .' he flicks through the glossy pages, '. . . reminded me of Hannah. Here.'

Frédérique comes closer, and together they lean over the catalogue.

'She's beautiful,' Frédérique murmurs. 'Mademoiselle Rivière.'

The pronouncing of the name gives Edward pause.

'Where? Where does it say that?'

'Here, look.' Frédérique points to the caption on the opposite page.

'God.'

'What?'

'Our name. Our surname is Rivers. That's what Rivière means, right? Miss River.'

Frédérique nods. 'That is . . . strange.'

They stare down at the picture, her round face framed by dark hair and dark, curving eyebrows; eyes that are almost black staring out hesitantly, the tiniest bit of colour flaring in her pale cheeks.

'You know . . .' Frédérique herself is hesitant now. 'You could go and visit her Edward. The painting, I mean. She's in the Louvre.'

'Yeah.' Edward nods. 'Maybe I will.'

21

News of the new neighbours' arrival flits around number thirty-seven like a bird in flight, wings carrying the whisper of it up staircases, dancing it along the windowsills. A removal van has indeed pulled up in the street and mysterious belongings are beginning to emerge.

Madame Marin returns to the salon, where she clucks around her customers and scolds her assistants.

'*Martine*, how many times, don't schedule two perms at the same time!' A serpentine smile and a deep, '*I'm so sorry, Madame*' to the waiting customer as the browbeaten Martine returns to her telephone and her appointments book.

'Now, what do we have here? A nice smart bob again, Madame Claré?'

Madame Marin runs her hands through the hair in front of her, false fingernails pulling it taut at the root, while her eyes follow the goings on in the street.

A youngish man has appeared beside the van. He might be thirty, he might be forty; his dark hair is as yet unpeppered and his eyes are bright. He has a beard, but not the kind César Vincent would be afraid of. In a white shirt and jeans he fumbles excitedly with his new keys, with the scrap of paper on which he's written down the door code.

A family gaggle accompanies him. A young woman, also in jeans, her hair wrapped in an orange scarf. An older man with a stick that he's jabbing in the direction of various pieces of furniture. An older woman in a loose-fitting dress, wringing her hands in excitement.

From his vantage point in the doorway opposite, Josef

smiles. Are they his parents or hers, this older couple? Hard to say, but in any case, it's the younger ones Josef's focused on. The tender looks they throw each other. The smiles. The tiniest moment in the doorway where the husband's hand flutters tentatively over the wife's belly and Josef knows that a baby is coming, and he remembers that joy. A muscle memory that creaks within him, quieter than the click of his joints as he stands, rubs his hands along his thighs, and slowly pushes his trolley down the street.

Up in the building, number thirty-seven's residents are watching too. The family itself is no longer in sight, but Isabelle Duval maintains her post at her window, wincing at every stomp of the removal men's feet, snarling to herself about the quality of the furniture being unloaded. They are moving into the apartment below hers and already she detests the laughter floating up from beneath her floorboards.

Beyond her nocturnal investigations, Isabelle also has a day job, though it is a job from which she frequently claims sick days. She feigned illness today when she caught wind of the news of the new family's arrival. On the days she does venture to the office, she's a human resources manager for an academic publishing house, a title her colleagues joke about, since Isabelle is known for neither her management skills nor her humanity. Her presence is enough to fill the office with a chill, everyone from the newest intern to the CEO steering themselves out of her way. They don't know, these colleagues at whom she snaps, that she has been battling for a decade with medication; that the pills that were meant to level her out have done everything but. Puffed up, shrunk down, pulled high as a kite and dropped lower than she would have believed possible, they've done everything except make the road even.

An even road. That was her father's job. A city engineer in Bayonne, roads and bridges were his purview, his expertise, and it has always seemed to Isabelle that it was his departure that sent her path off course. From the age of eight she railed against a mother who did not have the capacity to be both parents, to step into the newly vacant pair of shoes. Her memories of her father are warped and faded now, steeped in the smell of hot tarmac and the sight – can it have been true? – of a team of neon-jacketed workers making new road under his command. She has carried for some thirty years or more the feeling of what she saw, or thought she saw, that day: her father berating a man for his error, seizing the rake, spreading the dark mixture himself. 'I'll just have to do it myself!' he shouted, and that is how Isabelle has felt too, through all these years of managing alone. Fiercely independent, she would say, though she's heard 'nitpicking' and 'micro-manager' bandied about in office whispers.

She has learned the hard way that independence is not conducive to coupling, though she rarely lets herself think about the distinction between being alone and being lonely. In French they are the same word – *seule* – knotted together with a smug insinuation she detests.

Besides, she would argue if anyone were brave enough to raise the subject, she is not alone. Computer, phone, tablet, she is as connected as anyone to the events of the world, a damn sight more connected than many. The online world is her solace, her sword, a weapon in the armoury with which she's already decided she's going to battle the happy couple she can hear below.

Chantal Vincent has also heard the van pull up and has been watching what she can from her bedroom window. César is at work and she is glad of it. Glad she doesn't have to try and reason with him. Glad these people can move in unencumbered.

When she and César first lived together, it was in a tiny studio in the fifth arrondissement. A stone's throw from the river, they ate their dinners on the footpath by the Seine. They walked in the evenings through the Jardin des Plantes. They made the city their garden since the flat itself was tiny and César was forever knocking his head on the sloping ceilings.

They didn't have much, then, but she had loved that garret home. Loved standing with her head in the skylight in order to stir the pots on the stove. Loved sitting in their one armchair, feet up on the window ledge. Rain was celebrated in that apartment: a festive percussion that ran all along the rooftops, a drum solo reserved for them alone.

Chantal wishes it would rain today. Break the spell that's hanging over them.

The phone rings, and as she turns to answer it the first fat drops fall onto the windowsill.

'Hello?'

'Madame Vincent?'

'Yes, speaking.'

'It's the printers, Madame. We have your invitations ready for collection.'

The invitations. César's party. All that time she'd spent a month ago agonising over colour schemes – blue and gold? Green and bronze? – and what does it matter now, when the intervening weeks have wrought this rift between them?

'Thank you, I'll come today.'

She'll come today, but even as she says it she wonders if there is any point. If César is too far gone from her now to be brought back by a simple birthday party. She'd tried voicing her fears to her friend Marine over lunch; blonde, buxom Marine whose first husband had tried to kiss Chantal more than once, first when drunk, on subsequent occasions when terrifyingly sober.

'Men!' Marine had proclaimed loudly, blowing cigarette smoke over the diners at the adjacent table. 'There'll be some bit of skirt he's chasing at work. You *know* what they're like.' She'd gestured crudely with her little finger while Chantal blushed into her salad. 'But he'll be back – César's a good boy, he knows how good he's got it.'

But Chantal doesn't know what 'they're' like. César's never been like this before. It's more than just a woman, she's certain of that.

The rain is picking up pace and by the time Chantal reaches the street, the storm has started in earnest. All the pressure falls away and as she fumbles in the turquoise doorway for her umbrella, the first lightning rends the sky, the first roll of thunder crashes. Already water is coursing down the pavement, lapping up through the gaps in her sandals.

The drama of it takes Chantal's breath away. Two removal men hurriedly bundle a dresser back into their van, their shouts whipped to nothingness by the noise. A pedestrian joins her in the doorway, seeking shelter. He shouts at her, but she doesn't hear him. She is remembering another storm.

When the doctor told them they could not have children, you could have heard a pin drop. They were speechless, their words taken by that brief and bitter diagnosis, the stark, disinfectant certainty of it. Total quiet in a city filled with noise, and then, in the privacy of the rooftop apartment, César broke. He roared, he slammed his fist into the wall and smashed the plasterwork. He wept and above them the rain drummed like this, and the next day he had started looking for a new apartment, one whose walls did not know his pain.

He was silent then, in the days and weeks that followed, the least talkative he's ever been, and it comes back to her in a rush as rainwater sprays up from the street and drips down from the doorway.

'It'll pass.'

The man next to her is smiling now from beneath the safety of a plastic rain jacket.

'Yes,' she replies blankly, 'it'll pass.'

22

The storm does pass, almost as quickly as it came, yet there is something incomplete about its passing. The air has not been cleared. Rather, it is as a prelude to something larger. Once again the city is pulled taut with summer heat, a violin string humming almost imperceptibly beneath the sound of daily life, waiting to snap.

On the third floor of Bâtiment A, Ahmed and Amina wake for the first time in their new home. It is early. The floor is a sea of boxes that Ahmed, his muscles railing against yesterday's graft, is happy to ignore. His wife, by contrast, is skipping through them to the kitchen, rummaging for the frying pan, determined to make a celebratory breakfast. Eggs and tomatoes, just the way they like them.

'What're you doing in there?' her husband shouts, burying his head into the pillows.

'Breakfast!'

He groans. 'I can't get up, I never want to see another box again!'

'Ah,' his wife smiles back from the doorway, 'I think you'd shift a thousand boxes if it meant you got fresh eggs.'

And sure enough he is up and out of bed, and they eat from one plate, standing in their kitchen, a plastic spoon for her and a plastic fork for him because who knows in which of the forty boxes the cutlery might be hiding. They fling open their shutters and sunlight warms the tiles beneath their feet. If anyone were watching, they'd see the dance of newly wed affection – pecks planted on cheeks, raspberries blown against earlobes, the scrabbling for who gets to keep their one set of keys – because ownership is new and exciting; they haven't had any bills yet, the washing machine hasn't flooded, the boiler won't break for another month or two, and for the first time they are somewhere that is really *theirs*.

'Let's go explore!' Amina is already in the bedroom throwing yesterday's clothes on.

'Shouldn't we unpack?'

'It's too nice of a morning to unpack.'

Ahmed tries a different tack.

'You're meant to be resting.'

'I'm not going to rest for the next seven months!'

And so, as usual, Amina wins, and soon they are trotting down the staircase hand in hand.

It is not until they're on the street that they hear it. A sort of distant roaring. Faint drums beating out a rhythm, as if a medieval army might be lurking around the corner. They walk towards the sound and at the intersection of two large boulevards find the source: a protest, readying itself to march.

It seems to Ahmed that there must be a thousand people here. People waving heraldic flags. People with placards against the President. A group in black holding horrible pictures of foetuses that make his stomach clench and his hand grip Amina's tighter. There's a lobby with signs about the European Union. On the other side of the street, a teenager is trying to set fire to a rainbow flag.

With every minute the crowd is growing. Amina and Ahmed hesitate, each unwilling to make the first retreating step. What world have they woken up to? Seconds pass and they are jostled in the crush.

'Get out of here!' a man shouts as he passes, deliberately knocking his brawny shoulder into Ahmed's. Another follows this warning with a gob of spit.

Amina seizes her husband by the arm and drags them free

of the crowd, down a warren of side streets, until they are no longer in the flow of protesters. In the quietness of a dank, urine-scented alley they look at each other.

'You okay?'

'Yes. You?'

'Yes.'

And it is true, it's nothing they haven't seen before. Ahmed had a teacher once who called him a darkie. Amina had someone shout at her on a bus last week. And yet. This has shaken them more than either of them would care to admit. Gently, Amina reaches for Ahmed's hand.

'Come, love. Let's explore a different way.'

The Laribis wouldn't know it, but further down the boulevard, some of their neighbours are encountering the same protest.

Edward is with Charlotte near Montparnasse. He saw her last night, stayed over, but the seeds planted in his mind are quickly ripening to bitter fruit. She took a phone call from Julien late into the night, and there is, he feels, a perceptible difference between them, so solid he could reach out and cup it in his hands. There was no closeness to their sleep and this morning their world is most definitely out of kilter.

Riot police have closed off Charlotte's street. They stand across it in an unbreakable line, fierce and armoured and looking, to Edward's mind, like Ninja Turtles in their jointed Kevlar suits. He tries this joke on Charlotte but it falls flat. She is in need of a cigarette and the police line is blocking their route.

'For fuck's sake.'

She storms back towards a side street, face tense with nicotine exasperation. Edward has to run to keep up with her. Four streets later they find a *tabac* and, relaxing into the cloud of her exhalation, they watch the protest roll by.

'Abortion, gays, Europe, liberals . . .' Charlotte counts off the placards as if it's a shopping list of unpleasant political opinions. 'Oh, look, that lot over there are against immigrants too.'

'Is there anything they're not against?'

'Nope.'

They stand in silence for a while. A few others stop too to watch this tide of anger flowing past. The totality is bad enough, but Edward finds the particulars more terrifying. A group of sharply dressed teenage boys holding banners wanting to ban abortion; families who've kitted out their children in anti-gay regalia; an old white man on the back of a float screaming into his megaphone about women's bodies.

He leans towards Charlotte, and for all the dissonance between them there is still the lavender smell of her hair, its softness against his cheek.

'This is fucked!' he shouts over the noise.

She shrugs and edges away from him. 'This is France.'

Amidst the crush of bodies, the noise and heat and fury of it, César Vincent is in his element.

This is the protest Sylvain had first told him of, and he is brimming with schoolboy excitement to be here. César has never been part of the gang before. He wasn't popular at school. At work he had colleagues, not friends. He and Chantal have lived their life with a pleasant rotation of pleasant acquaintances, the occasional dinner party, but he has never felt so completely part of something before and it thrills his fifty-year-old bones.

Beside him, Sylvain has dressed for the occasion: all in black, his head freshly shaved, boots polished to a fierce gleam. But, like so many people caught up in the wave of it, César doesn't see the menace.

'Come on César!' Sylvain shouts above the roar, nudging him in the ribs. 'FRENCH JOBS FOR FRENCH WORKERS! FRENCH JOBS FOR FRENCH WORKERS!'

César fills his lungs and they chant in unison, to the beat of Michel's drum and the stomp of their boots against the hot tarmac.

All day, the city rings with their cries. The sun bears down on them, burning the protesters, but this only makes their shouts louder. It is sunny and God is smiling on their anger.

Eventually the crowds disperse. The metros fill up and the bars spill out, beer and urine mingling in the streets as blows are exchanged between those who love France and those who don't.

At number thirty-seven, there is an uneasy quiet.

In the entryway, Chantal Vincent bumps into Frédérique.

'Terrible about these protests, no?'

Frédérique cocks her head, trying to gauge from the other woman's response whether her husband is there, whether Edward's extraordinary claims are right. But Chantal seems sincere; she looks more sad than guilty.

'Yes, terrible.'

'Just terrible.'

As these exchanges are taking place, Edward appears from the street. He left Charlotte ages ago and the hours of hot, aimless wandering show on his face.

'Drink?' Frédérique asks him and Edward nods, and it is Chantal's turn to look quizzically now as the young man and the older woman wind their way up the stairs together.

In Frédérique's apartment, Edward collapses on the sofa, heat-soaked and exhausted. Head in his hands, he rubs his palms viciously into his eye sockets.

'I keep seeing her face,' he says.

'Go and see the painting, Edward.' Frédérique hands him an icy glass. 'Lay the ghost.'

23

Edward steps onto the train and into the crush of the morning commute, armpit to armpit with the city. Perfume and cigarette smoke cloy, and the proximity's uncomfortable: not just the press of unknown bodies or the rising heat, but the glances caught and quickly dropped again, the whole carriage retreating to its screens. Bone-ache, spine-judder, and the tap-tap-tap of thumbs against glass. Someone's breath falls hot and moist against his neck, and those who can contort themselves over the morning's newspapers, burying their noses in photos of the previous day's protest.

He is early to get to the museum, as Frédérique told him to be. One of just two or three milling around, he stands by the great glass pyramid entrance and tries to count the statues that decorate the vast building.

Quickly the line begins to grow behind him, snaking its way around the courtyard. Children run shrieking past the fountains, whilst tourists with selfie sticks lurch drunkenly back and forth, teetering precariously on the bollards near the road trying to snap a photo with their fingers on top of the pyramid's point. Men arrive with bin bags full of keyrings – 'One euro, one euro, one euro' – while anxious, unwieldy tour groups barrel past each other, bickering about who deserves first place in the queue, and the courtyard is a Babel. Noise, confusion, dust.

At nine o'clock, with more grunting than fanfare, a guard appears and heaves open the metal door. Immediately the crowd surges forward and the security team starts up a loud but tired chorus: BAGS OPEN, THIS WAY PLEASE, I SAID THIS WAY. Bagless, Edward slips through.

Inside the pyramid, it is quieter. Edward can hear his footsteps reverberate in the still air, though the noise of the crowd outside is mounting. Most people, he realises, are running straight for the Mona Lisa, jostling past him as though art were an athletic event and prizes given for the fastest visitor. He follows the directions Frédérique has given him ('The map might as well be in hieroglyphics!') and sets off alone for the second floor.

Scuff marks along the walls, paint cracking – this is clearly a little-loved part of the museum. Giant, echoing rooms stretch forward, covered in paintings no one but Edward has come to see.

Edward winds his way through the silent galleries, a half smile creeping over his lips when he recognises a painting from one of Frédérique's books ('It's like meeting old friends,' she'd told him once). But he is nervous, clicking through each of his knuckles in order.

Suddenly, he sees her. Mademoiselle Rivière in a small square gallery, and as he steps down into it he is glad to be alone.

The resemblance is all the more uncanny in the flesh, or the not-flesh, for this is paint on canvas but it is also his sister as if she is standing before him. Dropping onto a bench Edward's eyes fill with tears.

His sister. His hilarious, infuriating, wonderful sister. The only person who knows by a flash of the eyes what he's thinking, who can make him laugh without doing anything at all. Hannah, who shared every side-splitting childhood moment, who was there each time they stole the cake mixture raw from the oven because it was so much better uncooked; each time they blamed mud or mess or a broken bone on the dog; who was there for every game of hide and seek, every terrifying swing across the river, their mouths as wide as the tyre they flew on.

They were eleven-and-a-half months apart. Irish twins (how their mother hated that phrase). But if their bond was not forged in the womb, it was cast in the fields around the house, in feeding the cows and making daisy chains, panning for treasure in the stream, sneaking their first illicit cigarettes on the hilltop in the purple air as twilight encircled the valley.

It is not the usual way, for sons to go to university and daughters to stay on the farm. But Hannah was fierce and brilliant, as happy and competent as any man to plunge her arms into entrails and gizzards, blood and steam rising from new birth in the middle of a freezing night. Far happier and more competent than Edward would have been.

Happy, too, to lecture him. *Come home, come help, mum needs you, we need you.* Happy to take on the role of the older sibling, and he was happy to let her. Eleven-and-a-half months. He doesn't remember life without her and now he's having to relearn it, day by jarring day, her loss thick and substantial against his bones.

Tears course down his cheeks and his breath comes in noisy bursts.

It is the injustice of it that hurts the most. The stupid things they bickered about on the last day. That he'd lost track of the time in the pub and delayed dinner. About who was going to take mum to her next appointment. The worst thought to rattle its way around his brain is that, with the tables turned and sides of the car switched, if her feet had run like his across the street in time and he had fallen beneath the bumper, *she* would have been able to do something.

'You would have known what to do,' he tells her likeness, and Mademoiselle Rivière stares placidly back at him.

A middle-aged Japanese man wanders into the gallery. Audio guide on full blast, he doesn't seem to have heard Edward's words. Camera in hand, he snaps several photos before pausing to take in the young man sobbing on the bench. The tears unnerve him, for as quickly as he came he is scuttling awkwardly out of the gallery, 'sorry, sorry, sorry' under his breath, a flattened palm waving behind him.

The room falls silent once again, save the distant murmur of the air conditioning which whirs into action every few minutes to send an icy blast up out of the grates. Gooseflesh creeps along Edward's skin and he is back in that raw February day, the air so sharp it hurt to breathe, the world around them blanched and frigid, and he can see the clouds of breath as they huddle over Hannah's body, him and the driver and the passers-by who stopped to help. No white clouds from her mouth. No colour at all, save the dark blood in her hair that crept wet and glistening onto the road. And when the ambulance did arrive, he did not hear it at all, did not hear anything, saw only the blaze of lights against the leaden sky.

At first Edward doesn't register the siren that brings the Japanese man clattering back into his gallery. A tall woman in red appears in the opposite doorway, looking at them quizzically, and gradually his ears adjust and he can hear the neon wail of it now. A muffled announcement is being broadcast, but Edward understands less of the English than he does of the French. It sounds like an enormous bearded man in the highest corner of the museum, a microphone warped and distorted by masses of facial hair.

In silence, Edward and the Japanese man and the woman in red walk tentatively towards the central gallery. They look uneasily at each other before a guard appears, puffed out and half-running.

'Come on, come on.'

He sounds more bored than worried to Edward's ears.

'What's going on?'

'Evacuation. Move it.'

And so they do, the three of them spiralling down a hidden staircase until they emerge into a slow-moving crowd in one of the museum's grand and ornately decorated halls. They inch forward, as if dragging their feet through treacle.

'Come on, come on!'

There are more guards down here, and along with numbers they've picked up urgency.

'Hurry it up!'

The crowd moves as one, its voice one polyglot murmur of concern. Somewhere in the mass of it Edward loses the Japanese gentleman. Almost to the exit, he can see the red dress of the tall woman ahead of him.

It is only when he is back under the pyramid that Edward realises the scale of the operation. There must be thousands of people converging on this space, hot, compressed, panicky. Some take photos to dissipate the tension – of themselves, the crowd, the pyramid. Still, the muffled voice booms over-head and looking up, Edward's eyes seize on the pinnacle of glass above him.

'Jesus Christ,' he thinks, 'if this blows . . .' And he has to stop himself thinking about how many shards of glass this edifice might shatter into, or just how that would play out for those stuck below. His tongue sticks to the roof of his parched mouth while sweat pours down his neck, springs from the creases of his palms.

Finally, it is his turn to climb the staircase and he can feel cool air beckoning him from its summit. At the door, two burly guards are shovelling people out into the courtyard. Dazed, bewildered, they stand around in little groups, or gape gormlessly at the entrance, holding out their tickets, seeming to query in the curve of their brows the possibility of re-entry.

Edward grabs one of the men by the arm.

'What's going on?'

'Keep moving, sir.'

A push to the shoulder but Edward holds on.

'Please,' he uses his best French this time, 'what's happening?'

The guard eyes him suspiciously, then yields.

'An attack.'

'Here?'

'No, Notre-Dame. All public buildings evacuated.'

Edward can see the sweat beading along the man's hairline, trickling down to his pale-blue collar. What must it be like to be this man, responsible for these thousands of people, his gun pressing firmly into his thigh, the possibility of attack at any moment?

'Please,' the guard's brown eyes fix on Edward's, 'keep moving.'

He does. All along the banks of the Seine, sirens race in the direction of the Île de la Cité. Between fleets of police cars and ambulances, Edward crosses to the bridge. He can see Notre-Dame's towers from here, can make out the point of its spire, stabbing sharp against the sky. Others stop to look too, and it is only as his fingers grip the bridge's rough-hewn stone that he realises he has been shaking.

His phone rings. Emilie.

'Oh thank god, are you alright?'

'Yes.'

'I was terrified Freddie had sent you sight seeing and you'd got caught up in it.'

'Almost. She sent me to the Louvre today.'

'Jesus!'

'It's okay, we've been evacuated. I'm by the river now.'

'Have you seen the news?'

'No, what's going on?'

'Gunmen in Notre-Dame. They don't seem to know how many. At least ten people dead. They shot up a café, too, as they went in.'

'Christ alight.'

'Yeah.'

There is a pause. Another ambulance tears past, its peals deafening the awkwardness of talking again.

'It's good to hear you, Ed,' as the wails fade into the distance.

'You too. It's . . . Thanks for letting me be here.'

'It's helping?'

He thinks back to the painting he has left behind, with a sudden pang of concern for its safety. 'Yeah, yeah it is.'

'Good.' Her turn to pause now. 'I should go, I've got a class waiting . . .'

'Yeah, of course. Thanks for checking in.'

'Take care, Ed. Get home safe.'

'You too—' but already she is gone.

On the corner of the Boulevard Saint-Germain, Edward stops to send his dad a text message. Sartre and de Beauvoir used to debate here, to read and write the greats, and all he can manage is a 'Don't know if you've seen the news. I'm fine. Love Edward.'

It will likely go unanswered, this message. Or, if responded to, his dad's words will come in one lowercase line, urgent and unaffected; a twenty-first-century telegraph.

All around, waiters are packing up, collecting cutlery and glasses from tables, slamming menus shut with a dissatisfied air. They've seen this before; they know no one is coming to lunch today.

Along the pavements, everyone is walking home. A nervy mass of people hurrying away from the city centre. Turning up towards Montparnasse and the skyscraper that looms grey and ominous over this quarter of the city, Edward, too, walks home.

24

News of the attack has reached number thirty-seven. The business of hairdressing has been abandoned, and instead Madame Marin and her two pink-coated assistants stand in the courtyard talking urgently, hands clamped to their cheeks. Monsieur Marin has taken it upon himself to pull his television into the doorway of their house. Its wires as taut as his wife's stockings, he tunes it to the news channel as a small group forms to watch the story unfold.

Frédérique leaves the shop and stares transfixed at the screen in front of her. She does not have a television, so the footage of the cathedral seen from the air, the whir of the chopper's blades, the urgency in the newscasters' faces and the facts they shout above the noise of the sirens hit her with unusual force.

Gilles, who has been perusing a catalogue on the Pre-Raphaelites, stands next to Monsieur Marin. They are equally silent, Gilles creaking his weight back and forwards, Monsieur Marin still, his arms folded in stony embrace.

Chantal returns home from the market. The news has flown around the stalls, blaring from hastily tuned radios and flashing up on people's phones. She could take her shopping upstairs and watch the television in her own apartment, but there is compulsion in the communal. Dropping a bag of meat and fruit at the side of the courtyard (a single peach rolling right up to Madame Marin's stiletto), she joins the others. No one has anything to say, but there is comfort in guttural exhalations shared, in shaking heads together, in speechless incredulity. Tiny Monsieur Lalande from the top floor is ushered to the front since everyone else can see above his bald and freckled head, and when he shouts 'This is a bad business' to no one in particular everyone nods in wordless agreement.

Images whirl in front of them, the same scenes over and over: terror in full Technicolor. The cathedral surrounded by emergency vehicles, lights flashing. Police officers standing at cordons. Terrified tourists running from the scene. Two Italian men gesticulate wildly; a German woman breaks down as she describes hearing the first shots. 'So loud, so loud,' she says, her voice wobbling as she turns from the camera, and even in their proximity the residents turn a little from each other as her tears fall.

It is, indeed, a bad business.

Up on the fourth floor, Isabelle Duval slams her shutters, causing the courtyard congregation to jump. She prefers to watch in private, in the gloom, eyes cycling wildly between television, phone, tablet, computer, all of which give her the same information. *ATTACK IN NOTRE-DAME, UNKNOWN GUNMEN, AT LEAST TEN DEAD, UNCONFIRMED REPORTS, MAJOR INCIDENT, HEAVY POLICE PRESENCE.*

'Come on, come on,' Isabelle whispers to the news reporters, fingertips pressed tightly together. 'Admit they're Muslims, just tell us that.'

'*We cannot at this time,*' comes the nasal drawl of the police spokesman, '*confirm the identity or affiliation of the shooters . . .*'

'Bullshit.'

'*. . . all efforts to bring a swift and safe end to the incident . . .*'

Isabelle slams a hand on the coffee table.

'*. . . we thank you for your cooperation . . .*'

She stomps up and down on the floor, hoping that the new couple below will hear her rage (in fact, Ahmed and Amina are both at work, in different parts of the city; both watching the news unfold on television screens, both as speechlessly horrified as their neighbours). Isabelle wrenches open the window on the street side of her apartment and, having checked that she is not overlooked, aims a fat gob of spit at the plant pots Amina has placed on the shallow balcony below.

It didn't use to be like this, Isabelle tells herself, pouring a large whiskey with an unsteady hand. Living in fear of your neighbours, in fear of attack.

(Of course, it did. The 1980s and '90s were as tinder dry and spark filled in France as anywhere else, the same maniacal rhythm of shooting down and blowing up and no one keeping a level head. But Isabelle is of the same mindset as the conservative news channels she watches and the blogs she reads, and it is easier for them to pretend this is something new, that this menace is alien and recent, so that in a few days or hours, when the initial coverage has quieted down, they can utter the war cry and call for the root cause, and causers, to be stopped).

Heaving the turquoise door open, Edward steps into the courtyard to find eight pairs of eyes trained upon him.

'Oh Edward, thank god!'

Frédérique rushes over and clasps him by both arms.

'Are you alright?'

'I'm fine, I'm fine. The Louvre was evacuated, but as far as I know it's okay.'

'You were at the Louvre?' Chantal fixes her eyes sharply on Edward's, her arms folded tight around her.

'Yes.'

'What's happening there?'

'Yes, what's the city like?'

The little group closes in on him so Edward relates the evacuation, his French surprisingly fluent in the face of danger. He tells them about the crowds, the helicopters circling overhead, the hundreds of emergency vehicles racing up the banks of the Seine.

'Everyone's coming home, it seems. The whole city walking home, walking in the roads even. Cars have been stopped, the metro's not running, no buses. So I just walked back,' he ends, self-conscious suddenly at his accent, blushing under the intent looks that crowd around him.

'Very wise.' Frédérique squeezes his arm again. 'Thank god you weren't in the thick of it.'

'Do they know who it is yet? Or why?' Edward pushes his hair out of his eyes and squints at the television.

'They just said Islamists,' one of Madame Marin's assistants pipes up grimly. She has kept her post by the television, where she is systematically biting at each of her fingernails in turn. Her boyfriend is a police officer in the suburbs and she's certain he's one of the ones being sped into the city. He's not answered his phone since news of the attack broke.

Everyone's eyes return to the television, where the reporters' fervent chatter goes momentarily quiet. Footage of a covered stretcher removing a body from the adjacent café is being shown for the first time. The café's windows are shot to pieces. Beneath upturned chairs and tables there are dark stains on the pavement. No one, not even the news presenter, knows what to say.

Frédérique clasps Edward's arm again, and he is sure she is also thinking of the family of that body. Remembering the grief of that anonymous body bag first hand. And how tiny, he thinks as the television lets the same horrifying image loop over and over, must a nine-year-old body have been. He shudders at the memory of those appalling child-sized coffins he had seen when he and his father went to the funeral home. White wood piped with blue or pink decorations, like grotesquely oversized cakes.

The noise of a siren rips through the air around them. A helicopter circles overhead and number thirty-seven's residents trace the arc of its noise with their eyes. The day is hot and close, and Edward can smell the dusty bookishness emanating from Gilles' cardigan, Madame Marin's synthetic scent, fear on the air and sweat on the skin. Chantal smells of cloves, somehow, while Frédérique, still at his side, reminds him as always of apples and cut grass.

They watch in silence until Edward's legs hurt, until his head aches with the repeated phrases. They watch again and again as that one body is driven slowly away (towards them, in fact), until they can no longer bear the suspense of it, time achingly unbearable as it stretches forward with nothing more happening. The gunmen are still inside the cathedral; the police have the cathedral surrounded.

Gradually the residents dissipate, promising to tell each other if there's any update. Heavy-hearted, they return to the business of the day.

25

Anaïs has missed the morning's events. She took Louis and Florence to nursery and although she has seen people passing anxious words on street corners, and pressing into bars to crane their heads up at televisions, she has taken little interest in it.

She woke this morning more convinced than ever that she is going to break. In sleep, Paul had slung an arm around her and, waking, her heart was in her throat with fear that it would crush her. She panicked, wriggled out from underneath it, and spent half an hour around four o'clock inspecting herself in the bathroom mirror. Checking her torso for cracks or crumble.

When Florence was a newborn, Anaïs remembers taking her everywhere as if she was made of the finest porcelain. Placing her down in the crib with bated breath, as if that perfect, translucent skin was a trick and there was no flesh or bone beneath, just air that might suddenly escape its paper-thin casing.

Now, the tables are turned. It is her skin that is perilously thin, pale and freckled and each wrinkle a hairline fracture that might bring the whole creation down. She dressed this morning as if she needed padding. She has kept the children at arm's length (they have noticed, and cling all the harder). She dances along a line, fearing and willing disintegration in the same moment.

She enters the courtyard as the group of television watchers is breaking up.

'Isn't it terrible, dear?' Madame Marin asks, clutching her by the arm.

'Yes, terrible,' she gasps in reply, eyes fixed on the five red talons pressing into her sleeve.

'At least you have the little ones to keep your mind off it.'

Yes, she has the little ones, but she is convinced that she also now has five deep purple bruises forming on her flesh. She shudders, because she knows that just a moment longer or a fraction tighter and part of her would have come off in Madame Marin's grip. She hurries away, desperate to get back to her apartment, to check the damage she can feel forming beneath her clothes.

At the bottom of the staircase, she is faced with the same predicament as when she left. It is her custom to lug the buggy up and down the two flights of stairs each day, but now each jolt into her flesh terrifies her. Tentatively, she begins to climb, wincing each time the buggy lurches towards her. The baby sleeps on, untroubled.

The journey is an eternity, and as the light dances in from the windows, refracting into miniature rainbows on the walls, warping the silhouette of the banisters into ghostly shapes, Anaïs's mind dances over everything that has led her here. The images flash before her in quick succession: her parents, her home, her first kiss with Paul. It was at a fairground, and the carousel in the background is now in her mind, light and sound whirling, and she remembers the babies, each arrival, the too-quick succession but then the surge of love, too; ten tiny fingers, ten tiny toes, and she remembers with Léo's birth just months ago how tired she was, how the hospital, with its disinfectant smell and the wails of other infants (and other women) offered a strange kind of comfort; how she dragged her feet to leave it and how, days later, with Florence and Louis and the new baby all in tears she had had to dig her feet into the ground to stop herself from walking back there.

Finally, the second-floor landing is reached. Their keys are horribly sticky, each entry a violent shaking of the lock, and it is as Anaïs is preparing for the fight that she jumps to see a figure on the landing behind her.

'Hello?' Anaïs's voice falters, her heart in her throat.

'Oh, hello.'

The woman's voice is soft and distant – the same young woman who Anaïs saw before.

'I'm Anaïs,' she proffers nervously.

Dreamily the other woman rolls the word around her mouth as if trying it out for size.

'Anaïs. That's a pretty name.'

'Thank you.'

In the buggy, the baby stirs, kicking his tiny feet against an unknown dream. The woman's eyes light up.

'Is that a baby?'

'Yes. My son.'

Anaïs makes to push the buggy towards the other woman, but already she is swooping over, so light her feet barely seem to touch the ground. She leans over, face close to his, her hair tickling his belly.

'He's lovely,' she breathes.

'Thank you.'

'I had a son here once.' Her tone is wistful now, and something of it sets a chill down Anaïs's spine.

'Do you live here, in this building?'

But the question goes unanswered for the woman is leaning even deeper over the buggy, and Anaïs is powerless to do anything but watch her eyes rove over his face, screwed up in sleep; his cheeks round and apricot-soft; his blonde curls.

'Hello sweetheart, hello sweet boy,' a soft whisper of greeting. 'What's his name?'

'Léo.'

'Hello Léo, little lion. I'm Sophie.'

'Sophie . . .' It is Anaïs's turn to let a name echo in the empty hallway. She's never heard of a Sophie in the building before. 'Which floor do you live on?'

Gesturing upwards: 'The top, the top.'

Suddenly, Sophie moves from the baby and comes to stand so close to her that Anaïs can see pale veins tracing invisible routes beneath the other woman's skin. She smells of earth and a coolness rises from her in spite of the heat.

'It's hard here, isn't it, Anaïs?' Green eyes so wide they look like fright. 'I felt you'd understand, I knew as soon as I saw you that *you* would understand.'

Anaïs is lost for words, tongue fat and limp inside her mouth.

'Everyone talks, don't they? In this building.'

Sophie is edging closer, bright reflections in her eyes. Anaïs nods in mute agreement.

'They talk, and sometimes it's not nice, what they say about you. Of course, no one knows what happens behind closed doors and I bet there's plenty, oh yes I bet there's plenty people wouldn't want talked of.' She catches Anaïs by the wrist, stroking her skin with icy fingers. 'And it's so hard, isn't it, with the babies?'

Anaïs nods, and she doesn't even mind about the grip because there is something about Sophie that isn't like other people, something that is good, and however strange the encounter she feels oddly safe in this hallway embrace.

'Hard, to find the energy, and the money, and to do it on your own.' Sophie's finger catches against Anaïs's wedding ring. 'Perhaps you're not alone, but I think we're all alone really, we mothers. No one understands, do they? Little heads and little hands and so much love, even when you have to let them go.'

They stand in silence for a moment, and slowly Sophie brings her cool cheek to rest on Anaïs's. Breath judders between them, each woman wracked with it, and Anaïs is filled with both fear and solace.

'Where's your baby, Sophie?'

Sophie pulls back with tears in her eyes.

'He's upstairs waiting for me. Such a good boy, he's always there waiting for me.' She clasps Anaïs by both hands. 'I wish you luck, Anaïs, you and your babies. Be lucky. Be safe.'

A kiss to the knuckles and she is gone, moving silently up the staircase.

Anaïs cannot move. Every cell in her body feels different, as if someone has run a magnet over her and sent each particle spinning to the other pole. She clasps the balustrade rail in both hands and looks up, but there is no trace of Sophie. No door opening, no footsteps padding along wooden boards. With trembling hands she touches her cheeks, the one distinctly cooler than the other.

The peal of her mobile cuts in on the thick air like a terrifying knife. She jumps, and is relieved in answering to find it is only Paul. Real, flesh and blood Paul.

'Ana, are you okay? I've just seen the news.'

'What?'

'There's been an attack. Are you okay, are the kids okay?'

'I'm fine, I'm home with Léo. The others are at nursery.'

'You should go and get them. You should all stay at home today, have a quiet day.'

Anaïs trails her eyes towards the silent floors above, looks down at her wrist where the clasp has left no mark save a slight tingling in the skin.

'Yes, I'll do that, yes. A quiet day . . .'

26

At three o'clock, the siege ends, four hours after it started. Armed police storm the cathedral, scattering postcards and offertory candles and guidebooks in their wake. Dozens of hostages are freed; the three gunmen shoot themselves in the fray. Excluding theirs, some thirty bodies are recovered from the scene.

After the initial relief of resolution, the talk turns to grief. Tomorrow will be a day of national mourning, again. There will be a presidential address, again. Across the country, flags are already hanging at half mast, and throughout the night there will be more of the emergency governmental meetings. There is something awfully familiar now about these reactions. The threat levels are still at their highest – there's no higher for them to go.

'I've never understood that,' Frédérique muses. 'Announcing the threat level. Who wants to know it's 'critical' now rather than 'substantial'? Who's comforted by knowing something is imminent rather than likely?'

Edward raises his head from a book, palm trees and tigers burned on his retinas. Pictorial escape. 'I suppose it's so people can be prepared, or something? Keep an eye out?'

Frédérique shakes her head. 'Call me a nihilist, but I'd rather not know. Go out with a bang. I can't stand this creeping fear.'

Edward closes his book and thinks back to the Louvre. Only this morning, but it seems a different age. He thinks about the glass pyramid and what it was like to be beneath it in the press of all those people. He shudders.

They have spent all afternoon in the shop, radio blaring.

Gilles came with them to return his book, though only after Frédérique shot him several pointed looks.

'National catastrophe, but not a free for all,' she'd said to Gilles's departing back under the glare of a slanted eyebrow.

'Cheeky bugger.'

'Gilles would steal the laces from your shoes if you weren't careful,' she'd warned, returning to her books and the latest news bulletin.

Now, though, it has been hours and Edward aches with it. Stretching out, he realises he's been holding tension in his body like a forgotten breath. His muscles creak and splutter.

'I can't listen to any more.'

'No, very sensible.' Frédérique leans across to flick the switch and they are plunged into silence so loud it reverberates in their ears. 'God, what a day.'

'What a day.'

Edward's on an adrenaline hangover, a tension comedown, French news phrases rattling around his skull. If he holds them out there's still a tiny jitterbug to his hands.

'Come on,' Frédérique claps a hand on his shoulder. 'Let's eat. You look done in.'

Together they lurch unsteadily towards Bâtiment A, and Edward pulls up one of the kitchen chairs while Frédérique digs vegetables out of the fridge.

They do not speak much, the warm evening punctuated by the hiss of the gas, the gentle warble of water boiling, the vicious flare of a match as Frédérique lights candles, the cat's contented purrs as she settles herself on Edward's feet.

'Ah,' the slamming of the bread bin. 'No bread.'

'I'll go.' Edward is up, Mischa relegated to the corner, and there is pleasure in running down the dark staircase (a lightbulb blew today, and Isabelle has yet to yell at Monsieur Marin to fix it). Above him he hears the murmur of other people's evenings, the smell of unidentified dinners seeping out into the night.

'Edward?' Frédérique opens her door and shouts down the staircase.

'Yes?'

'Maybe a paper, too?'

The bakery is closing – just a handful of baguettes left – and the staff look haggard under the fluorescent light. Each customer receives an 'isn't it terrible?' with his bread, and a day filled with these stock phrases, these endless iterations of shock, has clearly taken its toll. Edward secures the penultimate baguette and pauses outside the *tabac* to tear off the still-warm end. He's not a great newspaper reader at the best of times – it's not something they grew up with, the rustle of sheets around the kitchen table – but somehow he wants a memento of this day too.

Inside the *tabac* it is clear that the rest of the neighbourhood also wanted one; there are only the tattiest copies left on the shelves. He buys one anyway, its pictures more use to him than any brilliantly incisive commentary. He turns back towards the apartment.

Opposite the turquoise door, Josef stops him.

'Evening. Frédérique ask you to buy that?'

Edward is taken aback.

'Err . . . yes?'

Josef, who's sitting on his customary step in candlelight again, gestures for Edward to hand the newspaper over.

'Can I read it? She always buys papers at night but never reads them. Ask her. You can have it back tomorrow morning, tidy as it is now.'

Edward hesitates. He knows they say hello to each other, but how can this man possibly know when Frédérique is going to read her paper? She specifically asked him to buy one, and how can he know if Josef will be here in the morning? But there is something magnetic about this man, with his honest, uneven eyes, the simple unthreatening way in which he reaches out his hand.

Edward hands the paper over.

'Thank you.' Josef tucks it carefully to one side. 'I'll be sure to give it to her in the morning.'

'Okay.'

Edward's feet don't want to move. He has so many questions. Josef looks up at him and says earnestly, 'I appreciate it, Edward. I've got my radio –' he gestures to the radio secured neatly at the front of his trolley – 'but it's hard only hearing things. People tell me what's going on, too, but you like to look, don't you?'

Edward nods.

'People think you don't care, if you're on the street, but in a way you care even more.'

'I can imagine.'

'Can you?'

Josef's tone is piercing and Edward is grateful for the cover of night as colour flares in his cheeks. It was a stupid thing to say.

'Anyway . . .' he makes awkwardly to go. 'Enjoy the paper.'

'Enjoy your dinner,' Josef replies, as if he knows the baguette under Edward's arm is also a purchase for Frédérique. It is only once he is inside the turquoise door and on his way back up the stairs that Edward wonders how on earth Josef knew his name.

'You don't mean it, about being a nihilist?'

They are sitting in the kitchen, in a circle of light cast by three squat candles. The remnants of dinner lie in front of them – a few slivers of beef, tomato pips swimming in vinegar, the dregs of thick, buttery lentils, the rind of a cheese.

'What, going quickly you mean?' Frédérique shrugs and tosses Mischa a scrap of meat. 'I don't know. I don't have vast numbers of people to say goodbye to.'

'There's Emilie. And me.'

'True.'

'I'm sure Gilles would want a last chance to steal a book or two.'

'Indeed!' Frédérique laughs. 'I don't know, Edward. I can't stand the thought of living in fear. Every time this happens now people get scared, they stay indoors, huddling at home for safety, but is it worth it? Are they any safer? It seems to me the rules have been broken now, and anything could happen any time, anywhere. Does it mean I shouldn't still enjoy a coffee on the terrace? Go to the shops? Eat out when I feel like it? That feels like letting them win, to me.'

He screws up his eyes. 'I keep thinking about those people this morning, just having a coffee when . . .'

She puts her hand around his, and he feels his own trembling subside. 'I know. And you're young, while I'm old—'

'You're not old.'

'Old*er*, then. And I think, in a way, when the very worst has already happened to you . . .' She shrugs. 'It doesn't make sense to be afraid. I'll be out at a café tomorrow with my coffee and my cigarette. I won't be cowed by this, but I don't have much reason to be.'

He looks her in the eye. 'You do.'

Frédérique smiles, rises, puts a hand on his shoulder. 'Come have a nightcap with me. Let's talk of nicer things.'

And so they decant into the *salon*, and the port slides easily down Edward's throat, sweet on the lips and a burn in the nose. Turning his glass in his hands, Edward begins uneasily.

'The man who sleeps in the doorway opposite . . .'

'Josef?'

'Yes. He asked me for your newspaper tonight. Asked if he could read it, give it back to you in the morning.'

'Oh, I'd completely forgotten about the newspaper – I never read them at night anyway. I assume you gave it to him?'

'Yes.'

'Good.'

'He knew my name, too.' Edward looks down at the amber

liquid, unsure how to put words to the questions swilling round his head.

'Yes, I imagine I told him.' As ever, Frédérique is direct. Looks straight at him with a mischievous smile. 'You find it strange, perhaps?'

'What?'

'That I talk to a man who lives on the street.'

'No, I . . . it's none of my business—'

'But you do. Find it strange.'

'Maybe?' Edward shrugs. 'Who am I to say?'

'Josef is . . . an old friend.' Frédérique leans forward, elbows on knees. 'We go back a long way.'

'I know, I know.' Edward is embarrassed. Not the admission so much as having sought it, having asked about this strange friendship that is so outside his understanding. He drains his glass. 'Thank you for dinner.'

'You don't have to go!'

'No, it's late, it's been . . . it's been a day.'

'I like this phrase. *It has been a day.*'

At the front door she catches him by the shoulder. 'Edward. We are so different, you and I, but I think we understand each other, no? Understand loss, at least. There's no question you can't ask. I want you to know that.'

He nods. 'I know. And I don't want you to go in a nihilistic bang. Be sure to say goodbye.'

'I promise.'

'Good.'

They embrace as normal, a kiss on each cheek. But the day has been anything but normal, and so they hug too, resting their heads for a moment on the other's arm.

'Goodnight, Edward.'

'Goodnight, Frédérique.'

It makes no difference: back in his room, Edward still feels mortified. Feels, with the slosh of port and wine in his stomach, a soupy blur of emotions. He *does* want to know about Josef. He wants to sleep. He wants to tell his parents he's okay; he wants them to have asked.

Actually, now that he's back in his oppressive cubbyhole of a bedroom and able to hurl his shoes across the room and slam his body onto the bed, he wants to hear from Charlotte. He looks at his phone for the hundredth time. Nothing. Almost without realising it, his drunk fingers press dial.

'Hello?'

She is out somewhere, the sound of voices crowding in on his ears.

'It's me.'

'You okay?'

'Yeah. You?'

'Yeah.'

A long pause.

'I was at the Louvre today. Got evacuated.'

'Shit.'

'Anyway.'

'Edward, I'm kind of in the middle of something.' A shriek of background laughter cuts Edward to his core. 'Call you tomorrow?'

'Sure.'

He doesn't wait for her goodnight. Grabbing his laptop, he tries in vain to connect to César Vincent's internet again, but the signal struggles to climb four flights of stairs and when he does reach a news website, all he can see, after an eternity of loading, are the faces of today's gunmen. Twenty-four, twenty-five, twenty-six years old. He stares at them until he feels sick, for what leads someone his age to do something like this is a gulf of understanding over which Edward cannot and does not want to pass.

Before long he is asleep; uneasy, crowded dreams, tigers and palm fronds and Frédérique smiling at him, and Josef refusing to meet his eye.

Across the courtyard, Frédérique stands for a long time at

her bedroom window smoking, looking up towards his attic room.

And in the street, Josef is laying out his bedding, cigarette dangling from the corner of his mouth. He has plenty of thoughts flickering through his mind as he settles in with a torch to read his newspaper.

27

The following morning is as grey as the national mood, and the city is on edge. People twitch and jitter in the metro, they look nervously over their shoulders and scurry head down from one place to the next with grim determination. The troops are out in force, fingers on triggers. Museums and monuments are closed indefinitely. The Eiffel Tower remains open, but the line is threadbare, only the most time-pressed tourists inching cautiously forward.

César is up in the north of the city, at Sylvain's request. 'Porte de la Chapelle, 9am' the message read, so César has dragged himself all the way to the end of the line, puzzled at how curt this text is when Sylvain's others rival *War and Peace* in length and detail. He was expecting the usual crowd at the metro station, but is surprised to find only himself waiting. His is the sole white face in the crush of morning commuters, and his lip curls in disdain at the smells he imagines on the North Africans rushing by.

He loiters by a newsstand, its papers all bearing the same photos of the three gunmen, the same scene outside the café of blood and glass. Like the rest of the country, he spent yesterday glued in horror to the television screen in his usual café. Even the waitress with the gelatinous belly was reduced to tears. She must be French after all, César had decided on his way back to the apartment, where he and Chantal sat in front of the television together in silence. He considered this silence her defeat, the grudging concession that his concerns about Muslims had been spot on. Vindicated, he puffed out his chest and set about waiting for her apology, when so ever it might appear. (It hasn't yet, for Chantal has kept herself stoically wordless).

César's phone rings. Sylvain.

'César, walk away from the station down the Boulevard Ney.'

'Left or right?'

'Right.'

'Why did you have me come to the station then?' César puffs, already somewhat out of breath.

'Secrecy is everything César. Never know who's listening.'

César rolls his eyes and walks, following Sylvain's instructions to turn right down the deserted industrial boulevard, ducking between the concrete arms of what looks like a multi-storey car park and down an unlit flight of stairs. He continues nervously down a long, dimly lit corridor, until suddenly two rough hands clamp down on his shoulders and it's, 'In here César' with a shove at his back.

'Jesus, Sylvain,' César wipes the sweat off his top lip. 'This is like being in the Resistance.'

Sylvain doesn't smile. 'No funny business today, César. I didn't invite everyone. I've picked you special; don't let me down.'

With that he swings open a door to reveal a largish concrete room in which thirty or forty men are gathered. The single strip of fluorescent lighting overhead lends the scene a menacing air, as does the smell of so many male bodies in a windowless space.

César is reminded of Van Gogh's *Potato Eaters*, of a trip – was it Amsterdam? London? – where by some extraordinary chance he and Chantal ended up in front of the painting alone for a few moments. He remembers the coarse features of the peasants, the griminess of their skin. The oppressive sense of dirt and poverty had shaken him, while Chantal stood at his side, so close he could feel her breathing, and she was enchanted, whispering about the magic of the brushwork and the way the light fell, and all that César felt was horror coursing up and down his backbone.

Sylvain hisses at him under his breath. 'César, get over here.'

César follows meekly to the corner of the room. He is surprised to see that Sylvain stays by his side. He is used to seeing him take centre stage. Today, that task is assumed by an older man, in his sixties maybe. He sits on a high stool at the centre of the room. Hunched over, all César can see is the curve of his spine and a mop of grey hair; in spite of the heat, he wears a big padded jacket.

'Friends,' his voice is a growl, brought low and rumbling by decades of smoke. 'What happened yesterday is an abomination. The government talks of mourning, of loss, but what we need is a *response*.' He raises a hand to quiet the enthusiastic murmurings this brings. 'A measured response. A response appropriate to this level of violation.

'There will be a march on Sunday, the government has said this. Events and candles and calls for unity. It's all very well, but we need *action*. We need to show we are not afraid.'

Again, a ripple of approval runs around the room.

'Jean,' the ringleader nods to a tall thin man standing with his arms crossed, 'I know you've got some things planned for the interim, but our main event will be next weekend. The Day of Anger, they're calling it. A day to express how we really feel.'

A cheer goes up and bounces deafeningly off the walls. Leaning back, César can feel condensation dripping down the concrete. Amidst the shouts and the claps, Sylvain leans over and says, 'You're in then, César?', and César nods as a bead of sweat runs haltingly down his back.

Chantal is at the library today but she is not, truth be told, doing much work. In spite of what he thinks, her silence is not a malice directed at César: she was struck dumb by yesterday's events. She spends her life reading, organising, ordering and cataloguing books, countless hours invested in the power of words, their ability to transcend the most horrific situations. And yet to see the bodies carried out of the cathedral yesterday, to feel how close it was, to see the helicopters overhead and hear the roar of the sirens and to know, on some level, that a couple of hundred metres this way or that and it could have been her, has rocked her. What can she say in response to this? There is nothing to say.

She is caught, too, in the paradox of feeling as if she's living through it, living for the next news report, breath bated in time to the syncopated rhythms of the headlines and the newscasters, heart pounding, when really, it was three kilometres away. She hasn't been to Notre-Dame for years. She'd never have gone to that café. It was her, and yet was so decidedly not her, who came under attack. She feels ashamed at the vicarious, sensationalist pull of it all at the same time as she scours the internet for the latest analysis.

'Good morning, Chantal. We meet again.'

It's Adrien, the handsome new head of library services. Tall and trim with field-green eyes and a gentle, soft-spoken manner that sets a tremble to the back of Chantal's knees. Their shifts have often been in alignment lately (which is not so much of a coincidence as Adrien might think). Their conversations are the favourite part of Chantal's day.

'Coffee, Adrien?'

'Please.'

She presses the red switch and slowly, slowly the water starts to percolate.

'Awful, isn't it?'

'Awful.'

They stand in silence for a moment.

'I feel . . .' Chantal begins but hesitates. 'I feel at a loss for what to say. I don't know how to put it into words. They're not adequate, somehow.'

'I quite agree,' Adrien murmurs. 'The gulf between word

and incident. How vast would a vocabulary have to be to touch on all these . . .' He trails off into a gesture, waving his hand vaguely around the room.

'How vast and how precise.'

'Yes.'

'They're imprecise, my words. Awful, terrible—'

'Yes, yes.' He pauses. 'Perhaps for some things there are no words.'

'Perhaps.'

The water hisses in the machine and Hélène from cataloguing appears. Hélène is not like Chantal and Adrien (at least not to Chantal's mind). Thirty, with wild unkempt hair and a nose ring, she bursts into the kitchen in a thunderclap of noise: boots stomping, tinny music blaring from the headphones around her neck, mouth going fifteen to the dozen.

'They've just released more information about the shooters,' she yells over her shoulder, head thrust deep inside the fridge.

'We were just saying how . . . terrible it is,' Chantal says quietly, smiling at Adrien, who smiles back; their own private joke.

'I don't know,' Hélène roars, tearing off a hunk of sandwich and chewing it as she talks, 'if you think how easy it is to get hold of guns and bombs and stuff, it's a miracle how rarely people *do* decide to blow each other up.'

She slams out again, leaving Chantal and Adrien to suppress their giggles.

'Well,' says Adrien, 'I suppose that's one way to look at it.'

'The youth of today,' Chantal replies, shaking her head.

'She's not that young, is she?'

'She makes me feel ancient.' Chantal is pouring the coffee.

'You are by no means that.'

Chantal blushes as Adrien looks away, and it occurs to her that cultivating a reputation for dreaminess affords one a lot of liberties. What freedom, when words are followed or excused or made possible by eyes that swivel pensively to an unseen middle distance. How freeing to be 'not of this earth', as colleagues so frequently say of Adrien. She herself feels the vehemence of gravity's tug.

At home that night César asks her, 'What do you make of all this, then?'

'What?'

'This, this.' He gestures at the television. 'What do you think of it?'

'What do you expect me to say to that, César?' It's photos of the victims up now on the screen. A nine-year-old from Toulouse who was visiting with her aunt. Two university students. Three Italian teens. 'It's horrible, horrific. Actually,' she pauses to recall the afternoon's conversation, 'I think there are no words for it.'

She expects him to argue with this. With César, there are always words, upon words, upon words. But he is silent, looking down at his phone which she can see is flashing with new text messages (Sylvain again).

'No, no words. Actions, not words,' he murmurs.

Only half listening to him, Chantal shakes her head. 'Anger, reprisals. I feel like something terrible is about to happen.'

'Yes,' César replies slowly, scanning his phone. 'Something is definitely going to happen.'

28

Edward is meeting Charlotte in a square near her apartment. Hot summer wind rips around the buildings, thundering dry leaves across the pavement and whipping flecks of grit into his eyes.

It is Sunday, and it is she who suggested meeting here. Edward tastes dust on his tongue and the whole morning has an air of finality to it. He cannot explain how or why, but things have shifted and rankled, buckled and bloomed, not in the way of roses but of cankers; ominous spores that have taken hold and crept secretly over them while they slept.

During their last meeting, at the bar, it was as if an invisible string between them had been pulled taut. The languorous, sensuous Charlotte was gone, replaced instead by a woman who twitched each time he touched her and spoke only in furiously quick French, with none of the tender English asides to which he has become accustomed. She rolled her eyes when he talked and Julien sat opposite, a broad smile on his face like a cat with cream. Late in the evening he came out with it, leaning across the table to hiss at Edward while Charlotte was deep in conversation with someone else.

'Charlotte and I, we used to be lovers. Did she tell you that?'

Edward felt a fresh wave of sweat prick across his skin. For once he was grateful for the dark, airless night, thankful that it would hide his reddened surprise. 'Yeah, she did,' he'd replied, but Julien had merely raised his eyebrows and leaned back with a knowing smile.

That was Friday, the day after the attacks. They had not

slept together that night, Edward making his excuses and Charlotte nodding brusquely, for all the world as if she were glad of them. He heard nothing from her, so spent Saturday in the shop with Frédérique, sharing two bottles of Chardonnay late into the night, noting, as he tumbled heavily into bed, the buzz of his phone and Charlotte's request to meet.

She is late, and it is not in Edward's nature to be early but today he is here on time. And as he sits on a bench in the square scuffing his feet in the dirt, with the white diamond-dazzle glare of the sun, he hears his mother say, 'Storm's coming' and suddenly she is so close it is as if she is sitting on the bench next to him.

'Storm's coming, I said.'

And he is home, and he can see the dark army of it marching towards them up the valley, but it is not the storm they think it is. His mother cannot remember names any more, cannot be left alone, but still she will not seek the diagnosis. She prefers it to creep up on them, like these clouds rolling ever closer, and even in the stale heat of the Parisian morning he can smell the lilac soap she uses; the whiff of fresh laundry she carries with her is carried to him on the dusty air.

'Morning.'

Charlotte is here, thrusting a cardboard espresso cup in his direction.

'Oh, thanks.'

For the first time, he notices the hardness in her features; the way her jaw juts in iron determination, the squint in her eyes that's not just from the sun. She lights a cigarette and wraps her arms around herself, steeling for a fight.

'You coming to République today?'

'What?'

'Place de la République. There's a demonstration. A march for tolerance. Didn't you see it on the news?'

'Oh. No, I can't. I promised Frédérique I'd look after the shop.'

And it's true. Frédérique asked him last night, the keys are digging into his thigh against the press of the bench. Not that he can move them now, it'd be too obvious a gesture to wave them in her face.

'It's important, Edward. Liberty, tolerance—'

'Yeah, I know, but I can't, I said I'd watch the shop.'

She snorts derisively. 'Who's going to buy art books today? The whole city's going to be at this thing.'

'Well,' he retorts defensively, 'if the whole city's there you won't need me, will you?'

'She asked you to watch the shop today?'

And in that question alone, some cog in Edward's brain slips into place. He doesn't think he's told Charlotte that much about Frédérique, actually. Not given that the two of them make up basically his entire Paris acquaintance. But the word 'she' grates on Charlotte's tongue. Slips dagger-sharp into the rough air.

'Yes, *she* did. Why?'

Charlotte shrugs and trains her gaze on a family walking across the square. Edward persists, feels the fight rising.

'Why?'

'It's *weird*, Edward. You come to Paris – what is this for you, some extended holiday? – and all you do is hang out with a forty-five-year-old woman?'

'Why should her age have anything to do with it?'

'It doesn't, but it's, ugh –' Charlotte waves her hands at him in frustration – 'what are you doing here? What are we doing? You don't care about the things I care about, you just sit around with your books and your old friend and all these *family problems*—'

'You don't know the first thing about my family.'

'I do know. You talk in your sleep, Edward. I know your sister is dead. But she's not coming back; you should focus on the living, on the things that need to be changed, to be fought for—'

He is on his feet.

'How dare you say that to me?'

'It's true!'

'How fucking dare you.'

He makes to go and she is shouting after him.

'Oh, you just walk away now? Like everything else?'

'Enjoy your protests, Charlotte, and your little group of friends who just sit and bitch about the world and do *nothing* to change it.'

'Julien was right about you!' she yells to his departing back. Another phrase follows but the wind snatches it, and all Edward will remember of leaving is her skinny black-clothed form standing in the sandy square, a stain on the sunlit day that retreats rapidly into the distance.

The memory is fabricated, for he does not look back. Instead he walks, feet pounding fierce against the ground, walks furiously, fingernails digging bloody half moons into his palms, until he is far enough away and there is a side street where he can hang gasping for breath against the side of a building and slam his hand repeatedly against the wall.

29

People do go to République. Hundreds, maybe thousands of them. The young paint *tricolores* on their faces and clamber up onto the statues. Their arms swing slowly, weighed down by the heat, waving French flags and banners that they've spray-painted with LIBERTÉ ÉGALITÉ FRATERNITÉ. People mill, directionless, in the square. The smell of McDonald's floats alongside cries for tolerance and peace. There are Christians and Jews and Muslims together.

But there are also those who stay at home. Those who watch the pictures on the news from inside their airless apartments; those who peer anxiously out from behind their blinds, afraid of or waiting for something to happen in the city streets.

It is a strange and eerie day, the kind where a billion dust particles lend the world an iridescent shimmer. The sky looms grey white over silvered streets, and were it not for the air, hot and damp as breath, it could have been midwinter, stone twinkling under first frost. The clouds bear down and the dust floats, and glimpsed down the right side street, it is as a spectre rising over the city.

Paul insisted Anaïs came to church. Insisted they wrestled all three children into clothes and into buggies and hauled them down the street for the ten o'clock service.

'Why are you wearing *that*?' he asked, sweat pouring down his face, as she gingerly slipped her arms into a padded winter jacket.

Padding. Protection. Insulation, she thinks.

'Just feel like it,' she shrugs.

The church manages to feel both cool and stifling. If its dark stone keeps out the sunshine, the press of people within drags the temperature up, the odour hot and bodily, as exposed flesh sticks uncomfortably to the wooden pews and bare limbs are pressed together. Florence lies on the floor between their feet drawing shapes in the dust. Louis sucks his thumb and moans. Léo flails like a salmon out of water, muscled limbs flying in her face as Anaïs holds her heart in her mouth, torn between opposing impulses. Trying not to let him fall, trying not to let him break her.

'Brothers and sisters in Christ, we have been attacked.'

The priest drones in the low monotone he uses to express joy and fear and loss and Mass. Anaïs closes her eyes, opening them as Léo grabs a handful of her hair and pulls. It falls out in his chubby hand.

'I'm taking them outside,' she hisses to Paul, who is rapt in the low, mumbling words descending from the pulpit. She stands up into a shard of light streaming down from a high-up window, and the hair floats, like golden feathers, to the ground.

There are a few other women in the playground, their children rapidly wilting in the heat but free here at least to run around and make noise. Anaïs smiles awkwardly at them and they smile awkwardly back. She sits down on a stone bench, drawing the padded jacket closer. Leaning over to set Léo on the ground, she can feel her hipbones digging into her flesh. She thinks about Sophie.

Their meeting has had a profound effect on Anaïs. Someone has noticed her. And not just for the baby, the children, the dog – she is astonished daily at how many people will stop in the street to coo over one or other or all of them while she stands there vacant like a cipher, merely the vessel and not the content. But when Sophie looked her in the eyes it was the first time in months, in years even, that she felt someone understood her. Could see into her, not just through her.

She has tried, since, to seek her out, this strange new ally in the building. Trailing up the staircase and down the hallway, waiting for a sense of the other woman, a foot on a stair or the swoosh of her long skirt. And she has played down, in her head, the stranger elements of the meeting: the intensity of her gaze, the absent child. But the top floor has yielded no answers. Anaïs crept up there the other day, knocked timidly at two of the four doors. Called tentatively, 'Sophie?' but no one came and, feeling foolish, she hurried back down to the second floor.

Louis giggles, smearing ochre dirt across his face, but Anaïs is not looking. Across the street, she can see the Marins walking along, the husband beiger than ever against his wife's cerise skirt.

'Excuse me!' Anaïs is on her feet. 'Madame Marin!'

She rushes to the edge of the playground.

'Could you . . .?' she gestures to the children, and a startled-looking woman nods dumbly that yes, she will watch them while their mother darts in front of passing cars and runs across the street.

'Madame Marin! Madame Marin!'

Finally, the head of flame-red hair turns, painted eyes wide with surprise.

'Madame Lagrange! Is everything okay? How are the children?'

'They're well, thank you.' Anaïs struggles to regain control of her breath. 'Madame Marin, I wanted to ask – the woman named Sophie, where does she live in the building?'

'I'm sorry?'

'Sophie, which apartment does she have? She introduced herself last week and she said she lived on the top floor, but I'm not sure which apartment.'

The Marins stare back at her with blank eyes.

'Sophie? There isn't anyone named Sophie, dear.' Madame Marin smiles kindly, a sense of trouble dancing on her lips. 'Augusto, we don't have a Sophie, do we?'

Her husband takes a forefinger and slides his glasses back up his nose.

'Gusto!'

'No.' The reply is as slow and monotonous as the man himself. 'No Sophie. Had a Sofia, summer of '83. No Sophie.'

Madame Marin smiles nervously, her gums rippling in and out of view beneath bright pink lips.

'I'm sorry, dear. Perhaps you got the wrong name. There's a young girl on the top floor, a student—'

'No, she wasn't a student. She had a baby.'

'A baby? Oh no dear. You're the only one with babies!'

Anaïs feels a surge of panic pulse around her ribcage. Cold sweat prickles her skin. She turns from the Marins and sets off, half running, towards the building. She does not think about the children, or about Paul. She has to find the woman from the top floor.

Crashing through the doorway to Bâtiment B, the hallway is perfectly still, dust motes suspended in the air. She climbs the stairs, hand trembling against the bannister. On the top floor she calls, 'Sophie?'

She knocks on the first door, then on the second. Louder this time.

'Sophie? Sophie!'

As she reaches the end of the corridor, the fourth and final door opens. Anaïs's heart leaps with fright, but it is only Edward.

'Hello?'

He looks awful, dark circles round his eyes and a bloodied tea towel wrapped around his hand. To his eyes, she looks awful too; gaunt and afraid, breath rattling around her tiny frame.

'I'm sorry. I was looking for Sophie? Do you know a young woman named Sophie up here?'

'No, sorry.'

'She's young, long brown hair . . .' Anaïs is desperate.

'No, I . . . sorry, I don't know anyone, really.' Edward makes to close the door, then hesitates as he sees the woman's face fall. 'Is everything okay?'

'Yes, yes,' Anaïs is already wobbling unsteadily back towards the staircase. 'Everything is fine.'

Edward's door slams shut in the wind and moments later Anaïs's does too. The dog flops down at her feet and she rests her head on the wooden table, thoughtless, void. Sometime later the door slams in its frame again and Paul appears in the doorway.

'What is wrong with you?'

It takes all her effort to heave her head away from the cool wood.

'I said, what the *hell* is wrong with you? You left our children, Anaïs! You left them!'

She notes, vaguely, how cross he must be to use the word 'hell'. And sure enough, when she looks, she sees that Paul cannot contain his rage. It throbs at the veins in his throat, pulses through the hands that he balls into fists and claws back out again.

'I asked a woman . . .' she begins, 'there were people there with them.'

'This is it, Ana.'

For once the children are sitting quietly in the living room. Wide-eyed, all three watch Paul storm past them to their bedroom, where he starts shoving clothes and nappies into a bag.

'I don't know what is wrong with you but you are a *liability*. You are putting our children in danger. And I won't have it.'

'Paul—' she reaches out to touch his arm but he pushes her back. Losing her balance she lands against the wall with such a smack she is certain she can feel her bones splintering into kaleidoscopic fragments.

'No! I won't hear it. I'm fed up. Fed up with the sad faces and the moping around, as if I don't do enough for you, for this family. *I feed this family!* That's what I'm out doing every day, Ana, and the Lord only knows what you do because this place is never clean, there's never food, I have no idea if you even bother feeding the children—'

'I do!'

Hot corrosive tears are sliding down her cheeks now but he doesn't stop.

'You clearly don't bother to feed yourself.' Looking at her as if in proof.

He returns to the living room and bundles the children back out into the hallway. Beau whines and scrabbles down the corridor ahead of them, determined not to be left out, but soon there is the barked order of 'Beau! Basket!' and the terrier slopes off with mournful eyes.

'Paul, please! Where are you going?'

He turns in the doorway, looking at her in sorrow now, not anger. His voice falls back to almost-normal, though even as she thinks that it occurs to Anaïs that nothing may ever be normal again.

'I'm taking the kids to my aunt's. Taking a few days. Ana,' his voice is cracking, on the verge of tears, 'I have tried everything I can think of. I've given you space, I've tried talking to you, I've prayed, I've done the dishes in the middle of the night, and none of it's been enough. I don't know what else I can do. But the kids, the kids have to come first.'

With that, and with an infant on each shoulder, leading Florence by the hand, he takes them slowly down the stairs away from her. At the last moment, Beau makes a bid for freedom and joins them, wagging his tail, and Florence's wide blue eyes stare back at her until the troop of them disappears from view.

30

As night falls, the trouble starts.

Across the city, Jean's gang is at work. Bricks are sent through the windows of a Halal butcher on the Rue du Faubourg Saint-Denis. Red graffiti bleeds down Muslim-owned shopfronts at Barbès – Rochechouart. Just for good measure, a fire is started outside a synagogue in the Marais and a homeless man has his teeth beaten out of him, bloodied enamel clattering across the pavement.

Once again, sirens wail and people turn their eyes to the television news reports. Most breathe a sigh of relief to hear that these are just reprisals – nothing against them, this time. What's a window, a mosque, a shop or two?

Up on the fifth floor of number thirty-seven, Monsieur Lalande's sparrows have not come. Scared away by the new din of the city, the shrieking peals that rip the air, so hot and thick and tangible it really could be rent in two by the noise or the shards of blue light that illuminate the emergency services' trail.

With a shaking hand, Monsieur Lalande has turned off his radio, his constant companion these long years since his wife died. He does not like silence, but he cannot listen any more.

Even with his pale skin, he has been here before; felt the hateful gaze of strangers on the street, dodged the names that were flung at him, the spit, the punches. A woman on a bus in the second arrondissement once told him he smelled. Another shouted at him to go back to where he came from, so that he was left wordless on the pavement, wanting to tell them, 'I come from *here*.' Where do you go if your home is no longer your home? If you are always out of place within a place?

His wife Eva was a wise bird. 'You mustn't be troubled by such things, Haki.' Haki – the name reserved for their most private moments, for his deepest insecurities. 'We have each other and we have our boys. What's one woman on a bus?' And it was true, they had their boys and each other. And the boys grew and found wives of their own, as boys are wont to do, and moved out to more spacious apartments in the suburbs. 'There's people like us here, dad!' they'd tell him, but he stubbornly shook his head and refused the offer of a new apartment outside the city. *Like us?* Henri Lalande felt like nobody else.

Then Eva had died, quite suddenly, and now, between his sons' visits, there is nobody else. Nobody to tell him not to mind the insults, the slurs. He is sad and scared tonight to hear the same words returning. But he has also lived long enough to know that most things pass, eventually. With meticulous care he breaks the end of his bread and lines his window-sill, readying crumbs for when his friends return.

In the depths of Picardy, the Lagrange children are sleeping. Paul's aunt has opened her house without questions, for which he is grateful. Florence asked enough for all of them – *where's mummy, when is mummy coming, when are we going home?* – placated only by the promise of feeding the chickens at the bottom of Tante Marie's garden.

Now it is dark and the children are quiet, hot little arms and legs flung across each other in the spare bed. Paul leaves Marie watching images of the violence in Paris and wanders out into the garden. The night is wet with meadow scent, the air at once lighter and heavier than the city's smog. He walks down the familiar paths, the whisper of verdant growth invisible around him. Away from his daughter's prying eyes, Paul lets his shoulders slump. He digs his feet into the grass, thinks of his wife, of what she is doing.

(Anaïs is where she's been since they left this afternoon, lying on the hallway floor.)

In the insect-hum, breeze-ruffle pitch of the country night, Paul can admit his faults. That he should have seen this coming. Should have done more. Should have realised. He thinks back to the old Anaïs. The young Anaïs, in fact. Cheeks pink, eyes bright, nervous but excited to move to the big city, endlessly twisting her shiny new wedding ring around her finger. He fears it is he who has drained the light from her, he who has reduced her to her current shell. With bare feet in the wet grass and the breathy rustle of cattle in the next field, he can admit to himself that the children were a bigger drain on her than him. That watching her tiny frame wax so impossibly huge, standing helpless next to her in the fraught battle to birth them, he was terrified that she would break.

And now she has. His lovely girl. Brittle and broken, and he does not know how to fix it. To fix her.

For the first time in his life, Paul really prays. Not the rote prayers of thanks or praise – this is enormous, desperate prayer. It comes from a place of absolute lack. Utter help-lessness. *Please God, please God . . .*

He is too lost to even finish the sentence.

Walking along the dark streets, Isabelle purrs with pleasure. Her phone has been buzzing incessantly since the violence started, reports of disturbance in this or that area, such-and-such street closed, fire here, glass broken there, and she has cheered and whooped at it. While Paul is on his knees, she stands tall with pride and certainty, heart pumping in her chest, blood as red as the paint she is about to fling over the greengrocer's doorway.

Dirty little Arab, she's never liked his manner with her. She's seen him save the best fruit for other people. Watched silently as that bloody Frédérique gets everything discounted, just for flashing a smile at him. Watched him hand out tangerines to the local kids, his hands dirty and earthen against their pale skin.

Well, she tells herself, he can wash his hands tomorrow morning, wash them raw trying to scrub this paint off.

The rush is the greatest Isabelle has felt in years. Creeping along the street, paint can in hand. Waiting for a quiet moment, until she is sure she is not overlooked. Heart hammering in her throat as she bends down with a screwdriver to prise the lid free.

She is about to do it, seconds from launching her liquid missile, when a group of people turn the corner. They barely see her, full of their own noise and chatter, but her heart threatens to explode nonetheless. She waits, but there are a few stragglers out on the streets now, a local bar is shutting up, a metro has just pulled into the station.

Tomorrow, tomorrow, she tells herself, resolving to return earlier in the evening. And the paint will be flung not just at that one man, she reasons on her way back to the apartment, trying to temper her disappointment. Not just that one man, but at all the Arabs. All the immigrants. All the people different to her who are here and shouldn't be. In her heart of hearts though, alone in her bed in the silent moments of the night, she will grudgingly acknowledge for the briefest of seconds that it is thrown against other fears and disappointments too. For Isabelle, like most people, thought she'd end up with a husband, children. She thought she'd have little hands in which to place tangerines.

'Evening, Madame Duval.'

Startled by the figures of Chantal and Madame Marin in the doorway, Isabelle's left hand flies up momentarily while the right hides her paint can at her side. Although she is proud of her planned exploits, she doesn't want to share them just now.

'Good evening ladies. It's a lovely night.'

They stare quizzically at her retreating back as she hurries to the doorway of Bâtiment A. Chantal scans the street again.

'I just thought César would be home by now.'

'And I Gusto.'

'I hope they're not caught up in anything.'

In an unusual gesture of intimacy, a breach of the usual rules of boundary and proximity, Madame Marin puts her hand on Chantal's shoulder.

In the darkness of the stairwell (because that bloody man still hasn't fixed the broken light), Isabelle's hand pulls a can of spray paint out of her pocket. And as Madame Marin's red fingernails make contact with Chantal's skin, Isabelle's paint makes contact with the Laribis' door.

Ahmed and Amina are curled up on the sofa with mint tea to ward off the nausea of early pregnancy, with their shutters closed to ward off the violence of the outside world.

'Can we just watch something funny?' she'd asked, nestling her head into that nook in his neck that seems to have been made just for her. 'I can't bear watching the news any more.'

So yes, they are watching a rom-com they've seen three times before, and Ahmed is really watching her more than he's watching the screen, tucking the blanket around her toes, which are always freezing, whatever the weather. They will finish the movie and take a bath, go to bed and lie whispering sweet nothings until they fall asleep. They will not realise until the morning that this violence has sought them out, been brought right to their brand new door, an angry red scrawl that tells them to

GO HOME

31

'Edward?'

Frédérique raps her knuckles on the door again. It is stifling, this attic space; baked all day by the sun and suffocated in the evenings by everybody else's heat rising skywards.

She hasn't seen Edward today and just wants to check in on him, or so she tells herself. Her head clouded with the memory of the wine they shared, she'd felt a prick of disappointment coming back to the building this afternoon and finding the shop shut up, untended. He must have forgotten her request, yet last night they had laughed and talked and in the candlelight it had felt to Frédérique that they were the only people in the world.

'Let me cook,' he'd insisted, nudging her out of the way in the kitchen. She'd ceded and watched him slice potatoes as thin as pennies, frying them to a golden crisp. He paired them with cured ham from the Italian deli; clean, crisp endive; her favourite cheese from the *fromagerie*. He'd come unannounced bearing these gifts, which went unexplained, but it felt celebratory and special and delightful. She'd cut herbs from the window box to sprinkle on the potatoes, ducking in front of him to do so and feeling his breath against her neck, the warmth of his body behind her. She'd brought up two modestly special bottles from the basement, and they stayed at the kitchen table until the candles extinguished themselves, greasy smears at the bottom of their holders. They'd said goodnight, a kiss on each cheek as has become their custom, and then today, absence. She does not want to admit that she misses him. Wants to admit even less that she may have been a fool.

Frédérique raises her hand to knock a third time just as the door opens.

'Edward!'

Her eyes go first to the bloodied rag around his hand, then the inflamed circles around his eyes. He is standing in a wall of heat, his room even hotter than the corridor. The film of sweat across his skin glints under the electric light, lending his face a hollow, sickly air.

Frédérique has learned the hard way not to ask, 'are you alright?' She knows the carving out of loss, its perpetual absence-presence in the gut, the shallow depth it lends the heart knowing it'll never beat so full again. The heart is never alright, never righted. The world of loss is perpetually skewed, those who know sliding helpless from one side of the deck to the other, a ship rocked by eternal storm.

'What happened?' she asks instead, taking his arm as she enters the room.

He is silent for a moment.

'I was told today it was pointless living in the past. That . . .' – and his voice falters here – 'she's never coming back.'

Almost without realising, Frédérique raises an eyebrow. Edward hasn't talked to her of the girl, or girls, he's been seeing. She's momentarily surprised to hear that they know his history – it seemed a private, almost sacred thing between them – but she hides it, slowly unwrapping the rusty tea towel from his hand. Hot hours have allowed the wound to dry into the fabric and Edward winces as skin and blood are prised apart.

'Sorry,' she breathes. Leaning closer, she shakes her head. 'It's amazing.'

'What?'

'How quickly we begin to heal. Already your cells and this fabric knitting together, fighting for wholeness again.'

'There is no wholeness. Not now.'

Gently she leads him to the sink, where she washes dirt and brick dust from his swollen knuckles.

'There's a new kind of wholeness, Edward. Wholeness in absence.'

'I can't.'

'Look, look at these.' She holds his hands up between them. 'Fighter's hands. You're a fighter, Edward.'

She closes her hands around his, finger by finger, and their foreheads touch, and they are so close that she can feel his ragged breath on her skin, the way each inhalation wracks his body.

The bare light bulb above them fizzes and flickers, their joined shadow thrown into harsher relief against the wall. Then with a *phut* it blows, and the room is plunged into darkness.

'What the . . .?'

'A power cut?'

Holding their hands out in front of them like drunken sailors, they stagger through the exaggerated darkness towards the window and look out onto a deep, velvet black. Number thirty-seven has been plunged into darkness, and it is not alone. There is no light to be seen in any direction.

'Does that happen often here?' Edward asks.

'Not often, no. I wonder what caused it.'

'The heat?'

'Maybe.'

Neither wants to think that it might have been something more sinister. Slowly a few glimmers of light appear. Candles in the apartments below, two windows offering dim smudges against the newly encroaching night.

There are no blushes in the dark. When sight is whittled down to mere outline, there's nothing to be lost in seizing a hand and saying, 'Come out here.'

'Onto the roof?'

'Yes.'

'Is it safe?'

'You haven't been out here yet?' Frédérique laughs. 'Come on Edward, I've been doing this for years.'

And so he follows her as she kicks off her shoes and clambers onto the windowsill. Muscle memory, she reaches round to the right – 'there's a ledge, just . . . here' – and swings herself up onto the roof's slope. Above Edward's window there is a flat space, enough for two to perch on, to let two sets of feet dangle off.

Edward joins her, and they lean back against the curve of the roof. It is drenched with the day's heat, soaking into their flesh, leaving tessellated imprints of its tiles along their skin.

'Normally you can see the Eiffel from here. The dome of the Panthéon.'

'Strange to think of all those people down there, bumping around in the dark.'

'Yes.'

'I love blackouts.'

'Me too. There is freedom in the dark.'

Frédérique fans out her silvery hair and lays her head back. In the distance a siren sounds, but it could be a different universe for all she hears is the rise and fall of Edward's breath, the rustle of his clothes as he lies down next to her.

Their arms touch, skin searing a line of electricity between them. Up above, the stars prick slowly into focus, as if the dark is pulling away a cloth that has kept the heavens secret. So many balls of light hidden from the city's view.

'I feel like an astronaut.'

Edward's words come out of nowhere.

'What do you mean?'

'Terrified of re-entry.'

Frédérique pauses.

'Is that what this has been for you? An exit?'

'I don't know. Is exit the opposite of entry?'

'An astronaut.' Frédérique smiles. 'I imagine you now, suspended in space. Free floating . . .'

'Free falling.'

'Let it, then.'

'What?'

'Let yourself fall.'

'Strange thing to say to someone on a roof.'

'Something will catch you. Always does.'

'You caught me, Frédérique.'

His words hang for a moment, unseen in the centimetres between them.

'And you me, Edward.'

And in the darkness, there are no firsts or seconds. Fingers wrap around each other, and there is no sight with which to question who moved first, whose ligaments made the initial tentative stretch. And time's passing is unmarked up here, under the vastness of the unlit sky that seems to curve and bend and stretch its arms around them. It is measured only in heartbeats, in the thud of one pulse against another. The mysterious, lumpen city down below them, the city of light now the city of dark, muted by this lack, and two lost souls holding each other on the curve of a tiled roof.

A breeze skitters over them, whispers across the skin, and they are in their own heads together; Frédérique in the south in a field baked by summer sun, Edward on the hill of home knee-deep in wet grass, and both of them together, here.

And he is still holding her hand when he whispers, 'Let's go down', and downstairs the lights are still out and there is no question of staying in his box room. Barefoot they pad along the hallway, boards creaking under their weight. They traverse the silent courtyard unseen and tiptoe up the stairs to her apartment.

Later, she will not be able to recall who led the way, which one followed the other's feet up the winding staircase, nor who reached out first once the apartment door was shut. Their fingers urgent, exploring, and in the morning she will find blood from his hand on the sheet, a rusty smear of it across her stomach. But for now there is the touch of lips, the salt taste of summer skin, the luminous tangle of white flesh and white sheets as their wide eyes adjust, finally, to lightlessness.

And when finally they rest, the tips of his fingers in the hollow of her collarbone, the sky is tinged with the beginnings of light.

32

Across the courtyard, strips of daylight have already crept through the blinds and up onto the bedclothes by the time César wakes. It is a rude awakening, his heart in his mouth, brain short-circuited by the violent screech of the buzzer cutting through his dreams.

He stumbles to the front door, sleep-slackened lungs gasping for air. Wheezing against the shock, against the sudden weight of his body forced upright and onto his legs, he picks up the intercom.

'Hello?'

'César, it's Sylvain.'

'Christ, Sylvain, what are you doing here?'

César looks anxiously over his shoulder, where Chantal is visible now in the bedroom doorway.

'There's been a change of plan, César. I need you to come with me now.'

'What . . . I . . . what time is it?'

'No time to explain, César. Just get down here.'

'Okay, okay.'

César replaces the phone and holds his head in his hands. His hair is thick with yesterday's grease, his cheeks sandpaper abrasive to his hands.

'Who on earth was that?'

He does not know what to say.

'César?'

In the moment in which he turns towards her, time takes on a different quality for César. He is aware, suddenly, of the changed tone of Chantal's voice these last few weeks. Her concern has gradually been superseded by frustration and it grates in her throat. He sees, too, her folded arms; the way they wrap tightly around her, as if she is scared, as if to keep him out. He knows Chantal of old and knows that anger is a front for fear in her. He knows that he is making her afraid, and he is afraid, in these long, dazzling morning seconds as the light rushes towards him down the corridor, that she is going to call him out.

'A friend, my love. He needs my help.'

Seized by panic, César does not know what to do besides rush. Rush at a half jog down the corridor, rush past her, back into the bedroom so that she is left reeling in the doorway. Rush to trousers to shirt to shoes, because if he stops he will have no excuse for not answering her questions, and he is aware of just how sorely they need answering.

'A friend? What friend? César!'

'Just a friend, Chantal.'

Why, oh why, do his trousers stick around his knees? Why don't his socks roll gracefully up from the tip of his toes to his ankles? Why is he this half-dressed clown, hopping madly around their bedroom while his wife stands shaking in the doorway.

'I don't believe you.'

'What?'

'I don't believe you. A friend,' she scoffs, 'what friend? What friend calls at six in the morning?'

'Chantal, please, it's a friend, he's in trouble—'

'César Vincent!'

That gives him pause, even as he's frantically knotting his shoelaces. She never calls him by both his names.

'I swear to god, I cannot live with you behaving like this!'

César hangs his head, voice as low as his heart, which has just plummeted down through his ribcage.

'Chantal, I promise you, it's a friend—'

'Go, César, just go. Go knowing I don't believe a word you say to me any more.'

César stands and readies himself for departure. But thirty years is a long time, and he cannot go with her standing like that, head bowed and spirit broken at the end of their bed.

'My love—'

He reaches his hand out to her, but she turns away.

'Just go, César.'

The buzzer rings again, angry and urgent as Sylvain must be downstairs, and César has not even considered yet that Sylvain is downstairs, and that any number of prying eyes – Isabelle's prying eyes, even Chantal's own lovely, sorrow-filled eyes – will see them walk across the courtyard together. But again the buzzer rings, and Chantal turns further from him, and César has no choice but to turn from her and join his unlikely friend down in the courtyard.

'What?'

They are in Sylvain's car racing towards the suburbs. Sylvain is speaking, but above the roar of the engine and the pulsing of the radio, with Chantal's words and the buzzer's shrieks still etching themselves onto his brain, César cannot hear him.

'The Day of Anger. Had to move it forward.'

Sylvain presses his foot down harder and they jolt forward in a thunderous roar of engine and motion.

'Why?'

'Problems, police, restrictions.' With a sudden flick of the wrist, Sylvain jerks them into a different lane, cutting off the white van that was barrelling up behind them. 'The people are angry, César. You can't stop progress.'

Even in his present state of discomfort, César is dimly aware that those are two different answers. He feels like a miner inside his own skull, holding up a candle and yet unable to see anything beyond the rock face in front of him.

'So what are we doing then?'

'You'll see.'

Gingerly, César leans his head back against the headrest. It is thick with the smoke of a thousand cigarettes. He feels drunk, that awful, legless, uncontrollable drunk made worse by the morning light and heat. It brings to mind the sickly, lemon-grey hangovers of youth, bile tickling his throat, the world spinning dangerously fast, like plates on sticks, and knowing even as you turn and turn that the crash is coming fast and you cannot stop it.

He closes his eyes, and soon they leave the waking city behind them. There are not many cars heading out of the metropolis at this time on a Monday morning. The opposite lanes are already backed up, bleary eyes over the tops of steering wheels, some drivers trying to stifle yawns, others letting rip in flashes of flung-back heads and slack jaws as Sylvain and César speed past.

Soon enough, they turn off the motorway onto smaller roads. There are planes low in the sky, and endless light industrial units, interminable lots of boxy rectangles, roof after corrugated metal roof. The music stops and the radio bleats out the morning headlines. Disturbances last night; shop fronts damaged, windows broken.

'Jean and his boys,' Sylvain says with a smile, flicking the radio off before the presenter can get into statements from the President, from the Mayor, all the political voices calling for calm.

They turn into a side street and creep along in silence until Sylvain pulls up in front of a row of abandoned-looking garages. Years of sun and disrepair have faded their painted metal doors to a variety of pastel hues; one pale pink, another the lightest grey blue. Paint flakes from them, and when Sylvain stoops to open one the key jams in the lock, the door finally opening with a screech.

It is dark inside, hot and dust filled. While César coughs

into his sleeve, eyes watering in the gritty air and with the effort of expelling this microscopic dirt from his lungs, Sylvain is already rooting around inside various boxes.

'Come on, César. Quick sharp.'

A heavy box is thrust into his arms. The dim light doesn't reveal much, but he can make out what looks to be a truncheon, hears the metallic clunk of something else beneath.

'Sylvain . . .'

'What?' Sylvain doesn't even look up.

'What is this stuff?'

'Don't get soft on me now, César.'

'I'm not being soft, but this is . . . this stuff looks *brutal*.'

Sylvain puts down his box and turns to him. Turns on him, maybe, except that his tone is butter soft, his voice low, his arms loose by his side.

'You came to me, César, saying you were fed up. About immigrants coming in and stealing our jobs. About France being a black-brown mix of everything but French. French jobs for French workers, you shouted it with me, we shouted it together. And now, after *terrorists* come again into the heart of our city, into our greatest cathedral, and shoot our citizens, now you say to me that this looks brutal? They're not listening to us, César. The government, the press, the world – it's all immigration this and integration that, and this, *this* is our chance to tell them otherwise. So don't stand there with a crisis of conscience about whether this is the way to do it. I'm telling you it is, and I'm telling you to pick up that box.'

For a moment they stare at each other, blank eyed, two men from different worlds whom fate has thrown together. And César does pick up the box, and the next one, and the one after that. He blocks out what it is he's carrying, arguing in his head that it was Sylvain who approached him. Sylvain who picked *him*. And as the car rolls slowly, heavily back towards the city, César wonders for the first time how many other desperate-looking men Sylvain has picked up in the city's more desolate cafés, how many other middle-aged ex-bankers there are, despondent and dispossessed and waiting to be preyed on.

In silence, they slide back past the city limits.

33

At some point in the night, Anaïs crawled up onto to the sofa. Pulled the blanket around her shoulders, inhaled the scent of the children – talcum powder, lotion, teething biscuits – wrapped herself in it.

She wakes stiff and sore, her joints rusted over. Her fingers creep out from under the blanket to prod her phone screen. A blare of artificial light, and no word from Paul, just a picture of their smiling faces, from a time when the family all smiled together.

Heaving herself upright, creaking like a ship trying to make even its keel, she staggers to the kitchen. *Water, water*. She pours glass after glass of it down her throat, body and brain such arid deserts that she does not register the commotion going on in the courtyard below.

She does hear a tap at the door, though, and deep inside her desiccated body her dried-out heart leaps. Paul? Are they back? But even as she is padding down the hallway to the corridor, her hope slides down into her stomach. They would not knock; Paul would have a key.

As her fingers close around the latch, Anaïs wonders for a moment if she should just leave this knock unanswered. If any good can come of whoever it is on the other side. But her hands are in motion, independent of this sudden, unrooted hesitation and it is only as the door opens and she sees the figure standing before her that she understands the cause of her dread.

It is Sophie.

A cold wave pricks gooseflesh along Anaïs's skin and sets her lips to quiver.

'Hello, Anaïs.'

'Who are you?'

'I told you.' Sophie's voice is the same calm, smooth tone as it was before.

'No.' Anaïs's limbs are shaking uncontrollably now and she has to hold the door for support. 'You told me you lived here. But I checked, and I tried looking for you . . .' Her voice trails away as she takes in the long dress, the pale, pale skin. She can barely put breath to the words. 'Oh my god . . .'

'I used to live here.'

Sophie's fingers grip Anaïs's arms, and they're cold but substantial, real, and is this it, she wonders, is this madness? Is she losing her grip as Sophie's hands tighten their grip on her?

'I used to live here,' she says again, stroking Anaïs's arm with her forefinger. 'And I suffered, like you.' Sophie's eyes fill with tears, and they are so close that Anaïs can see herself reflected in the wet of the other woman's retinas. 'So I have to tell you not to give up. You are so strong, they need you to be strong.'

Anaïs is in tears now too, not the hot tears of yesterday, but ice-cold rivulets streaking silently down her face.

'What happened to you?'

'I left. People talked about me here, whispered and pointed. I hated it. I felt so alone, felt that anywhere would be better than here. So we left, and it was desperately cold that year, the flu was taking the old and the young, and my son, it took him.' She shakes her head. 'I should have stayed here. Should have been strong.'

Anaïs looks at the woman in front of her, so defined by loss that it makes her substantial, makes heavy flesh out of air and pain. She wonders again why Sophie has come to *her*. Why there was a Sofia in the building in 1983 and yet no one remembers a Sophie.

'Why me?'

Sophie shrugs. 'Because you want space, and I have it. I have all the infinite space and it is not what you want, truly, in your heart of hearts.'

'I'm afraid.' Her voice is a whisper now.

'Of what?'

Anaïs closes her eyes at the enormity of the question. She sees the village where she grew up, her parents in stony silence in front of the television, silent in their separate beds. She sees herself, waxing round and bountiful, and the bright lights of the delivery suite in the hospital; sees, she is sure she can almost see, the red-hot pain of it, and the bloodied mess of her body afterwards, stitches and swelling. She sees Paul running across the courtyard to work, and the years of days spent alone. She sees the man in the church with his rotten mouth and his hand on her breast, and the children's hands, and she sees herself shrinking ever smaller, and the relentlessness of it; the carousel they met at and one they took the children to off the Place de la Concorde and it whirled round and round, an endless spin of light and noise and that is what she is ratcheted to, and she cannot make it stop, and a child throws something, she does not know what, but it splinters to nothingness at her feet, and *what if she breaks, what if she breaks, what if she breaks?*

'You won't.' Sophie's lips touch her cheek, and their chill imprint lingers long after Anaïs opens her eyes to find herself alone in the doorway. Sophie is gone. Anaïs looks down at her hands, and though trembling, she finds them more substantial than they were before. She herself is more solid. And as quickly as it came, the revelation of fracture and breaking seems to slip away, intangible in the August air.

34

Down in the courtyard, tempers flare and voices rise. Chantal is caught up in her own tempest, but she leaves Bâtiment B and walks into the storm of it.

Of course she watched César leave this morning. Watched him pant embarrassed across the courtyard with his 'friend', flicking his eyes up guiltily towards her window. His 'friend', with his hands thrust deep inside paint-splattered overalls. His 'friend', with the shaved head and the tattoos creeping out beneath his shirtsleeves. After they'd gone, she found herself shaking with the anger of it. She tried crying, a few rage-filled breathless puffs, but she couldn't do it. Anger, frustration, yes; but the truth of it is there's little sorrow in this change for her, though that realisation itself is tinged with a certain sadness. The levelling out of middle age she'd promised her twenty-year-old self she would not succumb to; the resignation, the acceptance, the way it settles on the shoulders like a sigh, feather-light but pulling everything down in its wake.

Instead of weeping, she sat at the kitchen table. She had toast and jam and licked the spoon (a habit César hates). She drank her customary cup of milky coffee and scanned yesterday's papers with a deliberately desultory, lackadaisical air.

'Fuck you, César,' she said to herself, running the line of her eye pencil along her lashes with a pleasing flick. ''uck 'ou,' with her mouth pouted to receive cherry-red lipstick.

She spritzed her perfume, and tugged at her dress to push her breasts into shape, and neatly shuffled the crisp pile of invitations. She is damned if she is going to let César spoil her party. His own bloody party.

And so she is heading to the bank today. Using her day off to deliver her calligraphic masterpieces in person. And it is with her ribbon-bound invitations in hand that she steps into the furore in the courtyard.

The new man from the third floor is stood, one hand waving wildly, the other tugging at his dark hair. Madame Marin flutters next to him, butterfly-bright in a new kimono, her hands flickering like insect wings through a series of placatory gestures.

'Monsieur, please, I am very sorry indeed—'

'Our door! In our own home!'

The man is shouting, his voice trembling with rage. When he sees Chantal, the focus of his anger moves.

'You!' he jabs an accusatory finger across the courtyard. 'Is it your husband who's President of the Residents' Cooperative? I want to see him, I want to see him right now!'

'I'm sorry, César's . . . out, today.' Chantal looks at Madame Marin, whose painted eyebrows are deeply furrowed. 'What's—'

'That's not good enough! We've been attacked! A vicious hate-filled attack – your husband has to do something about it! I want to talk to him. Right now, I want to talk to him right now!'

'There's been graffiti—' Madame Marin tries to explain.

'Graffiti? It's worse than graffiti! "Go home", it says, right on our door. Someone, *someone in this building* came and wrote that in the night.' He shouts these words up at the two walls of windows that rise above them, to the perpetrator sat behind a curtain watching his distress. 'Who? Who of you did this? What did we ever do to you?'

'Monsieur Laribi, please—' Madame Marin tries to calm him, and sure enough his voice does drop.

'Our first home, and we've just moved in, and my wife expecting . . .' He buries his head in his hands as Monsieur

Marin appears, beige as ever, from the courtyard house, bucket and scrubbing brush in hand.

'Come on, Monsieur Laribi.' Madame Marin takes his arm with a kind but firm authority. 'Let's get this mess cleaned up.'

Silently he yields to her, and the three of them troop solemnly into the building.

For a moment, Chantal stands numb in the courtyard, in the dazzle of morning light. Already the sun is hot, but there is a chill within her veins. *Could César. . .?* It is too horrible to think about, and yet all she can think of is the day of the meeting, the purple anger of him, the way he spat his rage at her once the other residents had left. He was shaking then, his rage trying to burst the confines of his body, and what if he had not been able to control his hands, his lovely hands; what if he has stooped this low, to terrorise people in their own building – the people he didn't want here in the first place?

Surely not, surely not, surely not, she tells herself, her thoughts swaying to the rhythm of the metro. And yet her heart taps against her ribcage as insistently as the *rat-a-tat-tat, rat-a-tat-tat* of the rails beneath her. She can't shake the feeling that her husband, her other half, might have had a hand in this. Can't stop her hands from shaking, her mind from replaying the neighbour's distress, the way he ran his hands through his hair, the half-voice that spoke of his wife's preg-nancy. She imagines the wife, alone, afraid, cowering behind the vandalised door. Chantal's own jittery hand skims her belly, and she imagines that kidney bean of new life, wonders whether it feels fear, whether its mother's tears stain its own tiny, formless features.

She gets out of the metro at Opéra, the station thick with summer scent. She'd forgotten the shoeless man always to be found on the way to the exit, singing to himself as he lays out with collector's care the rotting food he's foraged that day. A chicken carcass and disintegrating salad leaves, half of last night's kebab, other items more pungent and less identifiable, meticulously spread across a filthy bedsheet. Even underground the flies hover low beside him, and Chantal's eyes water as she clenches her nostrils against the stench.

Above ground, it is a different world: the opera house fat and gold and glittering, tourists swarming in all directions, Roma begging on the pavement, angular businessmen rushing past on their iPhones, couples salivating over the jewels on display in the windows of the Rue de la Paix. Chantal cuts down a side street towards the bank's city headquarters; a secret square of modern glass amidst the second arrondissement's elegant nineteenth-century facades. Something of the curve of it has always reminded Chantal of a whale's mouth; with the atrium shrouded in darkness it is as if, in entering, one were to be digested. She passes a huddle of workers in pinstripe suits and cigarette smoke outside the main entrance; *plus ça change*, she thinks.

'Good morning, Giuseppe,' she says with a smile to the security guard who has sat as many long years behind the front desk as César has at his.

'Good morning, Madame.' He smiles back – and does she imagine it, or is there a flicker of something she doesn't recognise behind the familiar square glasses?

'Is Guillaume in, Giuseppe? I just wanted to drop something off to him. I wonder if he might be able to come down? I don't want César to see me. Here,' she flicks rapidly through the cards in her hand, 'here's something for you too.'

Creakingly, Giuseppe rises from his seat to take the envelope. He is still looking at her, and there is something decidedly strange in it, something that pricks along the back of Chantal's neck.

'Are you well, Giuseppe?' Chantal smiles brightly, aware that her voice is just a little too loud. 'How's your wife?'

Without taking his eyes from hers, Giuseppe reaches for his telephone, punches the number, utters a few indecipherable words.

'She's well, Madame Vincent,' he says, replacing the receiver.

'Oh Giuseppe, please, you can call me Chantal.'

He nods, gruffly.

'Gosh, how many years has it been Giuseppe, since you and César started? Twenty-three? Twenty-four?'

'It'll be twenty-five come Christmas.'

'Twenty-five! Extraordinary.'

She runs a finger along the edge of the desk as if looking for dust, a nervous twitch of hers. Giuseppe does not take his eyes off her, and for long moments they stand in awkward silence, before all of a sudden Giuseppe sits, and he is staring at anything except her as Guillaume arrives.

'Guillaume, good morning.'

'Madame Vincent. To what do we owe the pleasure?'

Guillaume is ridiculously tall. Beanpole thin, his long-nosed donkey face dangling a good foot above hers, so that she has to crane her neck in order to speak to him.

'Well, Guillaume, César's birthday is coming up and I'm organising a party for him, so I've a few invitations for you and the team – top secret of course, that's why I didn't want to come up to the office.' She laughs conspiratorially.

'What do you mean?'

'Just that. That I didn't want to come up to the office in case César saw me. Now, here we are, here we are.'

She holds out a stack of invitations, her beautiful invitations, but Guillaume doesn't seem to notice the calligraphy. He doesn't take them. Instead, he puts his hand on her arm, ushering her away from the front desk and Giuseppe's desperately averted eyes.

'Madame Vincent . . .' Guillaume stares at his shoes, which is ridiculous to Chantal's mind, as his eyes are so far away from them he probably couldn't make out any dirt or detail anyway. 'Why would César be in the office?'

'What are you talking about?'

'Chantal,' he meets her eyes this time, 'César left the bank nearly eight months ago.'

The shock is so great that Chantal staggers, physically staggers backwards. He catches her awkwardly by the arm, but he might as well have thrown a punch at her, that is the force against which she is fighting to right herself.

'What? What do you mean?'

'I'm so sorry, Chantal. There was a merger last year, we've had months of reshuffles, and in January we . . . we had to let César go.'

'January? Did you say January?'

She can't hear anything. Everything is white noise and the plummeting of her guts through the floorboards. It is a landslide, and she cannot stay her ground.

'Yes. I . . . I don't know what to say, I can't imagine why he hasn't . . . Here, why don't we sit down for a minute.'

Guillaume guides her towards a suite of corporate armchairs. She drops into one, entirely limp, her envelopes slipping from her hands.

'Can I fetch you a glass of water?'

'Yes, thank you, yes.'

But when it comes she can hardly hold it, her fingers jolting uncontrollably, fat drops of water jumping up over the plastic edge and plopping down on the remaining envelopes like tears.

'I am terribly sorry.' Guillaume is crouching next to her now. 'Is there anything I can do? Someone I can call, perhaps?'

She bats him away like a fly, as if this is a minor upset, as if it's nothing.

'No, I'm fine, I'll be fine.' She can't look at him. 'God, this is mortifying.'

'As I say, I am terribly sorry.'

Guillaume stands up, knotting his fingers together in a gesture of consummate awkwardness. He waits through a minute or two of excruciating silence.

'Well, Madame Vincent, I should probably be getting back . . .'

'Yes, yes. Thank you, Guillaume, for letting me know. Obviously the, the invitations still stand.' She rummages in her lap, seeking through bloodshot eyes to read the addresses, which she realises now – and it comes to her in a moment of blinding clarity – are stupidly fancy. Illegible. Pointless.

He places a hand on her forearm. 'Thank you,' tapping his breast pocket, where a neat stack of envelopes protrudes above the pinstripe. 'Are you sure you'll be okay?'

'I'll be fine, fine.' She smiles broadly. 'I'll just take a moment to gather my things.'

He leaves her, and when she leaves she does not look at Giuseppe, though she can feel him staring at her through the same smudged glasses he has worn these last twenty-five years. She stumbles out of the giant glass maw and into the daylight, rushing along the pavement, knocking into other pedestrians with deliberate force that takes away what little breath she has left. She must not cry. She will not cry in public, not where someone could see her. She is sure Guillaume must be watching from the upper floors, and sure enough, if she were to turn, she'd see a beanpole blur against the blue glass.

She thunders down into the metro station, slamming her body into the ticket barrier when the machine fails, on first attempt, to accept her ticket.

'Fucking thing!' she screams, dropping the remaining envelopes and ramming the pathetic strip of paper into the mouth of the barrier so violently that it crumples beyond repair. 'What are you staring at?' she shouts at a startled couple she leaves in her wake. The metro attendant lets her through the end gate with a look of alarm, and it is only when she has raced down the first set of stairs that, finally, it catches her and she doubles over in grief and shame and anger, roaring so loud that even the shoeless man looks up from his private world, scurrying to pack up his precious, rotting goods before she turns on him.

35

In the other building, Edward wakes to her absence. The imprint of her head in the pillow, the puckering of the sheets where she has lain next to him. The light streaming through the muslin curtains bathes the room in silver; a metallic sheen on the large wardrobe, pearlescent glimmers in the mirror. The white sheets are thrown up around him like wild surf or snow-covered peaks, and though they cling to the skin he does not kick them off because they smell of her, of cut grass and cool gin, and he cannot bear to leave them.

Frédérique appears, a shadow in the doorway. She rose late today, only when the cat's yowling became too loud to ignore. She has not opened the shutters, or put the coffee on to boil.

'Good morning.'

'Morning.'

She makes her way across the room, stretches out an arm to pull back the curtain.

'No.' Edward puts his hand on her waist, his fingers amazed at the coolness of her skin as they pull her towards him. 'I don't want to see the world today.'

'When I was a kid,' Edward says softly, 'there was a haunted house outside our village. Big Victorian house, two bay windows either side of a red front door. We talked about it all the time at school. Supposedly the wife of the house had died in one of those big, bay-windowed rooms, and her ghost never left. Cats would hiss and babies would cry, dogs wouldn't go anywhere near that room, and on cold nights you could hear her ghost howling, pacing up and down in front of the window. So her husband cut the house in half – cut out the bay window and the room above it, like he was cutting a slice of cake.

'We'd dare each other, when we were little, to go and stand in the space between. Tempt the ghost. But we never did, because we knew – you know how kids just *know*? – that anyone who stood between those buildings would die. It was our folklore.

'There was an autumn, we were maybe ten and eleven, my sister grabbed my hand on the way home and pulled me up towards the house. Leaves crunching under our feet and the light was falling, we could see our breath in front of our faces, and Hannah, she just ran up there. She was fearless, hooting and dancing in the space in between, and I, I just froze.' He can still feel the wall beneath his hand, plaster crumbling beneath his fingernails. 'I was the one who ran away first.'

Frédérique takes his hand, winding her fingers through his and there is no plaster now but his words linger between them like motes in the still air.

'And now?' she asks.

'Now I wonder if I should have gone first. If things would have been different.'

She puts a hand to his cheek.

'I think there are magical places,' she murmurs, 'but I don't think they have the magic to change things.'

A door bangs in the courtyard.

'Do you believe in ghosts?'

'Oh yes.'

Frédérique stretches, long and lean beneath the white sheets, ghost-like herself in the half-light of their hidden day. A sudden gust of wind and the pale curtains rush up into the room, like phantoms crowding in on them. They look at each other, and Frédérique says, 'Oh yes, the ghosts are always here.'

Later she tells him of a city of abandoned temples.

'The middle of India, the middle of nowhere, and as far as the eye could see, temples and monuments in every stage of ramshackle and ruin. How do you say that?'

'Wrack and ruin?'

'Yes, that. God, it was hot. Makes this –' she gestures at the fierce sun pressing in through the curtains – 'makes this look like a spring afternoon. I was travelling with a friend back then, and we'd been there a few days but there was one temple in particular she wanted to see, a long way outside the village. Some special temple.

'So we went. Cycled out there, and it was nothing but dust and heat. The bikes were useless, weighed a ton, scratched us up no end. We got there bruised and bloodied and absolutely covered in dust, ochre dust, like some farcical face paint. No one there, of course. It was beautiful, perhaps the most beautiful place I've ever been. Rocky landscape, extremely harsh; no trees, no shade, and hewn from the rocks these extraordinary carvings. Chariots of stone whose wheels were supposedly able to move. Pillars with fruit and flowers, monkeys, gods. It was silent and empty and magical.

'But there was a man. When we left, just as we were heaving out the bikes, trying to get the bloody things to move. He wasn't violent, wasn't malicious, he just walked up to me out of nowhere and took my hand, traced the lines of it.' She holds her hand in front of her, and now it is Edward who traces its folds, its curvatures. 'He looked at these lines here, around the little finger, and just said – so matter of fact – "Only one baby. Take good care of him."'

Frédérique pauses, eyes closed. Her breath is heavy for a moment, Edward can feel the rise and fall of it against his skin, but then she opens her eyes and resumes her story.

'"Only one baby. Take good care of him." Well, my friend was scared by this, she wanted to get out of there as quickly as possible.'

'And you?'

'I wasn't scared. It was strange. But we turned to go, and he wanted money. For the reading, for reading my palm now he was holding his out. But we hadn't asked for it, we didn't have much on us, my friend was panicky, really wanted to leave, and so we did. We didn't pay him. And like you, I've wondered. Would it have been different if I'd given him a few rupees? Would it have changed things?'

'What is it you said to me?' Edward asks, tapping her lightly on the temple. 'You know logically that's not true.'

She catches his hand. 'Ah, and what did you say to me? There's here and there's here.' She places his hand on her heart, and he feels the muscle's beat below the skin.

'Touché.'

'Touché indeed. Oh Edward,' she sighs, 'the myths we make for ourselves.'

They cling to the bed as if it were a life raft; as if the swoosh of drapes against the floor were waves, as if the floorboards might swallow them up. There are fleeting missions to the kitchen, bare toes barely touching the ground as they run between rooms to land breathless against the countertops in kisses. There are berries, placed delicately on lips, staining them red. Water with cucumber in it, and, later, gin. Tartines whose crumbs fall around them in prickly constellations, to be dug out from the sheets and from the skin.

If it would not occur to Frédérique to feel self-conscious, the younger, shyer Edward is surprised to find how light and carefree the world is this day. As if, in this pale cocoon of light, he is wrapped up and unwrapped all at once. Safe from the world and yet as bare and exposed as he has ever been. And there is no artifice, no pretending. They lie draped in the sheets, draped over each other, as if they had been there all their lives. He leans over to kiss her silvery blonde hair, damp at the forehead, and she runs her fingers along his freckled forearms. They talk of everything, and lie in silence too, languishing in the bed, in the day, in the other. Trailing fingertips over hot skin as the sun arcs above them in a sky they cannot see, burning brightest at its apex before beginning its slip down across the sky.

36

Out in the city, Anaïs is dazzled by the heat. Stunned by the weight of the peerless sky pressing down on her from above.

With Sophie gone, she walked around the apartment as if discovering it anew. A window banging in the children's bedroom – so strange that she had not heard it in the night, that it would bang just then when there was not a breath of breeze – and as if some gauzy film had been lifted from her eyes she saw the children's sweet clothes again, the beloved toys, the threadbare sheets she'd been meaning to replace for months, the shoes that were too small for Florence's feet. She caught sight of herself, too, as she picked up a favourite teddy from the floor and pressed it hard against her breastbone. Gaunt face, lank hair, purple smudges beneath her eyes. She resolved then to start over. To wash and dress and set her small corner of the world to rights.

She set off dizzily, giddily from the apartment to buy her daughter flowers. Florence loves flowers, has loved them wildly, dearly ever since she was tiny and Anaïs used to wander the flower market with her. So fixed is she on her mission that she has not noticed that the streets are quiet, the pavements empty. She reaches Notre-Dame to find it surrounded by a wide cordon, her usual route across the Île de la Cité barricaded with police tape and officers on motorbikes. No sirens, today, but their lights keep spinning, the lurid blue and white at odds with the bored stares of the officers at the periphery, chewing gum as they sweat through their shirts and direct hapless tourists back the other way.

'What's going on?' Anaïs asks one of them. He looks at her as if she is stupid, his lip curling in disdain.

'The attack, madame.'

'Attack?'

'Jesus, don't you watch the news? People died. It's going to take a bit of time to get the roads open again. *Apologies.*'

Anaïs hears them laughing at her as she scurries away ('*putain de merde, ces femmes*'). Her guilty eyes scan every shut-up newsstand, every discarded newspaper. She has been so in her own little world, she cannot remember when she last stopped to consider the wider one.

She crosses the river and finally snatches a paper from a bench by the Tour Saint-Jacques. It is cheap, with many pictures, and she loses herself in the atrocity; images of tourists screaming, people crying, the fierce determination on the faces of the police officers, the panic as a second round of gunshots rang out.

'A child, there was a child . . .'

She murmurs these words to herself, rocking back and forth as she flicks through the pages, alighting for a moment on the reports of violence the previous evening. Pigeons scuttle away from her feet, in search of more tranquil pastures. She is the only person sitting in the park; the other benches are all occupied with people sleeping. Homeless, she assumes, to be wrapped in so many clothes and lying prone in the middle of a scorching day. The earth is cracked beneath her feet, the spindly trees visibly wilting. She looks at the street, and it does seem more thinly peopled today. Or maybe it's people's lips that are thinner, pursed with worry, their faces drawn, eyes flicking shiftily over those around them.

Anaïs leaves the paper behind and heads into the nearest department store. The air conditioning is fierce, the crowds thin, and she loses herself in the tiny children's clothes, the sweetness of printed cotton; blue and red stripes for the boys, tiny flowers for her girl. She wants desperately to make them happy, to show Paul that she does care, that she does have a heart. Her arms buckle under the weight of her haul, and there is something redemptive in the ache of them. It reminds her of being pregnant the first time, before she was sore and exhausted, and every evening she would show Paul her purchases and they would coo over the minute delicacy of the items, breathe in the smell of new clothes and the promise of what was to come. The purchases today are a going back, a getting back of what is hanging by so precarious a thread.

'My children have been away,' she tells the cashier, who raises a perfectly sculpted eyebrow at the quantity of clothes and toys passing beneath her scanner. 'They're coming back soon. This is to welcome them back.'

She receives no response, and heads bulkily back into the heat of the street. One of the busiest roads in the city and she finds it deserted. Anaïs turns her head, unsettled by the eeriness of the abandoned pavements, the absent traffic, the resounding echo of her footsteps in this parched and vacant world. She takes a tentative step into the road when a police car appears from a side street, swerving in her direction, sirens blasting through the hot air. It races off into the distance, and three men emerge from the street behind her. They are tall, dressed in black. As they shoulder roughly past her, one pulls out a balaclava, dragging black wool over his pale face.

'Better go home, miss.'

'Yeah,' his friend calls over his shoulder, 'better get yourself inside.'

They disappear down into the metro. Anaïs hesitates, looking around for anyone who might have witnessed their passing. But there is no one. She takes a few steps towards the station, but at the top of the stairs her heavy and foreboding heart gets the better of her. She turns on her heel, making her way instead across the silent street back in the direction of the river.

37

At key points across the city, the marchers mass. Heat and animal excitement. 'It's a Day of Anger!' they shout. 'We're angry!' they roar.

At the major stations, trains arrive from the provinces, disgorging raging protesters into the city. Some bring flags and banners. Others bring weapons. The streets ring with the stomp of heavy boots, the menace of shaved heads fills the boulevards. As day slips slowly towards night, the air crackles with the promise of violence. Electric heat, just waiting for a spark.

César has spent the day with Sylvain, waiting numbly outside cafés and apartment buildings in the very dregs of the city while boxes were delivered, enthusiastic handshakes and arm claps exchanged. Though he himself is mute, he learns, in bits and pieces, of the evening's plans. An official march along the Boulevard Montparnasse towards the Assemblée Nationale, and unofficial marches, too. While the riot police lock arms along the protest routes, private protest will take place at mosques and synagogues, at kebab shops and Kosher delis, and without the barricades there will be nothing to restrain it.

'Give those blackies a fright,' César heard one man boast, arms folded in cocky confidence over his enormous belly, and if his tongue had not been made of lead, if he himself did not tremble at the thought of Sylvain's weaponry smacking into his own skin, César would have pointed out that most of the city's Jews were pale skinned; that many of the Muslims were too.

César will long reflect on this paradox of a day. Starting so early, yet its heat-drenched, interminable hours spin forward like the hands of a cartoon clock, and no matter how slowly he thinks back to it, or how much he remembers the long minutes in hot streets waiting for Sylvain to re-emerge, he will get no purchase on it. It slides perpetually from his grip, and always, every time he thinks of it, there is Chantal, Chantal, Chantal.

The worst question, the one Chantal will not ask, is *how*. They will thrash out the whys and wherefores; he knows this, even as he leans back in the stained, smoky seat of Sylvain's car and pretends this day is not happening to him. But she will not ask *how* he could be complicit in these things. The question will lodge between them, unvoiced, present in every cold shoulder, every long and disappointed sigh. It will be the question that has César at the kitchen sink in the dark hours of the night, seeking a glass of water for a thirst he cannot quench. He has no answers for himself, and even as they leave Sylvain's battered car parked somewhere in the shuttered streets of the fifteenth arrondissement and begin their walk towards the action, César knows that each footfall is another indictment against him.

They join the crowd at Montparnasse. Many have already marched from Denfert-Rochereau. Others step newly into the fray, emerging from the concrete chaos of the train station shouting and hurling their arms in the air. 'We're angry, WE'RE ANGRY!' Under the pillars of the shopping centre, in the press of the crowd, they find some of Sylvain's acquaintances. César thinks he recognises some of them, from a bar perhaps or that secret meeting. Sylvain mutters something and they lurch as one many-bodied beast into the protest.

Everyone around them is wearing black. César is out of place in his pale sports coat, even more so when they pause to pull scarves over their mouths. He hadn't known he was coming here, hadn't known to hide his face. The crowd is packed with male bodies, testosterone and sweat pricking with excitement, and it is too crushed to find space to step, to breathe. César stumbles, but there's no room to fall in this frenzy.

It's as a firecracker goes off somewhere behind him that César sees the first arms saluting in the air, hears the first Nazi chants go up. Someone has a smoke canister and a haze of orange is rising in cruel imitation of the sun, whose evening rays lend a golden glow even to the crumbling McDonald's. As if in a daze César watches a group of teenagers jostle past laughing. One of them has a geometric shape etched on his cheek.

The riot police don their helmets, run from their vans, line the side streets in their cross-armed gesture of control, but outside their cordon the real violence starts. The swelling crowd in which César finds himself shouts 'Jew, France is not for you!', 'Go back to Allah!', but beyond its sweaty, black-booted reach fires are being set in the Marais, cars torched outside Muslim-owned shops, bottles thrown through carefully chosen windows. Buildings that had been picked out on maps in underground meetings, marked with a red cross, are now marked with blood and jagged glass. The batons Sylvain has carefully distributed crack knees and break noses. As César's eyes smart from the first wave of tear gas, the knuckle-dusters he carried this morning sink into unsuspecting, unprotected flesh. Parents and children scream and cower.

The violence is brutal. The police, who'd been expecting it in the suburbs, are shocked to find it in the heart of the city – to find swastikas spray-painted at Invalides, to see bricks flying through the windows of public buildings. And yet some neighbourhoods have no idea. The sixteenth arrondissement slumbers on in its gilt magnificence. Up in Montmartre, tourists pose for the same old photos outside Sacré-Coeur, fall for the same old tricks from the pickpockets on the church steps. Everything is the same and nothing is the same, for by the time the authorities understand the scale of the attacks there are homeless people lying unconscious in pools of blood, North Africans dragged onto the street to have their teeth scattered across the pavement, rabbis barricading themselves inside their synagogues, whole neighbourhoods of smoke and broken glass. As the word spreads people creep out of their apartments, some to watch and some to join, and the city's emergency announcements to STAY INDOORS fall on terrified, intoxicated, unhearing ears.

38

An explosion rattles number thirty-seven's window frames.

'What on earth was that?'

Frédérique and Edward have finally ceded the luxurious comfort of the bed for the *salon*, where he is mixing drinks. She is stretched out like a cat on the chaise longue, plaiting her silvery hair. She has donned an oyster slip, he a crisp towel around his waist. They have showered together, cool water breathing new life into a hot, mildly hungover end of day.

Frédérique rises and peers out behind the curtain. Edward joins her, but they see nothing, just the street in unpeopled darkness. Again, another explosion sounds, more distant this time but they grip each other nonetheless. There is a faint smell of burning on the night air.

'Oh god, oh god.'

Frédérique disentangles herself and rushes to the radio. It screeches from classical music through various adverts and Francophone pop songs before it arrives at the smooth, toffee-voice of the news channel.

'Major disturbances in Paris this evening. Groups protesting a "Day of Anger" have broken away from the main protest route. Several fires have been set around the city; cars and businesses have been torched. The mayor of Paris confirms that riot police are in position but the public are *strongly advised* to stay at home. I repeat, official channels are urging members of the public to *stay at home.*'

Edward and Frédérique look at each other in amazement, and sure enough they can hear sirens now, the roar of a helicopter circling overhead.

'Bloody hell,' Edward whispers.

'Terrifying.'

'What does it mean, a "Day of Anger"?'

'I don't know.' She turns the radio off. 'Fascists, extremists. People who want France to go back to what it was.'

'God.'

'I'm worried about Josef.' Frédérique returns to the window. 'His eyes, you know, he doesn't see too well. He wouldn't know to get out of the way.'

'He'll be okay, won't he?' Edward is wrapping his arms around her, resting his chin in the angular crook of her collarbone. It's stupid, but now, after this day, this night, he doesn't want to talk of anyone else. It is the two of them against the world in this apartment. He doesn't want to let the world in.

As Frédérique tilts her head up to answer him, there is a sudden thump at the door. They jump, and there is hardly time for Edward to turn around before, with a thunderous clatter, the door opens and Emilie enters the apartment.

Her eyes move from one to the other, from their respective states of undress, to Edward's arm around Frédérique's shoulders, her hand flat against his chest.

'What the . . .' Her words trail off, her mouth hangs open, bags dropping to the ground at her feet.

'Em, darling,' Frédérique rushes forward. 'What are you doing here? I didn't know you were coming!'

But Emilie's eyes will not leave Edward's and he cannot read what is in them. Shock? Betrayal? Is she thinking back to the night they spent together because she is grappling, visibly grappling, to comprehend finding him in the same state with her aunt. She reaches out to steady herself against the sideboard.

'I didn't know you were coming,' Frédérique says again and Emilie responds to the prompt, wrenching her eyes away from Edward's, dragging a bracelet-laden hand through her blonde hair.

'No, clearly. Fucking hell, do you never listen to your messages, Freddie?'

All three sets of eyes travel to the answerphone. Edward and Frédérique look guiltily at its red flashing light, and in the depths of his memory Edward recalls a phone ringing, the mutual decision not to answer it.

'Darling . . .'

Frédérique moves forward but Emilie sidesteps her. She is still more or less in the doorway, the door hanging open behind her, her feet caught in a dance between staying and going. Above them, the helicopter circles again and the sirens' wails are getting closer.

For a moment, nobody moves, but then Frédérique darts towards the door, slamming it shut so that this private drama is not on show for the entire staircase. Edward makes an exit towards the bedroom, desperately gripping his towel lest it should fall. He pulls his clothes on, though they're thick with sweat. He attempts to straighten the bedclothes. From the *salon* he can hear raised voices, though not what they say, and in the privacy of Frédérique's bedroom he sits on the bed, hands over his mouth to stifle a laugh. His heart is beating nineteen to the dozen, his legs shaking, yet there is something awfully, terribly funny about Emilie finding them like this.

Ears pricked, he waits a few minutes for the shouting to die down before he makes his return. It is only as he takes a few tentative steps into the *salon* that he realises he has no idea what to say.

Emilie is in the middle of hissing, 'My fucking *friend*, Freddie.'

'Em, it wasn't like that.'

They are sitting on the sofa now, heads conspiratorially close, even in conflict. One silver, one gold. Edward stops awkwardly at the room's edge. This is a private club, with Frédérique stroking Emilie's hair, Emilie held beneath the

216

curve of her arm, where Edward himself has so recently been.

A creaky floorboard betrays him and the moment of calm is shattered.

'And you! You're meant to be grieving! This was to help you get away, not get you into bed with my aunt!'

Emilie is up and by the fireplace now, her muscles shivering with anger.

Edward clears his throat. 'Maybe I should go.'

'Yes, maybe you should!'

'No, don't be ridiculous.'

They reply in comic unison, so that even in the midst of the upset they cannot help but laugh. Emilie presses her forehead into the cool marble mantelpiece and groans.

'I just wanted to come out and see you both.'

'Well, love, we're here.'

'I just, I had no idea it would be like this. And I've been lugging my bags across the city for fucking hours—'

Her shoulders slump, and she slouches back to the sofa, throwing herself onto it, cracking the muscles in her neck.

'Yes, tell us,' Frédérique shoots Edward a significant look, seizing the opportunity to change the narrative. 'What on earth is going on? The radio said fires, disturbances.'

Emilie's hands have been pressed against her eyes, but now she looks up.

'You mean, you don't know?'

'No.'

'It's absolute chaos out there. Mayhem. I've basically walked all the way from the bloody Gare du Nord. Most of the metros have been suspended. There's fires and lootings, apparently. The main protest has broken up and now it's just a free for all.'

'But what? Against whom?'

'I don't know, but a group of police officers stopped and told me to get the hell away from the Marais. I think it's been bad near Strasbourg-Saint Denis, too. I couldn't come down

Sébastapol, there were fires and cordons and god knows what else going on. It's crazy out there.'

'The Front National?'

'I'd say so. The ones I saw looked fucking scary.'

Frédérique rises. 'I should turn the radio back on.'

'I don't know how anyone could report it, really. Half the city's impassable. I saw a crew trying to get to the Hôtel de Ville and the police weren't letting them get anywhere.'

'Still.'

She is just about to flick the switch when the air is spliced by a sudden, urgent pounding at the door. The three look at each other in confusion. Another intruder on this already crowded night? A second burst of banging, and Frédérique moves quickly to the door.

It is Anaïs, her hands and shirt smeared with blood. She is doubled over, can hardly breathe to get the words out.

'Please, there's a man. Hurt. You must come.' Her hand clutches Frédérique's and their eyes meet now, there's no space for all the things they haven't said. 'He's asking for you, asking for Frédérique.'

For a few seconds time stands still, and they are frozen in a tableau of fear and horror. Breath catches ragged in Anaïs's throat, the blood drains from Frédérique's face. Edward and Emilie stare at her, and then at each other, helpless in the face of this news and all that it implies. Then everything is movement, and Frédérique is grabbing a cardigan from the coat rack, slamming her feet into sandals, Edward and Emilie are surging forward, each grasping Anaïs by an elbow.

'Are you alright, Madame? Are you hurt?'

She shakes her head. 'No, no, I'm fine, there's just, there's a lot of blood. We had to carry him.'

Seconds later they are flying down the staircase to the entryway, where a small crowd has gathered behind the great turquoise door. Monsieur and Madame Marin have emerged from their house to see what the commotion is; although they do not all register it at once, it is the first time any of the residents have ever seen Madame Marin without her makeup. Small and pale, like a dancer stepped out of the spotlight; gone the orange hair (a wig, it seems), and instead a cropped head of feathery blonde. She looks small, and frightened.

Behind the Marins, Isabelle Duval stands at a distance. Cold and haughty as ever, her long nose visibly curls in disgust at the sight in front of her. She thrusts her hands deep into her dressing gown pockets, for just twenty minutes earlier she executed her plan. A can of red paint over the greengrocer's shopfront, and there was no one to stop her tonight, no one to interrupt save those who would have applauded her efforts. Her hands are stained, her heart pounding.

Against the door, Chantal Vincent is crouched over. She, too, has blood on her; a dramatic streak of it up her cheek where she has brushed her hair out of her eyes. Under the bare bulb of the entryway light, the blood is black and ominous, her eyes white and wet and full of panic. In her arms, the collapsed body of Josef.

'Josef!' Frédérique throws herself onto the floor in front of him. 'What happened, are you alright, are you alright?'

She cups his face in her hands and he recognises her, they all see his eyes open, his lips mutter a secret message. For she has put her face close to his now, cheek to cheek, cradling his crumpled form as she might a sick child.

'Where did you find him?'

She addresses Chantal, who stands shakily upright.

'Near Denfert-Rochereau. I recognised him, because of the trolley, you know?' She looks around her, gesturing, as if the trolley might be here with them. 'He, I don't know who did it, but he's badly hurt.'

Edward cuts in. 'Has anyone called an ambulance?'

'Yes, Monsieur,' Madame Marin nods. 'But who knows how long it will be with the city like this.'

Silence falls over the group as the helicopter loops overhead, momentarily illuminating the courtyard with its ill-omened spotlight. The light bulb above them swings gently in the breeze and Edward is reminded of the medieval paintings he has pored over in Frédérique's shop. They are *Pietà* and nativity in one, with Frédérique whispering Josef's pain away as the rest of them stand helplessly by. The homeless man is both the crucified and the child, they the bystanders who have come to help but who cannot enter into the intimacy of this embrace. Edward watches Chantal put her arm around Anaïs in an act of shaky, bloody support. He sees the Marins, usually so distant, creep closer together. He feels Emilie's hand near his, and grasping it, feels her return the gesture.

Like this they wait, in silence, until eventually a vehicle groans its way up the street and the ambulance's blue lights flash beneath the turquoise door.

39

When Anaïs finally stumbles into the apartment, she scarcely notices that the door is no longer double locked. Her muscles are agony; the adrenaline has left a crevasse of exhaustion in her head and her heart. When she looks up to see Paul in the corridor, her brain cannot compute what his return means.

'You . . . You're here.'

'Where have you—' He stops dead. 'My God Ana, what happened? Are you okay?'

'I . . .' And she is too overcome even to formulate the words, to compute what the last hours have meant. All she can think about are Florence's too-small shoes, the things she had bought today, before . . . Resting her head against the wall she whispers, 'I lost all my shopping.'

'Your shopping? What are you talking about? Are you hurt? You're covered in blood!'

'I'm fine, I'm fine.'

He guides her to a chair in the kitchen. His hands feel so good and warm on her shoulders she could weep. In spite of the heat, she is shivering.

'Here.' He puts a blanket around her.

'Thank you.' She looks at him. 'You're back.'

He pauses. 'Yes. Ana,' more quietly, urgently now, 'what happened?'

'I actually, I had a good day. I went shopping. Got the things Florence needed, some new sheets for the boys, new shoes for them, but then . . .' She screws her eyes shut. 'Paul, it was terrible.'

'Come on, tell me about it in here.'

He leads her to the bathroom and starts running the bath. She turns to him in fright.

'The children—?'

'They're here, they're safe. Asleep, tired out with all the fresh air and running around. Come on. Let's clean you up.'

For the first time, she looks at herself in the mirror. From her hands to her elbows, she is caked in rusty blood. There are dark stains across her shirt. Her face is covered in the dark dust of city summer, her hair matted with it.

Gently, Paul removes her clothes. She is powerless to resist, remembering the first time he undressed her, the excitement then and the utter exhaustion now. The warm water is a balm. She closes her eyes and could almost float away.

'What happened?' Paul's quiet question reels her back.

'I went shopping. I wanted to show you that I do care. That I am a good mother. I wanted to get things for the kids because I'm not heartless, Paul. I'm not.'

He puts his fleshy hand on top of her bony one as she grips the edge of the tub. 'I know you're not.'

'As I was leaving to come home, there were these men heading into the metro. To a protest.'

'They didn't hurt you?'

'No, no, but I didn't want to go down the metro after them. So I walked, but then things started kicking off. It was okay until I got near Montparnasse, and then there were men everywhere, balaclavas and fireworks going off, or explosions anyway, and they were trying to overturn cars, you know, rocking them backwards and forwards until they tipped. It was terrifying. So I came up via Denfert-Rochereau, and at first it was a bit quieter but then near the station it was just craziness. People shouting and screaming and throwing things, the police going crazy too. And I bumped into Madame Vincent, you know, from downstairs. She was on her own like me so I ran over, said we should go home together, we'd be safer. It was the strangest thing, she was just standing in the street, staring at the rioters. Just standing, transfixed. And they're running around, throwing things, shouting. She wouldn't budge. So I'm calling and calling to her, "Madame Vincent, Madame Vincent, come on, let's go", and eventually she snaps out of it and we walk a little way together, out of the really awful part, but then we came across four men beating a man. I wanted to run, but she was really with it by then, said she recognised the man being attacked, that he lived on our street, she gave him money sometimes.'

Anaïs takes a gulp of air as if she's coming up from a deep-sea dive.

'Well, she runs up to them, screaming, and the men got scared, this woman yelling at them, and they ran off so we were left with the man, the homeless man. He couldn't walk, there was blood everywhere. His face . . . Paul, it didn't look like a face at all but he recognised us, recognised her at least, and he just kept saying, "Frédérique, I need to see Frédérique" – you know, Madame Aubry from the other building? I must have dropped all my bags because between the two of us we carried him back here. He was a deadweight, barely conscious, and neither of us, neither of us is that strong, really. But eventually we did it.'

'Where is he now?'

'At the hospital. The ambulance took forever to arrive. You didn't hear us all, down in the courtyard?'

'No, I was up here thinking about you, not looking out of the window.'

She looks down at the murky water. Wide seconds stretch between them.

'Are you going to leave again?'

'No.'

There is a silence in which the water lapping around her legs stills absolutely. She holds her breath; even breath, it seems, would disturb this fragile moment.

It is Paul who clears his throat first. Hesitantly, he begins. 'I shouldn't have gone. For better for worse, we said.'

'I want things to be better, Paul.'

He nods. 'I know. But there have to be changes, Ana. Not just you, both of us I mean. I, I know I'm not always the best husband—'

'You are.'

'No.'

'You are. But I have felt so lonely, these last months. And tired. I don't feel real, sometimes. Haven't felt human. Just really fragile, as if I might break.'

'And yet you made these three beautiful children. You carried a man across Paris. You are strong, Anaïs.'

She bows her head, shuts her eyes against tears.

'But I can help more. I can cut back on the hours at work, at church. And if the job doesn't work out, screw it, we can go back to the Auvergne, or move out to the country with Tante Marie.'

She opens her eyes. 'I can keep chickens.'

'Yes.'

'And wrestle livestock in my spare time.'

They smile tentatively at each other. They both know that this is a pipe dream, that it will not happen. But holding hands for the first time in months in this steamy bathroom, she wonders if maybe that is enough. Enough to have the intention. To share the same pipe dreams. To look at each other and remember why they are together in the first place.

Paul squeezes her hand a little tighter. *Maybe*, she thinks.

40

On the other side of the arrondissement, the hospital is a war zone. A neon-lit no man's land, with wounded sprawled across plastic chairs, lying prostrate or desperate on every available gurney. Doctors and nurses run up and down the corridors, barking orders at each other. There's a wild look in their eyes; this has been a wild and savage night.

Frédérique travelled with Josef in the ambulance; that this should be the case was obvious. Edward and Emilie set off after them at a run, quickly finding themselves breathless and doubled over. After that, they walked. The streets they took were mostly quiet, though they bore the evening's scars. Car windows smashed, paint hurled against shop windows, particularly brutal graffiti scrawls. One shopfront had been bludgeoned in, its shatterproof glass dented, kaleidoscopic, but just about holding.

'His name is Josef Bobek,' Emilie shouts over the noise of two drunk men staggering around the atrium. 'Josef Bobek!'

'How do you know his surname?' Edward asks, as the harangued secretary rolls her eyes and jabs a new number into her telephone.

Emilie looks at him quizzically. 'Why would I not know his surname?'

There is no time to reply, for a group of men surge in through the doors. Two hold handfuls of broken bones aloft, clutching their forearms and waving their disfigured digits in the air. Another buckles and falls to his knees, clutching at his stomach. A fourth lurches towards the reception desk, then vomits on his shoes. Edward and Emilie recoil as the receptionist rolls her eyes again, tells them 'north pavilion, fourth floor', and yells for an orderly.

The upper stories of the hospital are quieter, punctuated by low beeps coming from unseen rooms. Everywhere the warm, cloying smell of institutional food, the sharpness of disinfectant, the air hot and sickly sweet.

They find Frédérique crumpled in a chair in an otherwise deserted corridor. She starts to see them, rewrapping the brown cardigan around her. The fluorescent lights turn her skin to pearl, pale as the slip she is still wearing.

'What did they say?' Emilie asks, dropping into a seat beside her.

Frédérique shakes her head slowly. 'They're doing tests, but it doesn't look good.'

'What happened?'

'He's been beaten, badly beaten. I saw them remove his clothes, swollen footprints all up his spine, skin purple, blue.' She shakes her head, as if trying to shift these gruesome sights from her mind's eye.

'I'm so sorry, Freddie.'

'I said, didn't I?' Frédérique looks to Edward now. 'I said he wouldn't know to get out of the way, wouldn't know to find somewhere safe.'

'There's nothing you could have done, Frédérique.'

She snorts derisively. 'Oh, how many times have people said that to you, Edward!'

'Sorry.'

She hangs her head. 'No, I'm sorry. I just . . . I should have done something.'

A silence falls over them, and they wait, Emilie stroking Frédérique's arm, Edward leaning against the wall, staring at his shoes. There is a clock somewhere, at the distant nurses' station perhaps, that ticks out the time in ponderous, booming seconds.

Finally, a doctor appears. White hair, white coat, face washed into paleness by the lighting, the time of night, the type of night that it has been.

'Madame Aubry,' he holds out a stiff hand as Frédérique and Emilie scrabble to their feet. 'I'm Dr Ghesquière. Our team is still carrying out tests on –' he pauses for a second to look down at his papers – 'on Josef, but I have to tell you, the prognosis is not good. The damage suffered to the spine, the nerves. Madame Aubry, I'm very sorry, but it is possible your husband may not walk again.'

'Husband?' The word bursts, unstoppable, from Edward's lips. Dr Ghesquière looks confused, as Frédérique sighs and turns, time stilling for Edward until there is an eternity in that movement and in the moments before she says, 'Yes, Edward. My husband.'

'You didn't know, then?'

It is the first thing Emilie has said to him since they left the hospital. Dr Ghesquière took Frédérique to Josef's bedside, with the promise that they could make her moderately comfortable overnight. Emilie and Edward agreed to go home, to return in the morning with fresh clothes and anything the pair of them might need. Emilie agreed really, for Edward was still reeling, pressing his sweaty palms into the breezeblock wall as if the faux geological texture might ground him in this moment of suspended reality.

'No.' He is standing uneasy in the doorway while Emilie throws herself down on the couch. 'No, I didn't.'

'You might as well come in,' she says, kicking off her shoes.

He walks slowly to the chaise longue. He lies back, bones aching, and realises it smells of her. It is gone four, and already the morning light is creeping up on them. There is a glow beyond the curtains, the sun returning to assess the night's damage.

On the blue sofa, Emilie rolls to face him. 'They split after the fire. After Daniel died. She couldn't bear to be there any more, in Provence, and Uncle Jo—'

'Uncle Jo!'

'That's what I called him! Uncle Jo couldn't bear to be indoors. Couldn't stand it. He drifted around Provence for a while, but they've been together forever, those two. I don't think they could live together or apart.'

And Edward remembers them now, Frédérique's descriptions of Josef, of her mysterious 'partner'. The way she looked at him that night and said, 'There's no question you can't ask', as if she wanted to be found out. The way 'We knock around' had rolled off her tongue, and he had forgotten it, completely forgotten it until that moment in the hospital, because their existence was one of present not past, and he wanted her to exist for him only. Or perhaps, though he blushes to admit it, perhaps they were each so busy with the business of forgetting, each so steeped in their own grief, that these other histories, other stories, had fallen on ears that had no interest in hearing them.

Emilie props herself up on one elbow, eyebrow raised in accusation. 'You must have known. You didn't think it's weird how much they talk to each other, how much they know of each other's routines?'

Edward knows that if he looks at her tears will come. He feels hurt and stupid, yes, but it is Frédérique's loss that is suddenly so much worse, so much more real to him now that he knows. For the first time in months it's someone else he's hurting for. He sees grief that's doubled not shared, two people so utterly broken by it. At the back of his mind his own parents swim mistily into view, and he is almost overwhelmed, inundated by the magnitude of sorrow.

But he can't say that, so keeps his eyes firmly fixed on the ceiling, shrugging his shoulders in feigned nonchalance. 'There's plenty of stuff that's weird here.'

'True that.'

There is a moment's rustling as Emilie nestles herself between pillows, then quiet.

'I didn't mean to hurt you, Em.'

'What?'

'Tonight.'

'Not hurt. Just . . . shocked. I was coming here to surprise you and I never for a moment thought . . .'

Edward contemplates telling her how recent this development was. That had she arrived twenty-four hours earlier, she would have been in time to stop it. To catch them. But in the dim light of early hours, with the press of the chaise longue beneath him and the dark shapes of the *salon*'s furniture looming, he decides he will be selfish and keep this secret. Keep some part of it for him.

'It was definitely a surprise,' he says, his best attempt at being wry.

'Yes.'

She yawns, and it is not long before they fall into an uneasy sleep, a few hours' break from consciousness and all the pain and questions it will bring. Their heads loll to the side, each drops an arm from their respective pieces of furniture, and it is like this that they will stay, under the watchful eyes of Mischa the cat until their necks ache and the daylight is too strong to ignore.

41

César has only cried twice in their married life. Once, when they could not have children. A second time, more than two decades later, when his mother died. On those occasions he laid his head on Chantal's knee. She stroked his hair, twirling the tendrils at the nape around her fingers. She whispered words of comfort, and kissed his tear-stained cheeks.

She does not do that today. Today the sobs spill forth, fat and embarrassed, embossed with snot and spit. Today he must sit upright, alone, while she watches him weep. As Anaïs returned to her husband, was bathed by and reunited with him, Chantal returned to an empty apartment. Once she left the bank (it feels like an eternity ago), she decided she did not want to go home. In the bowels of the metro station she wept, blew her nose, tidied her makeup, and took the train to Saint-Germain. She bought a packet of cigarettes, took a table on the terrace at the Deux Magots, and smoked the entire pack one after another in a blank-eyed, unhurried manner, interspersed only with cups of milky coffee so that by the end of the afternoon her limbs were jittering uncontrollably.

Chantal had not smoked in years, but she needed the greasy suck of it today, the sharpness of nicotine in her nose and throat. She stayed all day, until the waiters, getting twitchy about the dinner service, pointedly asked her if she was planning to dine. She smiled at them with hardened eyes. The politest impoliteness in Paris, the waiters in the cafés along Saint-Germain.

By the time she left, it was clear that something was happening up at Montparnasse. She wandered towards it, felt a smack of dread in her guts to see the Front National out in force, men with the same shaved heads and tattoos as had walked across her courtyard that morning. She waded as best she could against the edges of the tide, searching hopelessly amongst the hundreds, the thousands, for César's face.

It was as Anaïs found her that she found him. At Denfert-Rochereau, right above the entrance to the Catacombs, where nineteenth-century ossuaries made macabre, skeletal walls out of the remains of some six million people. The poet in Chantal felt she died too, at that moment, seeing César across the darkness of the square. She could not move, but if she had been able to she would have liked to walk down into the depths, out of the stickiness of summertime heat; to lie below the ground amidst the cool, damp bones and stay there, untroubled. At the same time the less poetic side of her thought, 'I bought that bloody jacket!' as she watched her husband, her portly, sports-jacketed husband, amidst this group of thugs lobbing bricks into a shop window.

All night she sat, blood-spattered, in the living room. Nicotine, caffeine, adrenaline, she wasn't a bit tired. She sat and waited, and in the grey murk of early hours, as the church clock strikes a mournful five, César returns.

He sees her immediately and his shoulders slump. She does not wait for him to take off his jacket, nor to enter the living room before she begins.

'I went to the bank today, César.'

'Oh god.'

'Eight months, Guillaume said. Eight months since they let you go.'

César turns his face to the doorjamb, eyes screwed shut.

'Chantal . . . I don't know what to say.'

'Funny isn't it? You've always had the gift of the gab. Seems there's a lot of things you've not been telling me recently.'

Tearing himself away from the safety of the wall, he looks at her. Eyes adjusting in the gloom, panic-stricken.

'Chantal,' he points, 'the blood . . .'

'It's not mine, César. A homeless man. Beaten up by a gang of your cronies. Or maybe you got in first, before I got there. You like giving a defenceless man a good kick in the spine nowadays, do you?'

'You must think I'm a monster.'

'Yes, I do. But I want to know why. Why you've been lying to me. Why you let me be *humiliated* turning up at the bank like that. Why you spend your time with skinheads now, beating people up and doing criminal damage to people who've never harmed you in their lives—'

'Chantal, I don't—'

'*I saw you, César!* I saw you at Denfert-Rochereau! The only one not in black, the only one in a sports jacket, the only fat, middle-aged, middle-class one!'

He hangs his hand, clinging desperately to the wall as if his whole world is subsiding. Which, in a way, it is.

'The game's up.' Chantal has regained the icy cool of her voice now though her heart pounds in her chest. 'I know. But I want to know *why*.'

Slowly, slowly, César prises himself away from the wall. He crumples, cringes, bends himself as small as possible in a futile bid to take his shame away. He falls into a wooden chair. Hard, sharp-edged, it is purgatory for tired and shame-filled bones.

'I didn't know,' he begins falteringly, 'how I could tell you.'

He looks up at her, in hope of a response. Receiving none, he continues.

'I felt worthless. As if everything I had worked for, everything that gave me value had been taken away. They said it was because of the merger, but I could see all these bright young things being brought in. People who knew nothing about the bank. Weren't even born when I started working there. Certainly weren't born here.'

He steadies himself, hands on the arms of the chair, breath catching in his throat.

'I should have told you. I know that now. I knew it then, but there was never a good time, and the longer I kept lying the better I got at it and the harder it seemed to turn back. You never suspected, so I was never brave enough. I'm a coward.'

'And the Front National?'

'I started going to this café out near the Porte de Vincennes. It was somewhere to go. Somewhere to be where no one would see me, recognise me. Eventually this man, Sylvain, started talking to me. He had a lot of friends who'd lost their jobs too, lost them to immigrants especially—'

Chantal snorts derisively but César perseveres with his telling of it. Redemption in truth after so many months of deceit.

'At first it wasn't violent. Just meetings, people to meet with. I was so lonely, Chantal, and it felt like these people understood me.'

'I would have understood you.'

'I know,' he whispers. 'But they were strangers, in the same situation, and it was . . . easier, somehow. I didn't have to justify myself to them. I thought it was just so much talk. Something to busy themselves with, not something they were actually going to enact. But then, after the attack, everything just snowballed and suddenly I was out delivering weapons to people and, oh god I wish I'd had the courage to stop but I was lost, Chantal. Completely lost.'

He is on his knees now in front of her, sobbing. She cannot look at him, keeps her eyes firmly fixed on the window where the grey sky is becoming brighter.

'Please, please believe me. I'm not a bad person. I didn't hurt anyone, didn't beat anyone up. I would never kick anyone in the spine like you said. Please believe that. I'm an idiot, yes, a stupid fucking fool who got caught up in something, but I'm not a bad person, my love.'

'Get off me, César.'

He returns broken to his chair, sits blubbering, convulsing

while she gazes out at the morning light. It is starting to rain. No burst of thunder this time, just the attrition of heat on cloud, plummeting pressure making the sky wet. No storm, no tempest, just slow, fat drops that fall noisily on the roofs and the windowsills, splashing up against the glass panes like pathetic tears.

In this moment, Chantal does not feel anything. Her heart, her mind, they are entirely blank. Slates wiped clean, and nothing – neither sorrow, nor anger, nor betrayal – nothing sticks to them. She feels neither energy nor exhaustion, just an emptiness, a lack of being.

'You'll sleep on the sofa,' she hears herself say, rising and moving towards the bedroom. She shuts the door softly. No need for slamming or screaming, no need to act out the betrayed wife, the victim, the fool. That would be to seek something from him, and there is nothing that she wants.

She steps into the shower with her clothes still on. She is pulled down by the weight of wet fabric, flecks of brown blood gathering on the tiles at her feet. She leaves her dress and underwear in a sodden pile on the bathroom floor. In the morning they will have that faint, pond-like smell that makes her think of damp childhood holidays in Normandy, swimming costumes and towels that never fully dried between each day's dip in the cold Channel.

Crawling into bed, she refuses to acknowledge the space next to her. Blocks out the noise of César sobbing in the living room by grabbing his pillows, plumping them up into a padded fort against her back. She lies down, but gets up again to open the blind. The rain is falling steadily now, and she watches it, hypnotised, until sleep finally overtakes her.

42

Paris wakes to an uneasy quiet, its residents slowly lifting their heads above the parapet, nervously stepping out into the world to survey the damage.

Number thirty-seven is no different. The rain has slowed to a steady pace now, a rhythmic drumming against the cobbles and the skull. In the courtyard, Monsieur Marin is out early with his mop and bucket, washing Josef's blood from the entryway's stones. Up on the top floor, Monsieur Lalande keeps his shutters closed. He has seen too much of this before; he will stay at home today.

Only Isabelle Duval appears in Technicolor spirits. She walks triumphantly to the *tabac*, the bakery. A group of people stand huddled outside the greengrocer's. The greengrocer himself has his head in his hands, his wife and daughter at his side. Isabelle jingles her coins loudly as she passes. She's not going to let this portrait of grief upset her day. But it rankles just a little though, even more so on her return when she sees neighbours – 'not even Arabs!' she exclaims to herself – appearing with buckets and cloths to scrub her handiwork clean. She grits her teeth, but it is as a tiny pebble dropping to the bottom of her heart, grating against tissue with each susurration of the blood.

'I hope that's not going to stain,' she snaps at Monsieur Marin, still down on his hands and knees as she re-enters the building.

In the Laribis' apartment, Amina banishes their phones and computers to a kitchen cupboard.

'It doesn't do any good to keep looking at it, love.'

All night they looked at it, TV-screen views of riots, broken windows, police, the news only interrupted by the seemingly endless network of family and friends calling – 'Are you alright?' 'We're fine. Are you?'

'Come on.'

Ahmed looks up aghast to see his wife slipping on her shoes.

'You're not thinking of going out?'

'Yes, we are. This is our city, Ahmed, our home. I want paint for the front door, paint for the nursery.'

He's incredulous. 'Today?'

'Yes, today. Today of all days.'

'This is madness,' Ahmed mutters as they emerge onto the street. But there is comfort in seeing other people out and about; to see people in shock, people being comforted, the group of neighbours banding together to scrub the greengrocer's facade clean.

And later, there is comfort in slapping fresh paint on their own front door, a particular pleasure in painting the spare room blue.

'Are you sure you picked the right colour?' he asks for the hundredth time. 'How can you know?'

'I just know,' Amina replies, her hand on her belly.

In Bâtiment B, Anaïs wakes to Paul's whispered declaration that he is going to take a sick day. This is the stuff that romance is made of. Miraculously, there are whole minutes to be shared between them before the baby stirs. Hundreds of seconds in which to look into the other's eyes, to plant gentle kisses on lips and cheeks.

Downstairs in the Vincents' apartment, there is no such tenderness. César wakes with a start, stiff and sticky, the fabric of the sofa tacking to his skin, his heart sinking even as it leaps into wakefulness.

Being an only child, César did not learn early the art of apologising. In their dark Belgian house there were no other children's toys to steal or hair to pull. César was rigidly well behaved around his grey and frosty father, indulged by his mother, and 'sorry' was a word that rarely entered his vocabulary. When it did, later, explaining poor school reports to his father or a particularly low grade on an exam, it carried with it an air of injustice, of falsehood, so that César struggles now to say it in a way that holds meaning. Which leaves him adrift in a situation as grave as this.

Timidly he opens the bedroom door. He cannot distinguish Chantal from the lumps and bumps of bedding. There is a pang in his heart to see his side of the bed unrumpled, his pillows seized to build a wall whose only intention was to keep him out.

'Can I fetch you anything, my love?'

But his words go unanswered, and the silence is worse than anything she could have said. It hangs leaden between them, drapes itself around his shoulders. Quietly he closes the door.

In the kitchen, he sets about the washing up, knowing even as he plunges his hands into the soapy water how stupid it is to imagine such an inadequate gesture might help. Once, when they had been married five years or so, one of Chantal's close friends had become engaged. César and Chantal had struggled to keep their faces straight when the lovebirds told them, in all seriousness, that they were taking marriage classes with the Catholic Church. Bursting into fits of smug laughter as soon as they were free of the restaurant, César and Chantal had ridiculed the idea. Marriage wasn't something you could teach with lessons. It didn't come with a textbook. And yet on this rainy morning so many years later, César wishes that there was a manual, a source of advice to fall back on. How to mend a catastrophe, how to bridge a gulf. But he feels old today, and unimaginative, and all he can think to do is carry on. To clean the house, go to the shops, do everything he can while biding his time until, maybe, one day, she will be able to forgive him.

Edward is also making amends. He goes out early to the bakery. Croissants, *pains au chocolat*, a fresh baguette; apologies in bread for the previous evening's distress. Emilie makes the coffee, which burns; feeds the cat, who grumbles at being given her least favourite food. They put together a bag for Frédérique: clothes, soap, toothbrush.

'What shall we do for Josef?' she asks, and Edward doesn't know.

They walk through the rain to the hospital more or less in silence, retracing last night's steps in the light of day. Handfuls of people are out and about, sweeping up broken glass or staring wide eyed at the damage. The President was on the television and radio early urging people to stay at home, and most seem to have been happy to comply. The hospital is calmer by day, order restored, its patterns and protocols back up and running.

They take an elevator to the fourth floor and find Frédérique slumped over the foot of Josef's bed. He has been moved in the night to a private room, and despite the syncopated beeps and whines of the various bits of machinery to which he is attached, their footfalls wake her from her sleep.

'Hello, Freddie.'

'Hello loves.'

'Any progress? Any news?'

Frédérique shakes her head. 'Not really. He's in and out of wakefulness.'

'Here,' Emilie extends the bag towards her, 'we brought you some clothes.' Then, less easily: 'I can stay here, if you two want to talk.'

Frédérique rises slowly, stiffly. 'Come on, Edward.' She takes his arm as she passes. As the door swings shut behind them, Edward sees Emilie take Josef's hand, hears her say, 'Hello Uncle Jo.'

Edward and Frédérique walk the grey, featureless corridor to the full-length window at its end. They see no one, hear no noise emerge from behind the uniform blue doors. The glass in front of them is rain spattered, a mix of beady drops and rivulets that run in slow motion into each other, mixing, becoming something larger than themselves until they slow or slip again.

'I should have told you.' Frédérique's eyes are fixed on the drab city in front of them, ashen buildings against a colourless sky. Her fingers trace the raindrops on the other side of the glass. 'I told you so many other things, you deserved to know this.'

'It's okay,' he half-whispers, in the hushed tone reserved for hospitals and churches. And Edward is surprised to find he means it, not just as a platitude, but with a kind of sweeping recognition, a great calm laying itself gently over him like a gauzy embrace.

'No. I should have told you. Oh, Edward, Edward.' He watches her close her eyes and press her forehead against the glass. 'I've been running by standing still, trying to escape by going nowhere.'

He thinks he understands that. Thinks of home: the farmhouse, his parents, the dog, the bedroom with all Hannah's things exactly as they were the day she left and did not return.

'I'm going to go back.'

The words are out of his mouth before he thinks of them. But they feel right, even as they cling to the muggy, artificially citrus air.

Frédérique nods slowly. 'That's good. Josef will have to come and live with me.'

'Will he walk again?'

She shakes her head. 'They think not. There's always the miracle, but no, they think not. Imagine. Ten years trying to live separately, and failing, and now we're forced to live together again. It's all change, Edward.'

'A new kind of wholeness. You said that to me once. The going on in spite of.'

She smiles, a tired and teary smile. Allows herself a moment of resting her hand against his unshaven cheek. He places his hand on top of hers.

'Come back any time. Truly. You are always welcome here. Part of the family now,' she laughs half-heartedly, 'whatever this strange family we make for ourselves is.'

'I'm not sure Emilie would like that.'

'Oh, she would. She likes you, you know.' Frédérique catches herself, remembers the gesture they are caught in, the catching out of the previous night. 'I'll bite my tongue. But promise me you'll come back?'

He nods and they embrace, tears running now down both of their cheeks, fiercer than those that streak against the windows. When she pulls her body away from his it is with a sigh that echoes long after she has retraced her steps down the interminable corridor, a sigh that echoes in his ears like the rush of blood in a seashell, the magnitude of ocean in a hand.

43

Drips. Drips from the crenelated tips of three different railway stations. Edward knows there must be people who can plan train journeys seamlessly, without the aching, hour-long gaps in between, but he has never been one of them. Three wet stations, three trains, three greasy windows from which to watch the murk of summer's-end weather. Smudges of red-brick houses first, then London finally peters out and it's motorway, the wet green of fields, tangles of hedgerow, mud.

The goodbyes were strange and stilted, both too quick and too slow, full of words and yet somehow leaving the most important things unsaid. He made his peace with Emilie, smoking cigarettes up on the roof. He did not tell her he had been there with Frédérique, even when she leant out and said in exactly the same voice, 'there's a ledge, just . . . here.' It was cool and damp, the summer spell broken, and they shivered in T-shirts through the smoke. He could see the Eiffel Tower this time, twinkling and distant, and he realised that for all these months in Paris he had not been to see it in person.

'I'm glad you've been here,' was the closest Emilie got to smoothing things over. 'For her, I mean,' she added quickly. 'She looks happy. You've been good for her.'

He was diplomatic. 'It's been good for me.'

'What will home be like?' she asked.

'I honestly have no idea.'

'Why go?'

'Why stay?'

She made to gesture to the building, herself, Frédérique, Josef – this strange world and its constellation of inhabitants. He cut her off.

'It's where I need to be. That's what I've realised here. You can't run from things forever.'

Now though, on the last stretch of track in a near-deserted train, he wishes he could have. He tried to drink in every last detail of the box room, the staircase, Frédérique's apartment. Every book in the shop, every painting in the *salon*, every now-familiar scuff and smear on the walls. But already the details fade, stealing away from him with every mile that he travels further. They float tauntingly just beyond his grasp.

He said goodbye to Frédérique at the hospital. Easier, cleaner, perhaps, than saying it at home. She was in the midst of animated discussions with the nursing staff about arrangements for Josef's care. There would be two different wheelchairs. She would be badgering Monsieur Vincent and the Residents' Cooperative about installing an elevator. She turned to Edward with wide arms and bright eyes, a smile that seemed somewhat forced as it wished him a safe and happy journey. For a moment, just a single second, she gripped him by the wrists as a tremor of sadness passed across her face. But it passed, and was that a glint of triumph in Josef's eyes as Edward gruffly shook his hand and wished him a good recovery? Or was it absurd to imagine such a thing in a recently maimed man?

Emilie accompanied him to the Gare du Nord (Frédérique had insisted on paying for a train ticket and not the cheaper, bone-juddering bus). The terminus was chaos: people shouting at each other, gangs of youths sloping around looking shifty, the police out in force, fingers on triggers, tourists lost and bewildered, children screaming and their mothers screaming back, pigeons everywhere, and rubbish, and as Emilie hugged him goodbye and waved to him, as he rode the escalator to the departure lounge stepping swiftly from the noise into the sanitised zone of British customs, it seemed to Edward that the city was as much of a mystery to him as when he first arrived.

Haltingly, creakingly, his train pulls into the all too familiar station. No crowds here, no roar, just flaking paint and slate grey puddles accumulating on the platform beneath the holes in the roof. At the front of the station, his dad, as grey as the landscape in which he stands, shoulders hunched and collar turned up against the rain. Edward realises, in a rush of tenderness, that he'd forgotten how small his father is. How vulnerable.

'Hello Dad.'

'Hello Son.'

Backs are patted, hands clasped, and then the inevitable wet minutes as his dad reorganises the car boot. The windows and windscreen steam up in the rain, Edward leaning forward to wipe them clean with the same cloth that's lived in the car for years. Nothing changes.

They speak in short, tentative sentences, uncertain of themselves and of the other. His dad asks how Paris was. 'Great,' he replies, 'really great.'

'Saw the shooting on the telly. Awful business.'

'It was,' Edward agrees, but he cannot go into the rest of it. Businesses attacked, cars burned, people beaten. He wonders if that made the news too, but his father doesn't mention it. A less attractive story, perhaps, to see white people inflicting damage. More compelling when they're the victims.

They stop in town, 'Just to get some bits and bobs', and Edward's missed that phrase, the cheery whistle his dad does when counting change for the pay and display machine.

The village shop is exactly the same, though even as he thinks it Edward wonders why just a few months would change it? The same bored girl behind the counter, the same tinny music piped through the speaker. Everything looks dull and sanitary compared to the riotous markets in Paris, produce piled into dirt-covered mountains, its sweet ripeness dripping in the air and off the tables. His dad buys a predictable loaf of white bread (sliced), pat of butter (salted), carton of milk (semi-skimmed). 'Just stocking up the cupboards.' Edward's eyes are overwhelmed to be able to read all the packaging, his ears drunk on the ability to eavesdrop. He steps in to help his dad with the bag and even the plastic handles feel alien after France's paper wrappings.

The light won't dip for hours yet, but the clouds scudding over add an air of evening to the afternoon, as if the sky is darkening for his arrival. The final journey is quiet. There is a lump in his throat that will not go away when Edward realises his dad is driving the long way round to avoid the spot where the accident happened. He closes his eyes, and soon enough it has passed and they are on the familiar road out to the farm.

As they slow to approach the house Edward's heart accelerates in his chest. It is still raining and the garden path is treacherous. Cold water slinks down the back of his neck, but in his head Edward is in summer, in the fields, on the last day that he was here. But that was leaving and this is re-entry, and already he is crossing the decades-old threshold, catching a handful of dog's saliva in the welcome, remembering to duck his head under the kitchen doorway.

His mother stands silently by the sink, looking out over the fields at the back of the house. She too is tiny, and Edward wonders how he could have sprung from such petite parents. She has not heard him enter, so he touches her arm, her cardigan, each knitted stitch familiar to him. She turns, looks at him, surprise, delight. She rests her head on his chest so that his nose is filled with wild hair, the scent, as always, of fresh laundry. It is as if he has never left.

'Edward.'

It is statement not question, said in pleasure not disappointment. His dad, who has been hovering nervously in the doorway, enters now and pats him on the arm as he passes. He moves to put the kettle on.

'It's good to have you back, Son.'

Afterword: The Building

Far back on the Left Bank, there is a secret quarter. A warren of quiet streets sandwiched between boulevards. Little traffic comes through here.

As autumn creeps into summer's shoes, number thirty-seven's residents begin to close their windows in the evenings. Daylight hours ebb and lights flick on earlier and earlier across the courtyard, cutting yellow squares into black night.

For some, life continues much as it ever has. Madame Marin trots from her house to her hair salon in increasingly improbable stilettos. Her husband hoses his bins and turns a blind eye when she trots out at night (and when she trots back in during the early hours). Isabelle Duval continues her indiscriminate discrimination. She grumbles about everyone – young and old, male and female, black, white and everything between. The frown lines on her forehead deepen, and with every passing day she travels further from the person she once wanted to be.

She leaves the Laribis well alone, though she resents the waxing of Amina's belly. The Laribis themselves have settled into their new home. Their front door is freshly painted, and but for a few drops of red caught on the floorboards, themselves only caught from a certain angle in a certain light, you would never know that anything untoward had been scrawled there. They are happy, and if Ahmed sometimes finds himself awake at night worrying – about more attacks, more fear, more Islamophobia – he is relieved to see that Amina's sleep is sound.

Across the courtyard, Anaïs no longer lives in fear of

breaking. She is in control of her days, however sticky and exasperating. A quiet happiness has returned to her, though she does occasionally catch herself listening in the hallways for the soft lilt of Sophie's voice. She still tastes the dusty air for signs of that mysterious friend's presence.

On the first floor, César Vincent greets autumn from his own side of the bed again. He wishes it had been forgiveness that had prompted Chantal to let him return to the marital bed, but the sofa was irritating his already grouchy sciatic nerve and she did not wish physical pain upon him, only what César has come to see as a sort of emotional retribution. Inch by inch he is making his way back across the bed. Chantal knows this and, in her heart of hearts, she doesn't mind. At first she could not imagine life carrying on in light of his deception, but later she found her quiet moments troubled by the realisation that she could not imagine life without him. Time has been her remedy, her prescription, her drug of choice. And as winter edges ever nearer, she feels in her bones that she will, somehow, learn to live with what has passed.

In late October, Josef returns home to the apartment that was never his. Frédérique has won the battle for Bâtiment A's elevator, and every afternoon she wheels him down the boulevards, racing that he might catch an auburn leaf in his pale hand.

'For luck!' she says, each time, and each time he smiles back. 'What luck I have,' he says.

Sometimes, Frédérique will glance across the courtyard and think back to the gentle young man who wandered into her life that June day. She hears from Edward sporadically, a postcard here and there between them, but she feels in her older, wiser moments, once Josef is in bed for the night and she has the *salon* to herself, that they shared what they were meant to. Learnt their lessons together, however fleetingly.

Without Edward here, the bookshop goes unloved, untended. Cobwebs creep across the bright and glossy covers, and even Gilles has long since stopped poking his head hopefully through the turquoise door to see if the shop might be open. But if the books are left to their own devices, there is care enough to go around. The neighbours all stop in to meet Josef, to wish him well. He likes to talk to Anaïs's children, who in turn like to clamber up onto his chair and ride around the apartment. He enjoys discussing Chantal's library projects. Little Monsieur Lalande brings chess and treats for the cat, and they spend many an afternoon chortling together.

In truth, the long afternoons with Josef are a solace for Henri Lalande. His sparrows are leaving now for the winter. He wishes them well, even as his heart is pained, waving them off into the high and icy sky. But he knows they will eventually come back. Everyone always comes back.

Acknowledgements

Perhaps some books are written without encouragement; this one was not. I owe a big debt to The Womentoring Project, and particularly to the amazing Lisa O'Donnell, who was the first to convince me that I could actually write a novel. I was fortunate to read many of the early vignettes set in and around number thirty-seven at Spoken Word Paris, and am thankful for all the feedback I received. Rob James-Robbins, Rob MacFarlane and Fabienne Bonnet are three wonderful teachers, now friends, who gave early support to my writing. Many other friends cheered along the way: special thanks to Greer Dale-Foulkes, Katie Dickson, Léon Digard and Rajvi Shah, and particularly to early reader and workshopper Anna Polonyi. Without the generosity of Liz and Bernard Carnell, I would not have been in Paris in the first place.

A big thank you to everyone at Curtis Brown, especially my wonderful agent Lucy Morris, and to the fabulous team at Hodder. I thank my lucky stars to have met Emma Herdman, who has shepherded this book from first draft to publication, and who has been its endless champion.

Finally, my family. Mum, Dad, Jess – your unwavering support means more than I can say. This book could not have been written without you, or without Alex Manthei; my great advocate, my great love.